D0458353

the LANGUAGE
of GHOSTS

the
LANGUAGE
of
GHOSTS

HEATHER FAWCETT

Balzer + Bray
An Imprint of HarperCollins*Publishers*

Balzer + Bray is an imprint of HarperCollins Publishers.

The Language of Ghosts
Copyright © 2020 by Heather Fawcett
All rights reserved. Printed in the United States of America.
No part of this book may be used or reproduced in any manner whatsoever
without written permission except in the case of brief quotations embodied in
critical articles and reviews. For information address HarperCollins
Children's Books, a division of HarperCollins Publishers,
195 Broadway, New York, NY 10007.
www.harpercollinschildrens.com

ISBN 978-0-06-285454-4

Typography by Alice Wang
20 21 22 23 24   PC/LSCH   10 9 8 7 6 5 4 3 2 1
❖
First Edition

the LANGUAGE
of GHOSTS

Prologue

It was the raspberry sundae that did it. Noa stormed across the banquet hall, dodging guests and servants. "Princess Noa?" more than one voice called after her. She bumped into a man carrying a tray laden with frozen guava. As he fell, the tray rose in the air in a spectacular arc, spraying horrified courtiers with ice shavings like pink snowflakes.

Noa didn't care. She ran up the black marble staircase, eyes blurring with tears, mouth aching from holding it in a stiff, calm, princess-like line.

If she had to listen to one more courtier tell her how sorry they were that her mother had *passed on* or *slipped away*, as if Mom were a tricky spy escaping into the night, Noa was going to throw up all over her horrible, funeral-appropriate dress. Her older brother, Julian—soon to be crowned King Julian—didn't see her leave.

The staircase wound around and around, offering a view

of the courtyard at every turn. The royal palace's architecture was typically Florean, with large, airy galleries built around a central garden teeming with cacti and vine trees and lava-wort. Normally, Noa stopped and said hello to the finches that liked to perch on the staircase railing, but right now there was a storm inside her, and she kept running until she got to her bedroom.

There was nothing particularly princess-like about Noa's room—no chests filled with jewels or fantastical chandeliers. It was messy in an organized way, piled with books and logic puzzles and model ships. She wasn't interested in ships, but she liked taking things apart so she could study them and improve the design. Reckoner, her brother's ancient dragon, was sprawled across the polished floor like a fat, spotty rug. Reckoner disliked Noa, though he disliked her less than he disliked most people, probably making a strategic allowance for the fact that her room had the best afternoon *and* evening sunbeams.

Noa went straight to the wardrobe and locked herself in. Then she collapsed in a heap of sobs and scattered dresses and coats.

Her mother, the queen of Florean, had been dead for a week. It was weird that this was the first time Noa had cried— that it hadn't happened when Julian had told her, or the first time she had walked past her mother's empty bedroom. No, it had been the sight of that towering raspberry sundae, a sundae so magnificent it took three servants to carry it out, piled with cream and chocolate and butternuts, the raspberries fat as chickadees. Her mother had loved raspberry sundaes, and Noa had turned instinctively to catch her look of astounded delight.

And that was when she had understood.

Noa stayed in the wardrobe until she thought the funeral guests had left. Then she stayed a little longer, for good measure. One of her mother's cats came in and meowed at the door in order to point out how difficult he was to fool. After a while, he got tired of bragging and went to nap in the sun with Reckoner. Noa's mother had loved cats and had accumulated sixteen of them over the years. She probably would have reached twenty if—

If.

Eventually, Noa ran out of tears. She occupied herself with cataloging by size and shape the dust motes dancing in the light that spilled through the wardrobe doors. Noa cataloged a lot of things, partly because it was calming and partly because it was useful, particularly in helping her win arguments with Julian. She was just wondering if tiny hairs from Reckoner's snout counted as dust when her bedroom door opened and two assassins stepped in.

Noa froze. She knew they were assassins immediately, even though she could see only a sliver of them through the wardrobe doors. They were dressed in all black like the funeral guests, but Noa had mentally cataloged the funeral guests and these two didn't fit anywhere. Their clothes weren't rich enough for courtiers, nor plain enough for servants, and they moved too quietly to be up to any good.

Also, the woman was holding a large dagger.

Noa's heart thundered so loud she was sure they would hear it. The assassins approached her rumpled bed. The woman relaxed her grip on the dagger when the man pulled the blankets back, revealing Noa's stuffed walrus.

"Odd," the woman said. She strode idly over to the wardrobe and pulled on the door, and Noa almost did throw up then, but of course it didn't open, for Noa had locked the wardrobe from the inside. She always did, to keep her sister out.

"We'll find the little one first," the man murmured. "Her bedroom is in the next hall."

Noa felt as if she had floated out of her body. As soon as the door shut behind the pair, she tumbled out of the wardrobe with a pair of pants tangled around her head. Reckoner was still asleep, of course, because he was the most useless dragon in Florean and wouldn't interrupt a good nap if a dozen assassins danced around him, tossing knives in the air.

The assassins had disappeared around the corner, and Noa ran in the opposite direction, because the assassins were wrong, and her sister's bedroom was next to hers.

Mite had already been put to bed, on account of her being only five, and several lavasticks had been left glowing on various tables in her room. She started to scream when Noa dragged her roughly out of bed, but Noa clapped a hand over her mouth.

"It's me," she hissed. "We have to find Julian. There are— there are bad people looking for us."

Mite's eyes were wide. Her dark hair stuck up, and there was something smeared on her cheek that Noa suspected was chocolate, because Mite was an expert at sneaking food into her room. "Bad people? Are they librarians?"

"Um—yeah," Noa said. Their mother had been in a long-standing spat with the librarians at the royal library, who had bitterly protested her habit of borrowing books indefinitely, even though every library in Florean technically belonged to her. "Mean, angry librarians. I heard them say you forgot to return something."

Mite gaped. Hans, the head librarian, had once scolded her for getting fingerprints on the card catalog, and she now lived in fear of him and all librarian-kind. "But I didn't!"

Noa dragged her out the door and down the hall. "Don't worry—Julian will sort it out."

They ran down the staircase, which was strangely deserted. Where were the palace guards? Where were the turquoise-clad servants? How had the assassins managed to reach Noa's room in the first place? Dread coiled her stomach into knots. They needed Julian. He was sixteen, and even better, he was one of the most powerful magicians in Florean—or he would be, if he ever bothered to practice his spellwork.

Noa stopped at the bottom of the stairs, pushing Mite behind her. There was a terrible clamor coming from the banquet hall, shouting and clashing swords. What was going on?

"Let's try the throne room." Noa still felt nauseous, and she prayed she wouldn't faint. She led Mite down a quiet servants' corridor. Mite was barefoot and kept tripping on the hem of her nightie, but at least she wasn't crying. They took the shortcut through the gardens—night was falling, and the sky was a deep purple curve like the inside of a mussel shell.

A black-cloaked figure came racing into the courtyard, and Noa's heart faltered, but it was only Julian. His cloak was singed, and he had a cut on his cheek. Noa leaped into his arms with a cry of relief.

Her brother drew back, and they examined each other. Most people thought Julian was handsome, so handsome that some bards had even written fawning songs about it, full of awful metaphors about his eyes that gave Noa no end of material to mock him with. He had the same olive skin and overlarge ears as her and Mite, but his eyes were blue like their mother's. He seemed fine, apart from the blood, though his gaze was cold and glazed over, like ice, and he was gripping Noa too tightly. "You're all right. You're both all right."

"What's going on?"

Julian didn't answer. He dragged them back into the servants' corridor and they found some oversized cloaks that the servants used while cleaning the chimneys. They smelled of soot and burnt cheese. Julian had to tie the bottom of Mite's cloak around her waist and the sleeves around the back of her neck. His hands were shaking.

"What's going on?" Noa repeated. "Julian!"

"It wasn't a fever that killed Mom," he said in a too-calm voice. "She was poisoned. Xavier was behind it."

Noa felt weightless, as if she'd become an echo of herself. Xavier Whitethorn had been on Mom's council. Noa remembered him as a pale and quiet and thoroughly dull grown-up, even by councillor standards.

"Xavier," she murmured. She should have felt angry, but since Mom's death, she'd been unable to feel things when she was supposed to. "Who told you that?"

"Xavier's assassins. Mages. They were waiting for me in the throne room."

"We didn't see any assassins," Noa said with a meaningful glance Mite's way. "But a couple of librarians dropped by. We must owe a pretty big fine."

Julian gave her a sharp look, but he didn't ask for an explanation. That was the best thing about Julian—he always understood what she meant, even when nobody else did. "I'll make sure they get it," he said. "We have to go. Xavier's turned most of the council against the Marchenas. He spread all kinds of rumors about Mom. That her power had corrupted her, that it was turning her mad, and that I was heading in the same direction."

Noa stared. "But that's ridiculous. How could anybody believe him?"

Julian looked ten years older. "Because we're dark magicians. That's how."

Noa let out her breath. Most magicians could speak only one of the nine languages of magic—they were born knowing how; it wasn't something you could learn. The common ones were Salt, the language of the sea, and Worm, the language of earth. Magicians who could speak more than one magical language could weave them together into complex spells, which was dark magic. Dark mages were rare, though no one knew exactly how rare, for many lived in secret—most people distrusted their gifts. Their mother had been the first dark mage to rule Florean.

Noa herself couldn't do any magic, dark or otherwise. She'd always thought that people hated dark mages out of jealousy, which she could understand, as she was jealous of Julian constantly. But it was true that a few dark mages had eventually gone bad—it was more common among them than regular mages. There was something about having all those kinds of magic inside you that corrupted some people, like fruit trees that rotted from too much water.

"The royal mages are on Xavier's side, and half the guards," Julian said. "I can't fight them all. It's a coup. They're taking over the palace as we speak."

"What's a coo?" Mite asked.

"It means Xavier wants to be king," Noa said. She felt a spark of fury, but it had nothing to catch on. "What about the navy?"

"He bribed the generals," Julian said. "General Albion's death last month wasn't an accident, either—he refused to side with Xavier, so Xavier sabotaged his ship."

Noa swayed. If the navy was on Xavier's side, what hope was there? None of the islands would challenge the takeover, because Xavier could reduce them to ashes.

"But Julian is the king now." Mite's lip trembled. "That's what Momma said."

"Maita." Julian drew her into his arms. "It's okay. I'll figure something out. But right now, we have to go."

"Where?" Noa said.

"We'll steal a boat. Come on." He pulled up their hoods.

Noa hardly recognized the palace—some of the rooms were on fire, and smoke hovered in the air, and everywhere there was fighting, fighting, fighting. It was difficult to tell what was going on—who was winning or losing, or even how many sides there were. Not all the guards had abandoned their posts—some of them were battling other guards in halls and stairwells and doorways. Servants cowered in corners or unlit fireplaces.

"Wait," Noa said as they passed the north courtyard. "I forgot something!"

"Noa," Julian hissed, but she was already darting through the greenery.

And there was Willow—on the bench just where she'd left him. Willow was a stuffed blue whale Mom had given Noa last month for her eleventh birthday. Noa and Mom were in agreement that blue whales were the best whale, and likely the best animal overall. Together they watched them migrate past the palace every spring.

Noa tucked Willow under her arm and ran back to Julian.

They escaped the palace without being recognized, though Julian had to blind a group of mages with a spell in Hum, the language of light. Outside, it was less of a mystery who was winning: the turquoise Marchena banners had all been taken down and replaced with bright red ones bearing an X that looked like a twinkling star.

The palace had been built atop a sharp crag of an island called Queen's Step, which was near the center of the Florean Archipelago. Queen's Step was so small that it was mostly all palace, with a harbor attached. Julian picked a fishing boat with a generous cabin at the end of the pier, and they clambered aboard. He pulled a lavastick from his pocket and blew on it to ignite the ember.

"What about my shoes?" Mite said. Her voice was so small that Julian had to ask her to repeat herself.

"We'll get you new ones, Mighty Mite," he said.

Noa hugged the whale to her chest, reveling in his stuffed-animal smell. "Where are we going?"

Julian blinked. He didn't look like he was covered with

ice anymore. His eyes were red, and he seemed closer to twelve than sixteen in the oversized, wet cloak. "Astrae," he said finally. "You remember—we used to go there on holiday before Dad died."

Noa didn't remember, or at least not very well—Dad had died when she was six. Suddenly, staring out at that dark sea, the ship seemed less like safety than it had in the palace. She wanted to go home. "Julian—"

His gaze sharpened on something behind her. Noa turned.

Clomping up the dock from the palace were at least two dozen royal mages. They stopped at the first tethered boat, and the lead mage shouted, "Julian Marchena, you and your mother stand accused of the crimes of murder and treason. You will surrender now to face justice."

"Why would anyone come out if you yelled that at them?" Noa whispered. She had her answer three seconds later. The fire mages chanted an incantation, and the boat burst into flames.

Julian, bizarrely, wasn't looking at the mages. He was staring down at the water, leaning over the railing as if he was about to be sick.

"Julian." Noa yanked on his sleeve. "*Julian*. What do we do? They're coming this way!"

"I have an idea," he said.

He began to murmur the strangest incantation Noa had ever heard. Julian was the only person in the world—possibly in history—who could speak all nine magical languages. Noa couldn't tell how many different languages Julian was speaking now, only that he was making a sound like a kettle full of boiling leaves that a porcupine was tap-dancing on.

Noa bit back a scream. Julian's reflection was moving—it skimmed over the water, and then it *jumped out* onto the dock, where it stood gawping at them like a nightmare. The reflection was Julian to a T—if you only looked at it out of the corner of your eye. If you *really* looked at it, which was a horrible thing to do, you saw that its limbs undulated like waves and its face was a mass of folds like ripples. Again Noa was almost sick.

Julian babbled another incantation at the reflection, and it took off. It sped soundlessly past the mages, who only took note after it made it past them. Then they started yelling various versions of what they had yelled at the boat, and running after the reflection.

That was when Reckoner chose to amble onto the dock.

Reckoner was about the size of a pony and nearly toothless. Julian had found him—or Reckoner had allowed himself to be found—when he had gone looking for dragons to use as familiars. Reckoner had been dying, skinny and shivering in a cave in the Halfmoon Islets. Mostly blind, the old dragon couldn't hunt anymore, and was hardly an intimidating sight with his cataract-clouded eyes and omnipresent drool, but Julian had taken one look at him and declared him the finest beast he had ever seen. Noa had never known Reckoner to protest his changed circumstances, and he spent most of his time hobbling around the palace sniffing at carpets or curled up at Julian's feet. He had become part of Julian's legend—the magician so powerful he had tamed a dragon with a word— but it was likely more accurate to say that Reckoner had taken a practical look at his options and decided that being tame was the best of them, particularly when it involved belly rubs, reg- ular applications of bloodroot salve to ease his arthritis, and a constant supply of cod.

Noa could see Reckoner from her elevated position on the ship, but the mages could not. The lead mage rounded the cor- ner, tripped over him, and went sprawling into the sea in an impressive somersault.

You would have thought that Reckoner would move out of the way. But the dragon just sat there like an enormous green barnacle, blinking his blurry eyes as the mages tripped spectacularly over his thick hide. Eventually, the mages at the back of the mob figured out what was going on and stopped to help the others, but by then Julian's reflection had escaped to wherever loose reflections escaped to. Maybe there was a spe- cial town where they lived, Noa thought dazedly, and walked around with their limbs flapping and their ripple faces grin- ning at each other. She tried to put the image out of her mind.

"You couldn't have just swept them out to sea?" she demanded, because if Julian could create a hideous water twin, surely he could handle a simpler—and far less flashy—spell.

Julian blinked. "I didn't think of that."

"Of course you didn't," Noa groaned.

Once the mages had all gone, Julian called Reckoner's name. The dragon's ears pricked up and he ambled over. He tried to jump onto the boat, but Reckoner's problem was that he never remembered how big he was, and he only made it halfway. He hit the water, sending up such a geyser that it soaked all three of them. Julian was too exhausted from the last spell to cast another, so they had to throw a net around Reckoner's flailing body and haul him up. It took a long time, and Noa was scared that, in saving Reckoner, Julian would get them all captured. But then she saw how Julian wrapped his arms around Reckoner as he sat dripping and sneezing on the deck, and buried his face in the old dragon's neck, and she didn't say anything.

Julian raised the sail and the fishing boat drifted out to sea. Noa helped him—they both knew what to do, for even princes and princesses were expected to learn how to pilot a boat in Florean—and then she sat with Mite until Mite fell asleep with her head in Noa's lap.

Mite cried a bit in her sleep, but Noa just stared straight ahead, her eyes dry. She'd cried enough. It grew windy as they reached the open sea, the waves stretching and pulling the thumbprint of the moon, and she was happy for the chimney sweeps' huge coat, even if it smelled like Reckoner's breath.

She looked at Julian. There was a cold expression on his

face that Noa had never seen before. He barely even looked like himself. Their eyes met, and it was one of those times when Noa knew they were thinking the same thing. She felt a rush of relief that she had Julian and Mite, that Xavier hadn't managed to take them from her, too. *We'll find the little one first.* If Noa met those assassins now, she would tear their hearts out with her bare hands.

The dark fishing boat glided on, and Noa watched the palace slip below the horizon. Something inside her hardened. The palace belonged to them, no matter how many banners Xavier strung up. It belonged to the Marchenas, and so did the rest of Florean.

And somehow, someday, they were going to get it back.

PART 1
Astrae

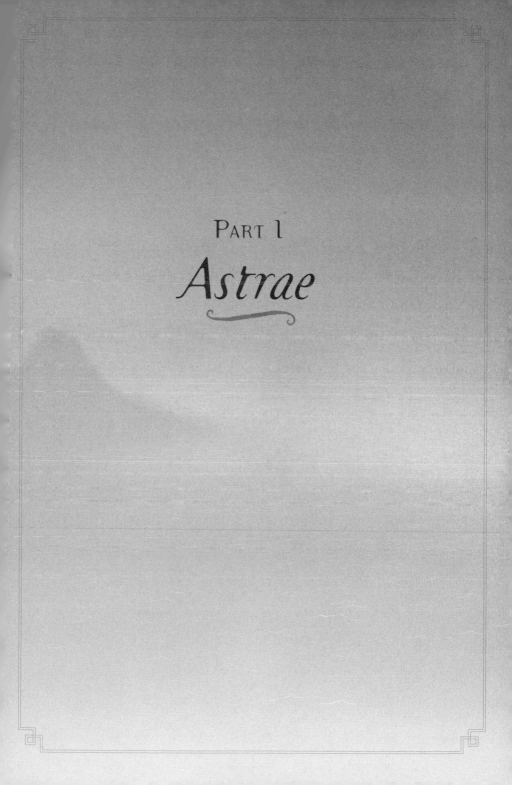

1

An Island Loses
Its Directions

Noa carefully arranged the map upon the sand, weighting the corners with rocks. She pulled two pencils, a ruler, and a compass from her cloak, twining one of the pencils through her long hair to keep it out of her eyes.

She had almost finished the map of Astrae. It had taken her several months—though the island was small, measuring only four miles in length and a mile across, Noa had wanted to be thorough. Maps were always useful. Knowing exactly where things were, and where other things might be, was powerful. Noa squinted at the beach, which was pebbly and dotted with tide pools like scraps of fallen sky, and added another mark.

The island gave a rumbling groan, and Noa's pencil skidded across the paper.

"What was *that*?" The island made a lot of strange sounds—it was an enchanted island, after all—but in the two years they'd been living there, she'd never heard it groan. Mite, crouched over something farther up the beach, made no reply. Mite was seven now, and had only two interests, as far as Noa could tell: insects and getting dirty.

"Look, Noa!" Mite held her hands closed in front of her, an ominous sign.

Noa grimaced. "If it's another spider with hair longer than yours, Mite, I don't want to see it."

Mite chewed her lip. "My hair isn't very long."

"Go put it in the grass."

Mite glowered, but she moved to obey, muttering to the creature under her breath. That was the other thing with Mite—she didn't just like bugs, she *talked* to them. Noa was certain Mite was going to end up living alone in a forest somewhere, cackling to herself.

Noa eyed the map critically, tracing the familiar contours of the island with a sandy fingertip. At the south end of Astrae was a dormant volcano called Devil's Nose, dark red and forested with a maze of scalesia trees that were home to hundreds of finches and geckos and lava crickets. The village on Astrae was also called Astrae, and amounted to seven shops and a few dozen whitewashed houses encircling a garden. The eastern side of the island was dominated by sea cliffs, the west by a reddish beach punctuated by little black coves.

Of course, "east side" and "west side" were now useless from a navigational standpoint, because soon after the Marchenas reached Astrae, Julian enchanted it so that the island could move about like a ship. This was exactly as complicated as it sounded, and the early days of Astrae's mobility had not been pleasant. The island would give an awful jerk at unpredictable moments, like a dog with fleas, and it rocked constantly. If you fell over on the beach during a particularly bad list, you would roll right into the sea. Once Julian got those things sorted out, the island began to spin calmly on its axis. The spinning phase was worse than everything before it, and for Noa it passed in a haze of nausea.

Noa tapped her finger against the map. Julian had enchanted the island to hide them from Xavier—now King Xavier—who wouldn't rest until he found Julian and killed him. But as the weeks passed, and Astrae went from cantankerous toddler to graceful denizen of Florean's thirteen seas, Julian stayed alive, and he began to set up a makeshift court on the wandering island. Some magicians who had been loyal to the old queen came to live on Astrae at Julian's invitation, ignoring the rumors Xavier spread about Julian being wicked and corrupt. Julian's plan was to recapture the islands of Florean one by one, and slowly, that's what he'd been doing, frightening away Xavier's soldiers and fortifying each island with defensive magics and his own magicians.

Astrae gave another groan, quieter this time. Frowning, Noa abandoned her map and went to the water's edge. She squinted through her spyglass at the islets drifting by. They were hard to see through the mist that lay over the sea in woolly tendrils. Mite skipped up behind her, pausing to examine clumps of seaweed for reasons Noa didn't want to know, because those reasons likely had too many legs.

The island gave a violent shudder. Then it went *wooshawooshawooshTHUNK.*

Noa fell over. Mite went sprawling into a tide pool. Astrae jerked a few more times, less dramatically, and then it stilled.

Noa pushed herself up. The island wasn't moving anymore, and a great rippling wave extended out from the shore like a wing. Noa's heart thudded—Astrae had hit something. But what?

"Come on, Mite," Noa called. Mite clambered dripping from the tide pool with seaweed in her hair, and they took off at a run.

They flew over the sand and climbed over the black rocks that bordered the cove. There the castle where they lived with Julian on the now-only-sometimes-west side of the island came into view. It had been abandoned for many years, and was rather tumbledown and woebegone, with pelicans nesting in the roof and layers of volcanic ash griming the stones. The beach below it was full of Julian's mages, some of them arguing with two strangers in a fishing boat. Looming above Astrae was the island they must have collided with, which Noa didn't recognize.

Julian himself stood talking to one of the mages, rubbing his hand through his dark hair and weaving it into ridiculous tangles. He faced the sea and began a complicated spell that calmed the fierce waves stirred up by the collision.

In the two years they'd lived on Astrae, Julian had thrown himself into his spellwork with a focus Noa had never seen in him before. Despite being the only person in the world who could speak all the languages of magic, he had never been particularly interested in mastering his powers, apart from a few showy tricks to impress the young lords and ladies at court. Now, though, he spent most of the time with his grimoires, practicing spells. He even traded in the colorful silks and jewels he had favored as crown prince for head-to-toe black, though he did wear a lot of impressive rings and had enchanted a dragon tattoo onto his face, curved around his temple. Noa considered this pointless vanity, but at least it was less pointless vanity than usual.

Noa squinted. The mystery island was perhaps twice the size of Astrae and densely forested. Astrae seemed to have collided with a sandy spit extending off the tip—Noa guessed that the first groan had been the sound of Astrae running over a shoal.

It wasn't the first time Astrae had gotten itself stuck. There were treacherous basalt pillars in Ripple Pass that the island had hit more than once, and then there had been the memorable occasion when it had plowed through the dust of a volcanic eruption and into a pool of fresh lava, melting one of the beaches. Banging into an island wasn't so bad by comparison.

They were probably only stuck because Julian had ordered Captain Kell to go too fast—he was always ignoring the advice of the sailors who steered Astrae.

But if that was true, why did Noa have a knot of dread in her stomach?

She watched Julian's magicians take up position on the sand, murmuring spells in Salt to detach the enchanted floating island from the ordinary stationary island it had run into. Astrae was reasonably safe—they were in the Untold Sea, which was full of pirates. Any royal ships that ventured into the Untold Sea were unlikely to come out again, which made it the safest place in Florean for fugitives. The pirates never gave Julian any trouble, probably because they assumed his heart was as black as theirs, if not blacker.

The fishermen were still yelling at the mages. Noa couldn't really blame them—if somebody nearly ran you over with an island, you were bound to be upset about it. But where had the fishermen come from? The other island looked uninhabited. As the men continued to shout abuse, Julian let out a frustrated noise and stormed down the beach, his black cloak billowing behind him. He spat out a spell that flung one of the unlucky fishermen into the sea—especially unlucky because it had been days since Beauty, Astrae's resident sea serpent, had eaten her last meal. The splash the poor man made was almost immediately followed by an awful gulping sound. Noa shuddered.

"How would you describe this?" she mused as she watched Julian stomp dramatically away. "You can't say we've run aground, because Astrae *is* ground. We're shipwrecked, but this isn't a ship."

Mite made no reply. She had quickly lost interest in the spectacle on the beach and had started overturning pieces of driftwood.

Noa knelt by the water's edge, brushing her hand through the lapping waves. The current was oddly warm— it swirled along the spit, which was now a causeway joining the islands. A school of bottlenose dolphins drifted past the beach. They chittered indignantly at Astrae, not at all impressed by a moving island.

Noa's brow furrowed as she eyed the undulating currents. She prided herself on being the practical one in the family— not that this was saying much, given Julian's penchant for drama and Mite's overall weirdness. She noticed things other people didn't. It had been her idea to capture the islet of Delphin before attacking its bigger neighbor, Gray Sisters, which had allowed Julian's magicians to simply wade over to Gray Sisters at low tide. The thought hadn't even entered Julian's head.

That was Julian's problem—he was the least practical person on the planet. Having more magic than anyone else made him think he could simply blast his way through obstacles instead of bothering with strategy. Well, Julian wasn't going to defeat Xavier and become the king of Florean by going about things that way.

And Noa intended to make him the king of Florean if she had to tie him down and beat some strategy into his head.

That was Noa's primary mission, anyway. She also had a secret mission that she didn't tell anyone about.

Specifically, stopping Julian from going bad.

It wasn't that Julian was cruel. It was more than he did cruel things without thinking—tossing fishermen to a ravenous sea serpent, for example. Julian used to toss people to Beauty only as a last resort, but these days, he didn't hesitate, and sometimes gave off the distinct impression that he was enjoying himself. Noa was used to hearing fanciful stories about Julian's black deeds. He was, after all, the Dark Lord that most people in Florean would only whisper about in low tones, or blame for bad harvests or other misfortunes. Those stories were no more Julian than his shadow was. But increasingly it was difficult to separate Julian from his reputation, as if shadow and brother were no longer distinct. And the fact was, as a dark magician, Julian was more likely to go bad than your average person.

In short, Noa had her hands full.

"Princess Noa?" a voice said. Renne, Julian's second-in-command, was hovering behind her.

"Yes?" she said coldly. She hated being called "princess." For one thing, it wasn't accurate—she wouldn't be a princess again until Julian defeated the king and all his mages and took his rightful place on the throne. Calling her "princess" was like saying her mother's death was something you could push aside and forget.

"Well," Renne began, stretching the word out. He fiddled with the edge of his cloak. Renne should have been intimidating—he was a big man and, like all of Julian's followers, wore the same ferocious dragon tattoo that Julian did. But there was something small about him.

"The island seems to have run up against a coral reef," he finally elaborated. "It's going to take a while to work our way free."

Noa didn't know why he was telling her—Renne usually seemed barely aware she existed. Then she sighed. "You want me to break the news to Julian."

"If you're headed to the castle," Renne said with a relieved smile.

"I wasn't, actually." But Renne was already walking away. Noa blew out her breath and turned her back on the strange currents.

"Mite," she called. Her sister bounded out of the tall grasses, her dark hair a bird's nest framing her tanned cheeks.

"Is it lunch yet?"

"You just had breakfast." Mite had three interests, Noa amended. Bugs, dirt, and food.

Noa didn't go to the castle right away. Instead, she followed the path from the beach to Devil's Nose. Noa and Mite had to step over several iguanas warming themselves on the dark soil. They just lay there, peaceful as logs.

"Where are we going?" Mite complained. She had to run to keep up with Noa's long strides.

"If you're tired, you can wait for me by the rocks," Noa said.

"No, I'm okay." Mite darted ahead, her bare feet quiet against the dirt.

Noa heaved a sigh. Looking after Mite hadn't always been her job—in the terrible first year after they fled to Astrae, it had been Julian's. But gradually, as he gained power and followers, Mite had become Noa's responsibility. Not that she had ever agreed to it. Not that she didn't sometimes try to give Mite the slip—after all, wasn't seven old enough to look after yourself, especially on an island as safe as Astrae, with so many magicians to keep an eye out? Noa had tried ignoring Mite, she had tried bossing her around, but no matter what she did, Mite followed everywhere she went, like a shadow that sometimes had bees in its pockets.

Noa spent most of her days exploring Astrae. As a princess, her life had been tightly structured into lessons with tutors, public appearances with her mother and Julian, banquets, and playdates with stuffy royal children. As a fugitive, though, Noa didn't have a schedule. She didn't have guards following her everywhere. At first she had found it strange, but then, once she got used to it, she drank in her new freedom like a cactus did the first rains of winter. She drew maps of Astrae's topography and flora and landmarks. She listed every tree and bird and animal that had names, and gave names to the ones that didn't. In short, she cataloged everything she could think of. The information wasn't just interesting; it helped Julian. When he needed a weird spell ingredient, such as bark from a lightning-struck tree or the feather of an aged parrot, she knew where to find it. She could tell him where the best viewpoints were on Devil's Nose, where the walruses slept on sunny days, and where the goldenberries grew fat and gleaming on the hillside like spilled coins.

Sometimes, particularly after a long day of tramping through tide pools and crunching over lava rock, with her hair wound into fantastical tangles by the sea winds, her old princess life felt like a dream. At other times, she felt guilty for enjoying herself at all, because it seemed like a betrayal of Mom. On those days, she shut herself up in her room with Willow and refused to talk to anyone.

After a lot of huffing and sweating, Noa and Mite reached the peak of the volcano. Noa took out the Chronicle and tried to pretend she was alone, a general surveying her domain. The Chronicle was a roughly bound notebook where she cataloged her daily observations about the state of Astrae and its defenses, like a ship's logbook.

She read over her observations from the previous days, which were neatly organized into categories like *weather* and *lookout rotations* and *miles traveled.* As she had suspected, the water temperature had remained steady, and there was no mention of strange currents. She squinted at the beach far below—she could just make out the tiny figures of the magicians, their hands linked as they chanted the spell to free the island again. The roiling currents were even more pronounced from above—they looked like dark snakes lurking beneath the water. The mystery island was densely forested with matazarno trees and bore no signs of villages or harbors. And yet they had run into a fishing boat, which could scarcely have come from anywhere else, given that there were no other islands within miles.

"It's too hot up here," Mite announced. "I want to go back to the beach."

"Then go back to the beach," Noa said. Mite sighed and kicked a rock. It rebounded off another rock with a crack. Mite kicked it again. *Crack. Crack. Crack.*

Noa tried to ignore her. She took out her map of Florean, which she kept tucked into the Chronicle.

The kingdom of Florean was made up of ten big islands and dozens of smaller ones, which jutted sharply out of the sea in a rough circle like bits of smashed plate. There were also countless islets, most of which were hardly big enough to fit a house and garden on. On the right side of the map was the edge of a blob labeled South Meruna, a huge, jungly continent of several kingdoms, all of which hated magic. Florean didn't have much to do with them.

Some of Florean's islands were basically just volcanoes and no good to anybody, coughing out ash and lava all day and night. Others were barren, with a lot of red rock and prickly pear cacti. The islands in the north of Florean were greener and often had forests; Astrae had been one of them before Julian enchanted it. Noa's map was more than three years old, so Astrae was still on it. The poor island hadn't known what was coming to it when the map had been drawn.

Noa tapped the map. Even if Julian had ordered Kell to speed up, they should be hours away from the nearest group of islands, the Nettles. It was possible they had run into an island that didn't appear on the map. Possible, but unlikely, given the size of it.

Crack.

"Mite," Noa said through gritted teeth. "Will. You. Be. *Quiet.*"

Mite's face darkened. She was quiet for a moment, and then she picked up a stick and began hitting rocks with it, making even more noise.

That did it. Noa snapped the Chronicle shut and marched back down the trail, even though she hadn't finished logging the day's entry. She walked quickly—she was tall for thirteen, and could move fast when she wanted to. Then, once she was certain she was out of sight, she stepped behind a tree. A gecko hopped onto her shoulder, and she brushed it off.

Mite came running down the trail, panting, her cheeks red. Noa waited until the sound of Mite's footsteps faded, then went back up to the top of the mountain and settled herself happily on a rock. It had been days since she'd had a moment to herself. She took out the Chronicle and continued cataloging in peace.

2

A Sea Monster Is Suspiciously Helpful

The magicians were still on the beach when Noa came down from the mountain an hour later. She felt a shiver of nervousness—she had expected Renne to have freed the island by now. The fishing boat was gone, whether because it had returned home or been devoured by Beauty, Noa didn't know.

As if in answer to her thought, the sea serpent lifted her enormous head out of the water. Noa paused on the steps that led up a narrow sea cliff to the castle and motioned to her.

The serpent's head dipped under the waves and surfaced closer to Noa. "May I help you, dear?" she inquired.

Noa tried to ignore the sandal stuck between Beauty's teeth. "What happened to the fishing boat?"

"There was a little incident." The sea serpent's elegant voice rasped in her throat, barely louder than the waves on the shore. Beauty never raised her voice.

"Ah," Noa said. "An incident involving the fishermen and

your stomach? That sort of incident?"

The serpent made a shrugging motion with her huge, horned head. "They were terribly rude men, shouting at dear Renne like that. I'm sure he didn't deserve it."

"I'm sure he did." Noa folded her arms. "Now, because of you, we can't question them. Where do you think they came from? Is anyone living on that island?"

"I'm afraid we didn't exchange pleasantries." Beauty coughed, politely covering her mouth with the end of her tail. Another sandal plopped into the water.

"Well, what can you tell me?"

Beauty seemed to consider the question. Her eyes were the oily all-black of a seal's, except that each one was as large as Noa's head. "The island isn't inhabited. The water doesn't taste of men."

Noa made a frustrated sound. "Then why was that fishing boat here? And for that matter, why didn't Kell see the island before she ran into it? It doesn't add up."

"Fascinating questions," Beauty said. "Forgive the presumption, but could I offer my help in investigating this mystery? I would be happy to circle the island to see if it's harboring any secrets."

"Somehow I don't think Julian would allow that," Noa said coldly. Beauty was magically bound to Astrae—she couldn't travel more than a mile from its shores. Sending her to explore the mysterious island would mean lifting the spell that kept her on a leash—a spell that also prevented her from devouring every living thing on Astrae that came within reach of her jaws. She didn't serve Julian by choice—he had bound her last summer, as punishment for eating three of his sailors. Noa had little doubt that the wily creature spent her every waking moment plotting her escape.

"Dear Julian," the serpent purred. "He does like to keep me close. Thank you for the reminder."

Noa held her black gaze. "You're welcome."

"Take care, dear." Beauty slid back into the waves. "Mind the stairs. They can be slippery."

Shaking her head, Noa climbed the last few steps to the castle. She wished that Julian would send Beauty away, but as he always pointed out, she was the best defense Astrae had. Half the sailors in Xavier's navy would sooner desert than face her. Noa couldn't blame them.

The castle was really more of a ruin, the remnants of a fort built centuries ago by some unknown lord. Julian had patched it up with magic, but it was still a sorry sight, even with his black flag flying from every battlement. Julian's flag had a dragon on it and the family motto, *Marchenas Are Always First.* It sounded dreadfully snobby, and the ancient Marchena kings and queens had probably meant it that way, but Noa's mother had said that, to her, it meant that a Marchena always puts their family first, not that they were better than anyone.

As she reached the front door, she tripped over a cat. She

knew it was a cat because it was invisible, and because there was another cat watching with a satisfied look on its face.

Noa picked herself up, muttering. She wasn't the only one who wished Julian hadn't given the semi-feral cats who roamed Astrae the ability to vanish at will. This was, of course, every cat's fantasy, and they spent most of their time that wasn't occupied with killing defenseless birds in getting underfoot. Julian claimed he had been testing a vanishing spell, though Noa suspected he had done it to spoil them. Julian was the world's biggest cat lover, after Mom. The cats knew this and took advantage of his indulgence as only cats could.

A scruffy tabby with a torn ear hissed as she passed. "Nice to see you, too," Noa said. "You know, in the South Sea, stewed cat is considered a delicacy."

She found Julian in his tower. To Noa's disappointment, Mite was there, too, happily helping herself to the food piled on the table: oysters, tomato salad, and seaweed pancakes. Mite glowered at Noa, then looked down at her plate, which Noa guessed meant she hadn't complained to Julian about Noa's trick. That was one point in Mite's favor, Noa had to acknowledge—she wasn't a tattletale.

Julian's tower room was large and open, the size of several rooms stuck together, which was how he treated it. A huge desk sat in the middle of the space, piled high with maps and sea charts, where Julian met with Captain Kell and her first mate to figure out Astrae's course. Against one wall was the fireplace, more accurately called the lavaplace, for it held an enchanted cauldron filled with bubbling lava that gave off a nice, even heat without all the smoke of a normal fire. And scattered everywhere were books and mysterious buckets full of dirt or coins or seawater—among other things—that Julian used to practice his spellwork. A flight of spiraling stairs led up to a loft where he slept. The round wall was lined with windows, giving an impressive view of the sea and the lay of the island in all directions. Noa could see the magicians down on the beach, and the lurking darkness beneath the water that was Beauty.

"There you are, Noabell," Julian said. "Off plotting and scheming, were you? You have that look."

Noa glowered at the nickname. A noabell was a tiny purple flower that grew in the cracks of dried lava. They were as close to ugly as flowers could get, scraggly and easy to miss if you weren't looking for them, and she used to resent the comparison. But Mom had said once that noabells were tough and grew where nothing else would, so Noa supposed it was a tolerable nickname if you viewed it from that angle.

Julian's chin was propped on one hand in a bored posture, which probably had something to do with the group of sentries standing before him, who must have been in the middle of giving a report. There was a calico curled up in his lap, and he seemed to be in a more cheerful mood, which was lucky for the sentries. One of them, a green-eyed girl about his age, was gazing at Julian in a familiar way. Noa smothered an eye roll.

Julian had grown taller in their two years on Astrae, though he was still too skinny to cut a naturally imposing figure. Yet there had always been something in his posture or the weight of his gaze that said *royalty*, even when he was demonstrating a party trick involving dancing napkins or wearing a particularly silly court hairstyle. Noa had often wished she could work out what this was so she could imitate it. As usual, he was all in black from his cloak to his boots to his flashing rings. Mom had worn black, too, which made her look intimidating, though that hadn't actually been the point. While a powerful magician, their mother was horribly clumsy, prone to spilling drinks (usually raspberry tea) all over herself. Black, she had often said with a wink at her children, was good at covering stains. When Julian had started wearing black, Noa and Mite had followed suit, without any of them discussing it. And so it had become a Marchena trait, like their hair and their crooked teeth.

Julian turned his gaze back to the sentries, and Noa sidled closer to listen. "How many this month?" he said.

"Four, we think," the man replied. "It's hard to know for sure. Our spies tell us there's a chance they've gone into hiding."

Noa knew immediately what they were discussing. It was widely rumored that King Xavier had begun quietly executing known dark magicians throughout Florean, and anyone who protected them—even if they'd never so much as looked at

anybody sideways, let alone gained a reputation for wickedness.

"One of them was only thirteen," the man added quietly.
"Her family's vanished, too."

Noa's heart gave an unsteady *thump-thud*. Julian's hand
briefly clenched the arm of his chair. He seemed to remember
Noa was there, and turned to her with raised eyebrows. "I was
expecting Renne, but I'm guessing he sent you instead, the
coward."

"He was probably worried you'd feed him to Beauty after
that tantrum you threw on the beach," she said. The sentries gave
the sort of chuckle you do when you hope someone is joking.

Julian smiled and waved the sentries out. "I can hear a lecture coming. Deserved, though—this whole thing is my fault.
I shouldn't have ordered Kell to go that fast. I suppose I was a
little excited after we conquered Gray Sisters—"

"About 'this whole thing,'" Noa said before Julian could get
going. He was nearly impossible to keep on track   his mind
flitted from one thing to another like a sparrow. "Don't you
think it's odd that a captain as experienced as Kell would run
into an island?"

"Not really. It's been foggy this morning."

"An island that *isn't on the maps*," Noa added.

Julian frowned at that, then shrugged. "The Untold Sea
is poorly mapped. Pirates don't take kindly to cartographers
poking around their hideouts with notebooks and spyglasses."

Noa forced herself to count to five. "Fine. What were those men doing out here in the middle of nowhere? Why are we so sure they were fishermen?"

"The nets and traps were a bit of a clue." Julian barely looked up from the spell he had been perusing. The calico hopped onto the grimoire. "No, darling, get down." The cat ignored him and folded herself into a passive-aggressive loaf.

"We need to get the island moving again," Noa said emphatically. "Can't you do it?"

Julian took up a different grimoire. "Renne and the others will have us underway in a few hours. Certainly I could do it myself, but it's a big spell, and I'd use up a lot of magic. Magic I'll need to conquer Thirial Island—which I thought we agreed was the priority?"

Noa stewed—it was hard to argue against yourself. Julian had a lot of magic, but like all magicians, big spells drained him.

"What if this is an emergency?" Noa said. "What if we're in danger?"

"From what, precisely?"

"I don't know," Noa said, frustrated. Why couldn't Julian just trust her? "But I have a feeling."

Julian was only half listening. His dark brows were knitted as he bent over the grimoire. Noa imagined the book snapping at his nose like a turtle.

She said sternly, "A *one-eyed pirate* feeling."

Julian's head lifted at that. *One-eyed pirate* meant something

Noa didn't remember, but Julian did. When Noa was a baby, their father, the king, had taken the two of them on a trip to the newly conquered Severo Islands. They had anchored offshore and waited for a boat to come get them, as the harbor was too small for their ship. That boat had been captained by the former ruler of the Severos, a weather-beaten pirate. At the sight of him, Noa had begun crying so loud that even the gulls fled, pounding her tiny fists against her father's chest when he tried to board the boat. The king had laughingly sent the boat back, and they circled the island until they found a bay. They discovered later that the pirate—an accomplished swimmer—had planned to sink the boat far from shore and leave the king, his advisors, and his two children to drown. Julian was still convinced that Noa had sensed the man was a traitor. For her part, Noa doubted it. She knew from having survived Mite's toddler years that small children often went looking for things to make a fuss about.

"Okay, Noa," Julian said. "Bring me some evidence that the island is in danger, and I'll get us moving. Something more than a gaggle of lost fishermen."

Noa tried to think of another argument. At that moment, though, Reckoner ambled into the room and flopped down at Julian's feet, immediately occupying all her brother's attention as he bent to scratch Reckoner's chin and assure him that he was a good dragon. She turned and pointedly stomped to the door. "Take Mite with you," Julian called, to her dismay. "I need to concentrate on this spell."

Noa thought fast. "Isn't she overdue for a magic lesson?"

"We'll have time for that tomorrow. She made progress last time."

"You mean she stopped blowing things up?" Noa said cruelly, because she was mad at them both now.

Mite's jaw fell open, revealing a mouthful of green pancake. "I haven't blown anything up in ages!"

"Of course. The playroom windows must have smashed themselves."

"I don't care what you say." Mite's face was flushed, her gaze hard. "You can't even do magic."

Noa stopped in her tracks. Her anger turned cold, as if her chest had filled with ice. How dare Mite bring that into it? Did she have any idea what it was like to be the sister of the most powerful magician in Florean, and incapable of casting the simplest spell?

No, of course Mite didn't understand. Because she could do magic.

"Mite," Julian admonished. The little girl stared down at her plate. He turned back to Noa, his brow creased with a sympathetic look that Noa didn't want any part of. She left, slamming the door behind her.

3

Mangoes
Lead to Disaster

Noa made it as far as the beach, where she flopped down on the sand. The waves lapped at the tips of her toes and then, a few minutes later, her ankles. She didn't move.

The tortoise sunning itself on the pumice rocks eyed her suspiciously. After a moment of consideration, it shuffled into the sea, as if it could sense her black mood.

There were now half a dozen magicians on the beach. They murmured to the currents, trying to rock the island free, their speech incomprehensible to Noa—the languages of magic could only be understood if you were a magician. To her, the language of Salt, which allowed you to speak to the sea, sounded like gargling bubbles.

She stared moodily at the horizon, which was speckled with tiny red islands only a few yards across. The last time Noa had visited the Untold Sea, Mite had been a runny-nosed toddler trailing at Mom's heels. Julian had been ill the entire trip—Julian had often been ill in those days, pale and small for a boy his age. Sickliness was common among magically gifted children; their power was like a living thing that ate them up from the inside. Noa had curled up beside him in the ship's hold and read to him, adding little details that weren't in the book to make him laugh. Back then, with their mother busy ruling Florean—and with a baby—it had often felt like it was just the two of them. Noa sometimes found herself guiltily missing the days before Julian had mastered his powers and grown strong and healthy.

It wasn't that Julian didn't listen to her. It was more like he didn't *trust* her, not the way he used to. She was just his little sister now—someone to protect, when they used to protect each other. As he became more powerful, Julian seemed to move farther away from her, as if they were on separate Astraes traveling in opposite directions.

Noa played with her bracelet. The charms were all blue whales—Julian had bought it for her after they captured an island with a jewelry shop. She wondered how she would have convinced Mom to listen to her. Mom and Julian were a lot alike, though Julian was flightier than Mom, who had been about as flighty as a bag of rocks. But they had the same laugh, the same twinkle in their eyes, and they looked so much alike that on her sad days, the days Noa missed Mom the most, she found it hard to look at Julian.

Noa sprang to her feet. Several figures were making their

way across the causeway that connected the two islands, one dragging a cart. Julian's soldiers ran to intercept them. There was some gesturing and waving, and then, to Noa's astonishment, the sound of laughter. The soldiers motioned for the strangers to come ashore. They unloaded their cart, accepted a purse from one of the soldiers, and then ambled back across the causeway.

Noa hurried over. "What in the thirteen seas is this?" she demanded, trying to sound coldly foreboding, the way Julian did when he was mad.

The soldiers turned from the sacks they had been hunching over, then snapped to attention. "Princess Noa," said Matias, the closest one. "The villagers have been kind enough to sell us their best mangoes."

He held out one of the sacks, revealing several dozen perfectly ripe fruits. The smell made Noa's mouth water.

She forced her gaze back to Matias. "Villagers? What 'village' did they come from?"

"On the other side of the island," Matias said, gesturing vaguely. "Said they noticed we were stuck and thought we might be hungry. Good thing they didn't see what King Julian did to their fishermen, else they might not have been so hospitable." The soldiers laughed heartily.

Noa pressed her fingers against her eyes. She forced herself to speak slowly and deliberately. "If any normal person saw Astrae on their shores, they'd run in the other direction, not come and give us fruit. People around here know Julian's reputation."

"Maybe they're not normal. One of them did have quite the twitch." He mimicked it, which got everybody laughing again. Clearly, the soldiers didn't have high standards when it came to wit.

"And you didn't bother to ask any questions?" Noa demanded. "What if those mangoes are poisoned?"

"Who'd try to poison King Julian?" one of the men said, looking bemused. Noa's heart sank. Most of the people in Julian's service thought he was invincible. Usually that was a good thing—it made them fiercely loyal, despite Julian's tendency to toss people to Beauty when he lost his temper, or, on one memorable occasion, turn them into a tree. But Noa realized this also made it impossible for them to believe that a group of humble villagers would dream of attacking him.

"There's nothing to fret about, Princess," Matias said mildly. He handed her one of the fruits. "See? They're just mangoes."

The soldiers gathered up the sacks and moved away, leaving Noa alone at the water's edge.

"You want me to do what?" Tomas said.

"Dissect it!" Noa thumped the mango down on the table for emphasis. "What's so confusing about that?"

"The fact that it's a mango," Tomas said, "not a science experiment."

Noa gave him such a glare that the boy hurriedly added, "But I can certainly do my best."

Noa had gone straight to Tomas with the mango. He was a baker, after all—or at least, he was a baker's son, and so should know his way around a suspicious fruit. Astrae's village had few shops, and fewer still that had remained open after Julian turned the island into a traveling lair. While the islanders had supported the old queen, not everyone was thrilled with their new living situation, and some had set sail for more stationary shores. But Tomas's father was a distant cousin of the Marchenas and fiercely loyal to Julian, and wouldn't be likely to leave Astrae even if Julian launched it into the clouds.

"This is dumb," Mite announced. She had met Noa on her way to the village, having been watching her from Julian's tower. Noa should have known Mite would never pass up a visit to the bakery—her mouth was already smeared with sugar from the cookies Tomas's father had plied her with. They were in the kitchen behind the shop, which was clean and cozy, with a clay floor and the black mouth of an oven taking up the entire back wall. It smelled faintly of octopus pie.

Noa ignored her sister. "Well?" she said to Tomas.

He shrugged. He brushed his hair off his forehead, streaking his dark skin with flour. Tomas was usually covered in flour. Only twelve, he'd decided that he was going to be a baker when he grew up, just like his father. He loved cookies and pies and bread so much that Noa suspected he might have flour in his veins, too. "I'll try cutting it up, I guess. See if there's anything strange about it. If not, well, it'll make a nice tart, or a mousse with some lime and chili pepper . . ." Noa folded her arms, and he stopped talking and went to fetch a knife.

Mite let out a long sigh. Noa ignored that, too. She hadn't spoken a word to Mite since leaving Julian's tower.

Tomas peeled the mango and cut it into small pieces, and nothing strange happened. It looked and smelled like an ordinary mango, and in spite of herself, Noa's mouth watered.

"Now what?" he asked.

Noa bit her lip. If the mango was enchanted, there should be some sort of flaw to it—an odd smell, perhaps, or a texture like sawdust. But she noticed nothing.

"Try cooking it, I guess," she said. "Maybe the magic will leach out."

Tomas's face brightened. "Good idea! Have you tried my dad's recipe for fried mango? Pairs beautifully with a nice sourdough."

He tossed the pit into the corner of the kitchen. A white cat winked into view and snatched it up.

"That's just Ghost," Tomas said. "Don't mind him—he eats everything. Here we go." Humming, he lit the stove and plopped the mango into a frying pan with a generous pat of butter. "It's not going to explode, is it?"

Noa sighed, sinking onto a chair. She felt stupid. Maybe Julian had been right not to trust her instincts. Maybe she was just a little girl with an overactive imagination.

"It's probably not going to do anything," she said. "I think I'm wasting your time."

"That's all right." Tomas took up a rag and wiped his hands, only succeeding in smearing more flour on them. "If Julian wants me to cut up—er, dissect—an orchard of mangoes, I'd be happy to help."

Noa winced. Tomas had an enormous crush on Julian, and while she hadn't said this was her brother's idea, she also hadn't said it wasn't.

"The truth is," Noa began, "when I said the island might be in danger—well, Julian doesn't actually agree."

Tomas nodded. Sweet-smelling steam was rising off the pan. "That makes sense. I mean, even if the king's navy is lurking on the other side of that island, Julian could take them. I wouldn't want to watch that." He shuddered, then darted a glance at Noa. "I don't mean that I'm afraid of him. But he's so powerful. And clever. And—"

"Please don't go on," Noa interrupted. She would rather cut off her own ears than listen to another person gush over how handsome or special or charming Julian was. For some reason, they all seemed to think this was something Noa would want to hear, or perhaps some thought she could put in a good word for them. She never did, of course—given how catastrophically Julian's last romance had ended, she hoped he never kissed anyone again. Also, it was gross.

"I guess we'll just go home," Noa said. She headed for the door, but an odd clattering sound froze her in place. One of the heavy trays of bread had overturned, and the loaves lay strewn across the floor.

"Oh no," Tomas moaned. "Dad's going to kill me."

Noa bent to help him gather them up. Mite screamed.

Noa whirled. An ugly row of red cuts bloomed on Mite's leg. Before her crouched Ghost—or something that looked like Ghost. The cat's eyes were all white, and his mouth seemed to have widened and grown extra teeth. As Noa watched in horror, Ghost's hiss deepened into a guttural, unnatural roar. Mite scrambled to get out of the way, but before she could reach Noa's side, the cat lunged.

4

Julian Almost Destroys the Island

Noa seized the nearest large object—a mound of bread dough proofing on the table—and hurled it at the cat. It connected with a wet thump, and the cat toppled over, while the dough fell to the floor with the imprint of a cat's surprised face in it.

"Oh," Tomas breathed, but he wasn't looking at the cat. The pan of mango was emitting a rust-colored steam, which gave off a foul smell. Tomas extinguished the stove and tossed the pot, mango and all, into a sink filled with water. More steam erupted, but now it was clear.

Noa, Mite, and Tomas stared at each other.

"Ghost," Tomas murmured, kneeling at the cat's side. Unconscious, he looked like an ordinary cat again, but Tomas didn't protest when Noa picked him up by the scruff and shut him in a closet.

"I have to get back to the castle," she said. "I have to warn Julian. He'll know how to undo the spell cast on those mangoes—whatever it was, it's definitely dangerous. Tomas, you stay here and look after Mite. Have your father close the shop, and don't let anyone in. By now, who knows how many people the soldiers have given mangoes to."

"I'm not staying here," Mite said, indignant. Noa opened her mouth to argue, but there came a series of shouts in the street outside the bakery, followed by several loud crashes, and then an ominous silence.

Noa swallowed. "All right, let's go. Hurry."

The three of them slipped out the back door. Rather than heading through the village, Noa led them up a narrow path through the hillside. Looking back at the village, she couldn't at first see any signs of trouble, but then the wind stirred and she caught the smell of smoke.

"That's the cobbler's," Tomas said, his face gray. Noa watched as flames spread from the shop at the edge of the village to the shed beside it. People ran helter-skelter along the streets, but she couldn't make out what they were shouting.

"Come on," she said.

The trail eventually petered out, and they had to fight their way through salt grass and prickly pear cacti. Mite, for once, didn't insist on stopping to turn over rocks. Her face was blotchy, and she was blinking rapidly.

"We'll be all right," Noa said awkwardly. She didn't know what to do when Mite was upset, because Mite didn't get upset like other children. She got all quiet or went off and hid somewhere, like a cat with a stomachache. Besides, Julian was usually the one who handled Mite when she was like this, not Noa.

Tomas, meanwhile, was chattering away about magical poisons. He couldn't speak any magical languages himself—most people couldn't, as magic was about as common as left-handedness—but like many Floreans, his parents occasionally bought spells from magicians, or, these days, requested them from Julian.

"My mom's sister had a healing spell go bad once," he said. "Made her see things that weren't there. Maybe this spell is something like that—you know, blood magic gone bad. If so, Julian'll put it right. Isn't blood magic his specialty?"

"Every magical language is his specialty," Noa said. "He's good at healing, but that looked more like magical possession, and I don't know if there's a cure for that."

"There's a lot of smoke," Tomas said, panting now. The hillside was growing steeper, and they had to scrabble forward on hands and knees. "I hope the fire hasn't spread to the harbor."

A chill settled in Noa's stomach. "I don't think it's coming from the village."

They came to the brow of the hill. Before them was the beach and the row of outbuildings that held supplies for the castle, as well as a dock lined with colorful fishing boats and dinghies. Now many of the boats were adrift, and the end of the dock had sunk below the water, with broken boards tumbling in the waves. These were enormous, the breakers reaching at least six feet, pounding at the beach like angry fists, despite the clear sky and still air. Smoke poured from several of the castle windows.

"Where's the island?" Mite asked.

With difficulty, Noa tore her gaze away from the castle. The mysterious island they had run into was gone, leaving no trace that it had ever been. In its place was a neat row of three royal warships, their enormous sails billowing in the wind.

They were flying the flag of King Xavier, and they were heading straight for Astrae.

"No," Noa murmured. Suddenly she was back in her wardrobe again, watching assassins pace toward her bed. She was shivering in the bow of a fishing boat, as home slipped below the horizon. Then she was running, ignoring the cacti that prickled her sandaled feet. She fell once, but was up again quickly, flying down the familiar hillside like a goat. Mite followed close at her heels, while Tomas huffed and stumbled some distance behind them.

The mystery of the waves was quickly resolved. Up to her knees in water near the broken dock stood one of Julian's salt mages, her hands raised as she screamed an incantation at the sea. The more she shouted, the higher the waves grew. The woman—Noa thought her name was Kearin—was drenched, her black hair a wild tangle around her face.

"What are you doing?" Noa shouted over the waves. "Did Julian—"

She faltered when the woman turned around. Her eyes were the same all white the cat's had been, and her lips were drawn back from her teeth in a horrible grin.

Noa shoved Mite behind her. "Go!"

The mage lunged at them, still screaming in Salt, but she didn't get far. A wave crashed over her, and a board from the broken dock struck the back of her head. She went limp, and the retreating wave drew her out to sea.

Mite's eyes were wide with terror. Noa grabbed her hand and dragged her along the beach like a doll, her sandals flinging up clumps of wet sand. Tomas, catching up at last, shouted a warning. A man in a black cloak was racing toward them, and Noa, panicking, turned and wrenched Mite in the other direction.

But it was only Renne, out of breath, his eyes wild but still their usual brown. "You can't be here— Not safe— Half the mages have gone mad—"

"We know," Noa said. "Where's Julian?"

Renne motioned to the castle. "I couldn't get to him. There are a dozen mages in the foyer, attacking anything that moves." Renne ran a hand through his hair. In that moment, he looked much younger than eighteen. "I came looking for reinforcements. Julian—"

"Can handle a dozen mages," Noa cut in. "You need to get the island moving. The king's warships will be within cannon range in minutes."

Renne rubbed his hair again. "I—"

"Find Kell," Noa ordered. "If she's been poisoned, look for one of her mates. The most important thing is to get moving again. Do you understand? Xavier wants to throw us all into confusion, then swoop in and capture us."

It was a mark of Renne's distress that he actually listened to her. "All right. But Princess Noa, you and your sister must hide before—"

His cloak burst into flames. Noa leaped back, but before the flames could engulf him, Renne shouted a command, and a fierce wind put the fire out. Noa whirled. Lurching toward them with jerky strides were two more mages, their eyes white and their mouths stretched into grins. Renne seemed to master himself. He stepped neatly between the mages and the children and barked over his shoulder, "*Run.*"

They ran. Noa led them toward the castle. Though she might have seemed confident before, Noa was worried about Julian. It was entirely possible that he was engrossed in spellwork in his tower, oblivious to the chaos unfolding below. If so, and the corrupted mages took him by surprise—

Noa swallowed. She couldn't let herself think like that. Julian would be fine. He'd found a way to slither out of King

Xavier's schemes to capture him in the past. He'd slither out of this, too.

The three of them dodged around an unconscious mage lying motionless on the beach, the waves licking his feet. On the basalt shelf that jutted out into the sea below the castle, a corrupted mage was confronted by three other mages who seemed to be trying to force her into the sea. Despite their numbers, the uncorrupted mages seemed to be losing. The corrupted mage kept rearranging the stone beneath their feet. As Noa watched, one of them stumbled and fell into the surging water.

Noa, Mite, and Tomas thundered up the winding stair to the castle. Waves crashed against the cliffside, spraying them. Then Noa spotted a familiar black eye winking at her amid the froth.

"Beauty!" she shouted. "The island is under attack!"

"Is it?" The sea serpent lifted her head above the waves. "I hadn't noticed."

Noa dashed the seawater from her eyes. "You have to do something! You're bigger than the king's warships—could you coil around them, or—"

"Oh my." The serpent cocked her head. "You want me to attack the royal fleet? Really, dear, what sort of lady do you think I am?"

"The sort of lady who swamped one of our fishing boats

and swallowed the sailors whole," Noa snapped. "Not to mention all those other ships that went missing in your old hunting grounds. Do you think I'm going to believe someone else was responsible?"

"I think," Beauty said, "that you're the wrong Marchena. You see, only your dear brother can command me. Alas, I don't see him anywhere."

Noa stared. "But you're supposed to protect Astrae! That's— that's the whole *point* of you!"

"The point of me." An uncharacteristically sharp note entered the serpent's elegant voice. "I see. I have endured for over five hundred years, tasted the waters of all thirteen seas, seen the births and deaths of dozens of silly kings and queens who all, at one point or another, sought to destroy me, and will be alive to watch dozens more rise and fall, but now I understand that my entire existence can be reduced to my present servitude at the whims of the Marchenas."

"I'm sorry," Noa said hurriedly. "I didn't mean—"

"Apology accepted, of course," Beauty said in her usual purr. "Now, if you'll excuse me . . ."

"But you can't go!" Mite cried at her retreating head. "The king wants to kill Julian!"

"Oh, I won't go far, little Marchena." Beauty's black eyes gleamed. "I don't intend to miss a moment of this."

Noa grabbed Mite's hand just in time, as Beauty slipped

below the waves and slammed her tail against the staircase with an echoing crash. The stone shook, and Mite almost fell into the sea.

"Forget about her," Noa said grimly. She, Mite, and Tomas reached the top of the stair and flung back the half-open castle doors.

The castle foyer was a grand space, tiled with basalt and studded with obsidian tesserae that made the floor gleam like the night sky. Julian had ordered the cracked and faded walls repainted with bright frescoes—portraits of their royal ancestors; flamingos mincing across shell-strewn sand; killer whales charging through watery depths laced with sunbeams. Upon the huge staircase that anchored the foyer, Julian was in the middle of a battle.

"Duck!" Noa shrieked. She knocked Tomas to the ground just in time—Mite was smart enough to drop right away—and a magician went sailing over their heads, his cloak tangled around his face, out through the doors they had left open. Julian spoke another incantation, and another mage was blasted backward, her all-white eyes wide with fury. She landed in a heap at their feet, and Noa pressed Mite behind her. Julian called out a twisty incantation that reverberated through the hall, and before the corrupted mage could rise, roots made of basalt rose out of the floor and wrapped around her.

Julian's hair was disheveled, as it often was when he

worked on his spells, and his black cloak was inside out, as if he'd hastily pulled it on. With a slash of his arm and a word, he summoned a wave of water from the fountain splashing in the foyer and swept two more magicians out the door. There were still four left, but they hesitated on the landing, watching Julian like wary animals, still grinning their horrible grins. Julian descended toward them, a storm in his eyes.

"Don't hurt them!" Noa shouted. "They're not traitors, they're poisoned!"

Julian broke off whatever incantation he had been casting. With a sharp glance at Noa, he let out a stream of words that sounded to her like wind hissing through a tiny crack. The magicians were lifted into the air—no more than a foot—and drifted back down the stairs. They writhed about and bellowed vicious curses, but it did little good; they were like feathers caught in the breeze, unable to alter their course. Once they were out of Julian's way, he left them hovering just above the ground, thrashing uselessly.

"You have to gag them," Noa said. "They can still use their magic."

Julian spat out a command in Marrow, the language of blood, and the magicians fell silent, though their mouths still moved. He had taken their voices.

Julian knelt before Noa and Mite and swept them into his arms. "Are you all right?" He leaned back and examined them, murmuring a word that healed the cat scratches on Mite's leg. She buried her head in his shoulder and let out an uncharacteristic sob.

For the first time Julian seemed to notice Tomas, hovering awkwardly. "Noa, why have you brought Cornelius's son into this? Timmy, is it?"

"No time to explain," Noa said. "Julian, you have to get Astrae moving again."

"Yes, I was going to," he said. "But not a minute after I looked up from my books and saw Xavier's ships on the horizon, Louise ran in and attacked me. It must be some sort of magical possession—I've heard of spells that can cause an irresistible bloodlust in the victim. Then I heard Tyrone screaming bloody murder downstairs—he was unconscious when I found him, but I stopped them from doing worse. Being knocked on the head might do him some good, the scatterbrained—"

"*Julian*," Noa yelled. Even in a crisis, he was incapable of getting to the point.

"Yes, all right," he huffed. He lifted Mite, who was still clinging to him like an ant on a picnic basket, and hurried up the stairs, Noa and Tomas at his heels.

They passed the floor that housed the magicians—now eerily deserted—and raced up the spiral staircase that led to Julian's tower. Noa ran to the windows, but before she could check whether King Xavier's ships were within firing range, there was a thunderous roar, and the castle shook.

Julian caught himself against the wall. He snatched up one of his books, his expression black. "That was the west turret! The library! Oh, you will pay for that, you traitorous, cowardly—"

There came another thud, and the castle shook again. Two more thuds followed, but these cannonballs struck the cliff-side. Noa felt the reverberations pass through her sandals and into her bones.

She gasped as she caught sight of the king's ships, now massed just beyond Astrae's shoals. "Julian—it looks like they're preparing to launch boats! They're going to board us!"

"No, they aren't." He slammed the book down on a lectern and moved it to the window. "This is going to be a bit com-plicated without Kell at the prow—I have to weave together commands in Salt, Worm, and Eddy. Noa, hand me that bucket of seawater behind the—" He stumbled, letting out a sharp exhalation.

Noa raced to his side. "What's wrong?"

"I don't know." He pressed his hand to his forehead. "I feel—"

He swayed, slamming into the window behind him. Noa followed, but Julian said "*No*" in a voice that stopped her like a wall. His gaze, when he met hers, was oddly bright. His brow was shiny with sweat.

"You didn't—" Noa breathed. Slowly, nausea churning in her stomach, she scanned the room. Her gaze came to rest on the mango on the desk, half-peeled, from which a single bite was missing.

"Noa, take the others and go." Julian's voice was carefully even. "Get as far from the castle as you can. Find Renne—tell him—" He sagged forward.

"Julian," Mite cried. Tears streamed down her face.

"What do we do?" Tomas wrung his hands. "What do we do?"

"We can't leave him." Noa's thoughts were spinning. She saw the frenzied salt mage on the beach, summoning waves to destroy the pier. Julian could do more than destroy the pier—he could destroy them all, and save Xavier the trouble of doing it himself.

"Noa, go," Julian shouted. His eyes were white now, with only the palest hint of blue left in them.

"This is very bad, very, very bad," Tomas chanted.

"Get out." Noa shoved him toward the stairs. "Take Mite and go. I'll try to hold him off."

Tomas gaped. "How are you going to do that?"

Noa had no idea. "I'll figure something out. Mite, no!"

Mite darted toward Julian, her sobs broken and desperate, and Noa had to wrap both arms around her to hold her back.

"Mite, stop," she gasped. "That's not Julian anymore, he doesn't—"

Then two things happened at once. Julian let out a feral cry and lunged at them, and Mite screamed. There was a sound like a dozen cannons going off at once, and Noa was blasted off her feet. Then everything went dark.

5

Noa and Mite
Move the Prow

"Noa." Someone was slapping her face. "Noa, Noa, Noa—"

"Stop, stop, stop," Noa groaned.

Her head was one big ache. Her right arm felt worse—when she lifted her hand, the room briefly darkened again.

She was lying against the tower door. She brushed her face, and her hand came away muddy. Her clothes, too, were a mess of dirt and seawater and bits of singed leaves.

Mite leaned over her, her face wet with tears. Tomas groaned somewhere nearby. Noa clambered to her feet, leaning against the door frame for support. The tower was—well, calling it a ruin would be generous. Most of the windowpanes were smashed, and the spiral stair that led to Julian's bedroom lay on its side. Julian's desk was gone, the desk chair dangling out a window a clue to its final resting place. The cauldron lay on its side—fortunately, it was a warm day, so Julian hadn't melted the hardened lava. Many of Julian's books were in tatters, the wind idly twirling their pages around the tower, and the floor and walls were covered with the wreckage of his experiments: dirt, leaves, coal, seawater, and bits of metal that combined to form the impression of a mudslide that had just buried a village.

"How long was I asleep?" Noa asked.

"Dunno. A few minutes, I guess."

Noa limped to Julian's side. He lay sprawled on his back behind the toppled staircase, his breathing shallow. Blood trickled down the side of his face, making it look like the dragon tattoo had taken a chomp out of him.

"I didn't try to wake him up," Mite said quietly. "He has a big lump on his head."

"Good. Hopefully that'll keep him out for a while." Noa stood, wincing. Her wrist was definitely sprained, if not broken. "What happened?"

"I—" Mite bit her lip. She looked as if she might start crying again. "It was me. I'm sorry. I didn't mean—"

Noa burst out laughing. It turned into a cough—she had dirt stuck in her throat. "Mite. Are you saying you blew up Julian's tower?"

"Yes." Mite sounded miserable. "He's going to be so mad. Look at his books!"

"He won't be mad. Though I'd take an angry Julian over a magically possessed Julian any day." Noa hadn't thought she'd ever be grateful for Mite's habit of accidentally blowing things up when she got upset, any more than you could be grateful to have a volcano for a next-door neighbor, but she had clearly saved them all. Mite was a dark mage, too, and could speak two magical languages. Even more unusually, they were oppositional in nature: Worm, the language of earth, and Spark, the language of fire. This made her volatile, and while Julian had been teaching her to control her powers, he would likely be happy to learn that he hadn't succeeded yet.

Noa patted her awkwardly. "It's going to be all right."

"You said that before," Mite said. "And it wasn't."

"Fine," Noa said, annoyed. "It might be all right, and it might not be. Either way, there's no point moaning about it. Now be quiet and let me think."

Mite nodded. She didn't look in danger of crying anymore. "That sounds more like you."

Noa huffed. Tomas stumbled over, rubbing his head.

"Oh, Tomas!" Noa said. She had forgotten he was there. "Are you all right?"

"I think so," he said, though he sounded a little put out. "I hit my head, but I don't think anything's broken."

"Why are you holding your wrist like that?" Mite asked suddenly.

"Forget about it." Noa pulled off her backpack, but a lash of pain stopped her. "Actually, help me. Please."

Mite opened the backpack and placed the Chronicle in Noa's lap. "What's in there except a bunch of stuff about what the weather was like last month?"

Noa treated her to a dignified silence. She opened the Chronicle, savoring the familiar smell of parchment and iguana leather. Her neatly organized columns and charts soothed her immediately. She pressed it open to today's entry, creasing the pages just the way she liked, then allowed her mind to drift.

She traced the sketch she had drawn of the mysterious island. It had been large—large enough to conceal the king's warships. But it had been an illusion, and illusions were incredibly difficult magic. That made it likely that some of the king's most powerful magicians were on those ships. But the poison in the mangoes was so dangerous that it was a risk to have them transported with such important people. If the mangoes burst or exploded, which could happen when ordinary objects were imbued with magic, they could have infected Xavier's soldiers. Noa's thoughts drifted to the bakery, and the strange steam the mango had given off, which had turned clear the moment it was immersed in water.

"Bring me some water," Noa said.

Mite looked around. "There might be some left in one of those buckets."

"Not seawater. Get some from the tap."

Mite didn't ask questions. She dashed into Julian's bathroom and returned with a half-full cup. "Is this enough?"

"Let's hope so." Noa knelt next to Julian. Summoning her courage, she threw the water in his face.

He hissed something in a voice that wasn't his own, and his body twitched. Then he let out an odd sort of sigh, and was still again.

Noa gingerly pushed back one of his eyelids. A twilight-blue eye stared sightlessly back at her.

Mite let out a cry. She sat on his chest and began patting his cheeks hard enough to make his head loll back and forth. "Julian! Julian!"

"Don't you start that." Noa drew her off. "He's hurt worse than I was. He needs a blood mage."

Tomas gaped at her. "How did you know what to do?"

"It's obvious," Noa said, trying to sound nonchalant as her insides danced with relief. "The poison in those mangoes is so dangerous that King Xavier would have wanted the antidote to be easily available, just in case someone on his side accidentally came in contact with it. He wouldn't care that we might figure it out, because he didn't need the poison to be foolproof—he just needed it to infect enough of us to distract Julian and make us all run amok for an hour or two. Then he'd march in with his soldiers and take control. Speaking of which—" Noa darted to the window. "The king's boats have almost reached the beach. The waves keep pushing them back—maybe one of the salt mages is at it again."

Mite leaped to her feet, her eyes shining. "We can cure the others!"

"We need to get to the prow before we worry about curing

anybody," Noa said. "We have to get the island moving. Come on."

She turned and almost ran into Tomas, who was still staring at her. "How did you figure all that out?" he demanded, a note of helplessness in his voice.

"Noa always figures things out," Mite said in exasperation, as if it was the most obvious thing in the world.

"Stay here and look after Julian, all right?" Noa said to Tomas. "Lock the door and don't let anyone in until we get back or he wakes up."

They ran out, leaving Tomas staring after them.

Ten minutes later, they were clanking and sloshing along the path behind the castle.

"Hurry up," Noa called over her shoulder.

Mite's face was a brilliant red. "They're heavy!"

"Dump out some water, then."

They had stopped in the kitchen on their way out of the castle, grabbing the first things they saw that could hold water and filling them to the brim. Consequently, Noa held a stewpot with her uninjured hand, while Mite had two saucepans, one under each arm, and a cookie tin that was already half-empty, given that she had forgotten the lid.

Panting under the weight of the brimming pot, Noa was beginning to regret her idea. It was hot, and a bead of sweat trickled down her back. They hadn't encountered any corrupted mages so far, and the pots and pans were certainly slowing them down.

No sooner had she had that thought, though, than she heard a twig snap in the brush. She whirled and caught sight of a malevolent, grinning face. She barely had time to recognize Kell's first mate, Eron, before he lunged at her.

"Look out!" Mite shouted. She ran in front of Noa, flinging the contents of one of the saucepans in the man's face. Eron fell back as if he'd been struck with a bat, then sat down heavily. The color returned to his eyes, but he seemed dazed, swaying in place.

They didn't have time to make sure he was all right, so they ran on, water sloshing. When finally they reached the prow, Noa's left arm was aching almost as much as her injured wrist.

The prow of Astrae was composed of a wheel scavenged from an old pirate ship and a plain wooden box that Kell liked to sit on when she steered. There was also a pole from which hung a scrap of fabric that could have been a bedsheet, but was actually an old piece of sailcloth. That was it. The prow was currently on a hill at the north end of the island, but depending on their course and the direction of the wind, Kell sometimes moved it to another spot.

Noa looked up at the furled mast. The sailcloth was still as stone, despite the breeze brushing the hillside. Both mast and wheel were enchanted, of course, but there was one problem:

the island had to be moving in order for them to control it. Usually, Julian kept Astrae moving constantly, even when they docked somewhere, though then the island moved so slowly that it was almost imperceptible. But if Astrae ever came to a dead stop—if, for example, it ran into another island—the prow became useless. The fact that Astrae wasn't stuck anymore didn't matter. Julian called it a safety measure—if he needed to leave the island, or was ever captured, he could simply bring Astrae to a halt, and nobody else could take control of it.

Noa chewed her lip. Without Julian, how on earth were they going to move the island?

Cannons boomed in the distance, nearly a dozen shots this time, and Noa winced. She didn't want to think about the state of the castle. She tapped on the wheel, squinting up at the mast.

The sailcloth twitched.

Noa's jaw dropped. "Mite," she said, trying to stay calm, "look at the mast. Tell me I'm not imagining things."

Mite had been watching her with an expectant look tinged with impatience. She obediently turned her face to the mast. "What?"

Noa's heart fluttered. "I think the king's cannons may be moving the island! Only a little, but it might be enough—"

Voices behind them on the path. Mite spun around, her remaining saucepan held high.

"Mite, I don't think—"

The owners of the voices rounded the corner. Two men and a woman, resplendent in red tunics and bronze breastplates—King Xavier's colors—each with a sword held loosely in their hands.

Noa swallowed. Astrae had been boarded.

"Hey, kiddos," one of the king's soldiers said, and began to lower his sword. "Don't be afraid, we're—"

But Mite, possibly too emboldened after her earlier success with Eron, yelled "Yah!" and flung the water from the remaining saucepan in his face.

The soldier stopped in his tracks, sputtering. He drew a hand across his face. "Black seas! What in—"

"Run!" Noa shouted. She dropped the stewpot, which sent up a geyser that drenched her legs, and hooked the wheel with her arm. It was mounted on a post driven into the earth, which came free with a spray of dirt when she yanked on it. She pulled up the mast and tossed it to Mite.

Mite threw her empty saucepan at the man, which went wide. Frightened by her own courage, she let out a squeak and dashed after Noa, the ratty sailcloth flapping behind her.

The soldiers' voices drifted down the hillside as they ran. "Come on," the wet man said, sheathing his sword.

"Ah, let them go," the woman said.

"They know about the antidote," he hissed. "They must. Why else—"

"Those two? They're just kids, Ryland," the other man

said. "You could use a bath, anyway."

"What was that stuff they ran off with?" the woman said.

"Dunno. Looked like what you'd find in a scrap heap." There was a clang as the man kicked the abandoned stewpot. "No surprise the poor brats trapped on the Dark Lord's nightmare island don't have much to occupy them. . . ."

They reached a grove of trees, and the voices faded. Noa had no idea where they were going. The pathless bracken was rough against her bare legs, and also, inconveniently, it seemed to be a favored gathering place for iguanas. Noa began to feel like she was doing more hopping than running.

Finally, once her panic wore off, she made a beeline for the nearest hill. They were almost at the coast again, and to the south stood a row of basalt sea cliffs.

"Here," Noa gasped when finally they reached a patch of elevated ground that was relatively clear of lizards. Below them, a tangle of mangroves spilled into the sea.

Ignoring the stitch in her side and the black dots swimming across her eyes, Noa grabbed a rock and drove the wheel into the earth. She took the mast from Mite, who had been ineffectively banging it against the ground, and twisted it around until it stuck.

"All right," Noa said to the island grimly, taking the wheel. "Let's see if you have any life in you. Raise the sail, Mite."

Mite's hands moved to the rigging. Then she froze, her gaze fixed on something beyond Noa's shoulder.

Noa turned. Atop the nearest sea cliff, perhaps fifty yards away, stood Gabriela, Xavier's First Mage. Her long blue-black hair billowed in the breeze, as did the red cloak pinned with a golden star like a crossed X—the king's symbol. It winked in the light.

She was looking right at them.

Noa's heart thudded. She hadn't seen Gabriela in a year, since the day Julian had discovered that the talented apprentice who had snuck onto his island—and into his trust—claiming to be a supporter was in fact one of King Xavier's mages, and a spy. She'd been a spy from the very beginning, and if she'd ever returned Julian's feelings for her, she hadn't let it get in the way of her mission. Gabriela had spent five months on Astrae, all the while sending regular reports to Xavier about the island's defenses, Julian's followers, and everything he was planning. Everyone had expected Julian to kill her when he found out, but for some reason, he hadn't. Instead, he'd stranded her on Cortes Island, part of a remote chain barren of everything but black rocks and penguins. Somehow, she had survived, and King Xavier had rewarded her betrayal by promoting her to First Mage.

Gabriela's arms were folded, one hand resting lightly against her chin. In her red cloak, she was like a wound in the blue-gray sky. Her beautiful face was thoughtful, which Noa took as a bad sign. Though only seventeen, Gabriela looked years older, her face aged and scarred by a childhood lived on a fishing boat in often harsh conditions. She had been truthful to them about that part of her past, at least, but almost everything else she'd told them had been a lie.

Noa's face grew hot. Like most people on the island, she had liked Gabriela. But Gabriela had betrayed Julian to Xavier. Now she had attacked Astrae. Noa wished Julian had killed her.

Gabriela seemed to notice Noa's expression. Slowly, she raised a hand, but whether in warning or greeting, Noa didn't know. Gabriela knew how the prow worked, but Noa doubted she knew that the king's cannons had nudged the island into motion. Otherwise, she would surely have stopped them already. Gabriela wasn't a dark magician, but she was so good at Salt spells that she was widely considered the most dangerous mage alive, after Julian.

"Mite," Noa growled.

Mite raised the sail with shaking hands. In the same moment, a group of black-clad mages charged over the hill—Julian's mages, led by Renne. He must have rallied everyone uncorrupted to his side—now they were trying to retake the island.

Gabriela noticed their approach. She made a lazy gesture that reminded Noa of Julian, her lips moving in an incantation Noa couldn't hear, and a wave leaped up and flooded the ground between her and the mages. One of the mages was washed away. A salt mage shouted an incantation, and a wave surged up the side of the cliff. Gabriela whipped around, holding up both hands, and barely managed to force the wave back before it closed over her head.

"Noa, look!" Mite cried. The sail was stirring in the wind—faintly at first, but then it opened fully, and the island gave a lurch.

Several of the mages stumbled and fell. Gabriela swayed, but caught her balance. Noa whooped, throwing her weight against the wheel. The island gave another lurch, and then it began to turn.

The mages were closing on Gabriela now. Her gaze flicked from them to Noa and Mite, her expression unreadable. Then, dashing her hair gracefully from her eyes, she turned and dove off the cliff.

Noa and Mite ran to the edge of the hill. But Gabriela had already vanished beneath the waves, with only a slight ripple in the water to mark her passage.

6

Julian Discovers
the Lost Words

King Xavier tried to follow them, of course.

At first, it seemed like he might catch up. His cannons continued to bombard the island, though most of the missiles fell upon the beach. The captains of the ships put in a heroic effort, the ships' vast crimson sails puffing out like frigate birds, but nothing could catch Astrae when it got going. The island had the added advantage of being invisible if viewed from behind (meaning whatever direction it was moving away from), so the captains were basically chasing a ghost. They didn't have a chance.

Because it didn't matter which way they went, as long as it was away from the king, Noa let out the sail and kept Astrae running downwind. She had watched Kell sail the island so many times that she didn't even need to refer to her notes in the Chronicle. If the sail was properly trimmed, Astrae could outrun any ship in the royal fleet. It took only a few minutes for the warships to fade into the ocean mist. Islets whipped past alarmingly fast, and the wind was fierce enough to make Noa's eyes water. Astrae vibrated a little but otherwise settled into the galloping pace like a well-trained racehorse.

Noa found out later that only one of the boats had made it ashore. Still, the twenty or so soldiers on board, including several mages, managed to come close to seizing control of the island. They had easily subdued the frenzied, corrupted mages on the beach, then broke into search parties to track down Julian and his council. Noa and Mite had met one of those parties. Another had entered the castle unopposed and made immediately for Julian's tower. Poor Tomas had been so unnerved by their pounding on the door that he had hidden in the bathroom. Fortunately, though, an old spell Julian had placed on the tower door, barring uninvited entry to anyone not of Marchena blood, had kept them out until he woke up. Once that happened, of course, the invasion was over. Julian had ordered Beauty to capsize all the rowboats still in the water, and Noa doubted that many of those soldiers had managed to swim to safety.

Noa spent much of the next day writing in the Chronicle. She sat on the beach in the shade of a barnacly boulder, trying to ignore the racket the earth mages made as they shifted soil and stone to repair the castle staircase, which had fared the worst in the attack. Miraculously, Julian's tower had taken only a few glancing blows. Mite had done more damage to it than the king's warships had.

Noa turned to a fresh page, adjusting the tortoise shell she was using for a desk, which worked surprisingly well. In addition to recording yesterday's events in meticulous detail, she had also made note of everything they knew about what she had decided to call the White Fever—symptoms, incubation time, and so on—and the poison that had caused it, in case Xavier ever tried something like that again. She had also drafted a list of safety precautions, including hiring official food tasters. She knew from experience that Julian would roll his eyes at something as sensible as precautions, but she intended to bug him until he listened.

Noa took another bite of lemon-lime cake. It was possibly the most delicious thing she had ever eaten, crisp on the outside and bursting with sour custard that tasted like sunbeams. Tomas's father had been sending an endless stream of cakes to the castle as a thank-you for looking after his son. Julian had already sent a messenger to plead with him to stop, as the kitchen cupboards would soon be overflowing, but the man seemed impossible to put off. Noa and Mite didn't mind.

Noa took a break from writing to flex her stiff fingers. The tide was returning, waves lapping against left-behind shells and little pools of crabs and anemones. Gulls squabbled over a dead fish, and the wind brought the taste of rain to Noa's lips.

A volcano huffed and puffed in the distance, shrouded in a cloud of steam.

Noa went back to the Chronicle, but her skin was crawling. Something had changed. She looked again, casually, and she figured it out. The water close to shore had darkened, as if a thick shadow had fallen across it. Every few seconds, the shadow would undulate back and forth.

"Hello, Beauty," she called, trying to keep the nervousness from her voice.

The serpent lifted her head above the water. She was so close to shore that the waves broke against the back of her head. "Hello, dear. I hope I didn't startle you."

"Not at all," Noa said. "But I believe Julian warned you against creeping up on people. It's not exactly polite, is it?"

"You're mistaken, little Marchena," Beauty purred. "I was merely taking a nap. I didn't even see you there."

"Of course." Noa nodded, as if she didn't know that Beauty's favorite game was getting as close to someone as she could—especially nervous young sailors newly recruited to Julian's service—and then lunging out of the water with her huge jaws snapping inches from their head. "I'm sorry to wake you."

"Oh my, that's all right," Beauty said. "Do you know, I was having a dream about you. Dear Julian was there, too." She licked her lips with her black tongue. "It was a very good dream."

"It's not good to go to bed hungry," Noa said coolly. "Though I would have thought you were full after feasting on all those soldiers yesterday."

"It takes a lot to satisfy me, child." She sniffed the air. Her huge body made the beach look small. "Dear me, what is that delicious smell?"

Noa unwrapped the half-eaten cake. "This?"

Beauty's black gaze sharpened. "My, yes . . . Would you be so kind as to allow me a bite?"

"Be my guest." Noa didn't think she'd be able to eat with Beauty staring at her, anyway. She tossed the cake in the air, and the serpent caught it neatly on her tongue.

"Mmm," Beauty groaned. "Delicious!"

"I thought you only ate people."

Beauty gave a polite little laugh. "Oh, no. Actually, I don't really care for the taste."

"I'm not sure what's worse," Noa said. "Eating people because you like it, or eating them even though you don't."

"Your brother doesn't seem to object either way."

Noa looked away, and Beauty let out a low hiss of amusement. The truth was, while Noa and Julian's mission to retake Florean hadn't been much harmed by the mango attack, Noa's secret mission had experienced a setback. She'd been able to convince Julian to set the soldiers they'd captured free, but it hadn't been easy. He'd been all for tossing them to Beauty, or leaving them to starve on some barren rock. Seeing Noa and Mite in danger seemed to have hardened something inside him, and Noa could tell that he'd only given in because he was tired of arguing with her, not because he saw the point in being merciful to soldiers who, after all, were only following their king's orders.

Noa tapped the Chronicle. She had to stop Julian from doing wicked things; it didn't count if he simply refrained from wickedness when she was around.

"What's all this?" Captain Kell stomped into view, Renne at her side. Kell's silver hair caught the sunlight like a beacon as her gaze moved from the massive serpent to Noa, insect-sized in comparison, sitting only feet from Beauty's jaws. "Is this old snake bothering you, girl? If so, I'll give her reason to regret it." Her hand went to her sword.

Beauty paid Kell no attention. But then, she usually ignored everyone except the Marchena siblings.

"Let me know if you'd like to chat again, dear." Beauty licked her lips, spattering the Chronicle with spit. "Particularly if you have cake." Then, in an uncannily quick motion, she shot back out into the deep.

"It's fine," Noa told Kell, shaking off the Chronicle. "We were just talking. I gave her a piece of cake."

"Cake?" Renne repeated, blinking.

"Yes. Apparently sea serpents can't get enough of it."

Kell shook her head, her sun-darkened face creased with a frown. She looked halfway presentable, her wild silver hair tied back and her clothes relatively free of holes, which meant she must've just come from a meeting at the castle. Normally, Kell looked exactly like the ex-pirate she was—which is to say, like she'd just been rescued after a month on a deserted island, possibly with a tsunami thrown in somewhere. "What have I said about talking to that creature? You can't get pearls from an anemone. D'you know how many ships I've seen sunk by serpents, torn right in two with all hands lost? Leave her be, child. She's the king's folly and nothing to do with you."

Noa didn't bother to mention that it was Beauty who hadn't left *her* be. "I hope you don't mind that we moved the prow."

"Not one bit!" Kell's warm brown eyes grinned down at her. "Nice to have a change of scenery once in a while. Though I must point out, the spot you chose is lousy with lizards. Not a moment goes by without one running over my toes, which are fearsome ticklish. . . . Speaking of the prow, I've got you down for a shift tomorrow night. Up to it?"

"Oh, yes," Noa said with a stab of excitement. Taking a shift at the prow mostly just involved sitting around and making sure no storms blew the island off course. Still, Noa loved it. There was nothing like sitting at the wheel as the stars gleamed above you and Astrae glided through the sea like a ghost, knowing you had an entire island at your command.

"Thought I could teach you some mariner's knots, too. You proved yesterday you've got a knack for sailing. Where would we have been without you?"

Noa didn't think mariner's knots would come in handy on Astrae—after all, the only bits of ship the island had were the mast and the wheel—but she agreed readily. You never knew when something like that would come in handy. Noa was of the opinion that it made good strategic sense to collect as many skills as possible.

Reckoner limped into view, belly swinging from side to side. The old dragon sat down heavily and sniffed Noa's pockets. Finding them empty, he heaved an enormous snort, as if resigning himself to the injustice of the world, and slouched off to the grass to take a nap.

Reckoner's appearance was a sign that Julian was nearby, and sure enough, there soon came the sound of his light footsteps on the path. Kell and Renne bowed, murmuring, "Your Highness," and left them.

Julian settled himself gracefully on the beach beside Noa, unclasping his black cloak to use as a blanket. He had healed his injuries, but his eyes were shadowed from little sleep. Like most of his magicians, he'd been up all night, searching for mages and villagers who were still corrupted and assessing the damage wrought by the king's attack.

"Where's Mite?" Noa said.

"We just finished today's lesson. I made her take a nap, though she insisted she wasn't tired. She fell asleep halfway through the first sentence."

Noa snorted. Mite refused to sleep unless Julian read her

a story first. The last time he went away, she had refused to go to bed at all, and had driven her nursemaid to distraction by leading her on a chase through the castle, which had only ended when Mite fell into an exhausted slumber in one of the kitchen cabinets.

Noa didn't often get Julian all to herself these days—at least, Julian undistracted by his books and maps and experiments. She wasn't going to waste the opportunity, so she arranged her arguments in her head like soldiers. "I have some ideas—"

"Yes, I know you do," he said, regarding her with amused exasperation.

Noa hadn't expected this. "You . . . do?"

"You're like the sun, my Noabell. I know that it will rise in the east and set in the west, just as I know that you've already hatched a hundred plots and schemes to prevent another near-disaster like yesterday's. And you will badger me until I agree to all of them. Your arguments are unnecessary. That's why I came to talk to you."

Noa's surprise was slowly giving way to suspicion. "Is it."

"You don't have to look at me like that. What, do you think I came here to give you a lecture? After what you did yesterday?" Julian rubbed his head. "You saved us all. You saved *me* from—" A shadow crossed his face. "I won't ever forgive myself for how close I came to hurting you two."

"That's nonsense," Noa said huffily. "You weren't *you*."

Julian shook his head mournfully, and Noa knew that he was going to blame himself no matter what she said, which was melodramatic and thus entirely like him.

"And worse," Julian went on, "you were right about those fishermen. You tried to warn me, and I ignored you."

"Sorry, what was that?"

"I said I ignored you."

"No, the first part," Noa said. "Say that again."

Julian made a sound halfway between a sigh and a laugh. He placed his hand over his heart and made his blue eyes wide and tragically earnest. "You were right. You were right. You were right."

Noa leaned back on her hands, grinning. "You can go on."

His mouth quirked, but then his face grew uncharacteristically serious. "I need your advice on something," he said. "Something of a strategic nature. One of the mages we captured during the attack has confessed Xavier's plans."

Noa's jaw dropped. She snapped the Chronicle shut and gave Julian her full attention. "What plans?"

"Well, for one, he isn't just going after dark mages anymore." Julian looked at her for a moment, seeming to weigh something in his head before continuing. "He's sending out assassins across Florean to quietly kill other kinds of mages, and to make it look accidental. Not just the mages, either, but their families—you know how magic often runs in families."

Noa felt faint. "Why?"

"You know why. Xavier hates magic. Or rather, he hates that he doesn't have any."

Noa knew how that felt. "But how can he do that? His mages won't stay loyal to him if they find out what he's doing."

"Some of them already know what he's doing," Julian said. "They're still loyal."

Noa shook her head slowly. "That doesn't make any sense. They can see what he's doing to people like them, and yet they still follow him?"

"No, it doesn't make sense," Julian agreed. "But people don't always make sense. I'd guess there are two reasons his mages stick with him. One, it makes the mages he *doesn't* kill more powerful as their gifts become more rare. And two, they think that as long as they're fiercely loyal to Xavier, he won't come for them." Julian shook his head. "But he will. If he has his way, there won't be any mages left in Florean in ten years."

Noa shuddered. She thought of the assassins who had slipped into her bedroom at night. *We'll find the little one first.* She thought of other families, other children asleep in their beds. In her head, they all looked like Mite, down to the chocolate smeared on their chins. She heard the soft murmur of the assassins' voices, saw the light of a lavastick glint off the edge of a knife. She squeezed her fists around the sand.

"There's more, isn't there?" she said, reading Julian's expression.

Julian nodded. "The mage also told me that Xavier's looking for the Lost Words. Do you know that myth?"

Noa frowned. She knew more about magic than most non-magical people—she'd grown up surrounded by magicians, after all, and as a habit, she paid attention to things. "Something about long-lost spells, right?"

"More than that," Julian said. "The Lost Words are magical languages that disappeared a long time ago. As you know, there are nine magical languages. Briar, Worm, Gleam, Salt, Marrow, Eddy, Squall, Spark, and Hum. Each named for a different power. Plants and harvests. Rock and soil. Metal of all kinds. The thirteen seas. Healing. Air. Weather. Fire. And finally, light. Some mages believe there were once more than nine languages. That there were other powers that the ancient mages decided were too dangerous for anyone to wield. So they bound them and scattered them across Florean, concealing them with magic on various uninhabited isles."

"You're saying King Xavier is searching for a myth?" Noa frowned. "That doesn't sound like him. He's too smart to waste time chasing fairy tales."

"What if he learned one of the fairy tales was true?" Julian said. "The story of the Lost Words makes sense. Why can mages command the sea, but not the rivers and streams? Why can I summon light, but not darkness?"

"Um, because you can't do everything?" Noa said. "Maybe?

Besides, I don't understand why Xavier would want to unleash any more magic on Florean. If he hates magic, why doesn't he hate the idea of the Lost Words?"

Julian gave a short laugh. "He does. But you'd be surprised how people can learn to love what they hate if it will bring them power." His expression grew thoughtful. "You said it yourself—Xavier's smart. He doesn't waste time on wild-goose chases. If he truly thinks he's found a weapon that he could use to defeat me, he'll go after it. The mage said he found some ancient maps buried in the archives at the royal library, which gave him the approximate locations of two lost magical languages."

Noa chewed her lip, mulling it over. "Is that why he risked attacking us with those mangoes? Because he thinks we've figured out he's looking for them, so we're looking now, too?"

Julian blinked. "I— Yes. That's what the mage told us. Apparently Astrae came close to the location of one of the lost languages—at least, where Xavier believes it to be—a week ago. It was a coincidence, of course. How did you know?"

Noa shrugged. "It's an obvious guess. If he really wants these Lost Words so bad, he'd be terrified of us getting them first. You said they were a weapon. What did you mean?"

"According to the stories, the ancient mages trapped the Lost Words in books," Julian said. "One of the mages who could speak the language they wanted to bind would fill the book with all the words in that language, and trap them in it."

"Like a dictionary," Noa murmured. "Well, an evil dictionary. One that doesn't teach people words, it takes them away."

"I suppose. Anyway, according to the stories, all a mage has to do is read the book, and that mage will gain its power. They have to be born with the ability to speak the language, just like any other, of course."

Julian absently pushed sand into a tower. "So. If Xavier gets his hands on the Lost Words, he can pass the books around to his mages and acolytes until he finds one who can read it. And then—"

"Then he has access to a power we don't." Noa's mouth was dry. "A power we won't even know exists until he uses it against us."

Julian knocked over the tower of sand. "You can see why I came to you. We need to figure out what to do about this."

Noa's heart was pounding. "What's to figure out? We need to get our hands on those books before Xavier does." She pictured Xavier's mages wrapping Astrae in a cloud of darkness, or stealing the water from every well. Julian and his mages couldn't fight a power they didn't possess—they couldn't even protect themselves from it, because they didn't know what form it would take.

If King Xavier found just one of those books, he could destroy Astrae—and Julian.

But there was more. Noa's brain riffled through the possibilities. "Julian, you'll be able to speak those languages."

He frowned. "I don't see—"

"Don't you? You can speak all the others. It's likely, at least, that you can speak the forgotten ones, too—if we can find them first." Her words tumbled out in her excitement.

Julian's eyes glimmered with speculation, and Noa felt a prickle of unease. If Xavier found the Lost Words, it would be the end of them. But if Julian found them, he could win the war.

And yet, said a little voice at the back of her mind, Julian was already powerful enough. What would he become if he found the Lost Words?

"You're right, of course," Julian said. "The only problem is convincing the council. Most people think the Lost Words are a myth, if they've heard of them at all. They'll want me to continue with our current plan, capturing Thirial Island."

Noa shook her head. "You have to tell them that this is too important. If these Lost Words are just a myth, we've wasted a few weeks searching. If they're real, we'll lose this war—or win it."

"You can tell them yourself," Julian said with a smile.

Noa blinked. "What?"

"I want you to join the council. I need to listen to you more often, Noa—and so do my advisors."

Noa stuck her finger in her ear, as if to clear it.

Julian waved a ringed hand. "Yes, yes. I know you've asked once or twice—"

"Once or twice!" Noa cried. "I ask you to put me on the council every week. You always say no!"

"Maybe I would be more inclined to say yes if you didn't lurk outside the window every time we meet," Julian retorted. "I'd move the meetings to the tower, but I'm worried you'd try climbing up the side of the castle."

"I don't 'lurk,'" Noa said. "I'm not a thief. I just happen to be nearby sometimes."

"Yes, scratching away in your Chronicle so loudly you'd think we'd been invaded by termites."

Noa folded her arms. "I have to take notes. Have you even read your secretary's? He includes everything that isn't important and leaves out most of what is."

Julian massaged the bridge of his nose. "Noa, Noa, Noa. Do you want to be on the council or not?"

Noa's stomach fluttered. She could hardly believe what Julian was offering. A chance to be listened to, to have Julian's chief advisors—many of whom had as much common sense as he did—consider her ideas and evidence and all the plans she had tucked away at the back of her brain for taking Florean away from King Xavier one island at a time. A chance to be *helpful*, rather than left to roam the island with Mite or to have lessons with whatever stammering teacher Julian had abducted for them that month. Not only that, but she'd be able to keep a closer eye on Julian, which could only help her secret mission.

"I accept," she said in a dignified voice. "And as my first piece of advice as royal councillor, you should move the meetings to a different room. The current one's too easy to spy on."

Julian groaned.

7

Mite Goes on a Secret Mission of Her Own

A fierce wind blew across the island as it sailed north, lifting the salt spray from the waves and scattering it over the grasses and cacti. Waves hurled themselves against the shore, so large and glittery green that Mite's knees trembled. She hopped from rock to rock, pausing to examine a big piece of driftwood for woodbugs. She found a line of them marching purposefully from one hole to another, where there was a nest of tiny eggs.

Julian thought she was asleep, but Mite had only been pretending. She had something important to do, and she knew that Julian wouldn't let her leave the castle without Noa, and also that Noa wouldn't want to go with her. Mite didn't mind hiking across the island with Noa while she took notes in her Chronicle, but she wished that sometimes Noa would want to do what *she* wanted to do.

"You have so many babies," she told the woodbugs. "Can I borrow some? I'll bring them back when they're grown."

The woodbugs didn't seem to mind. March, march, march went their many legs. Like her, they were clearly in the middle of something important. Carefully, Mite took a blade of grass and scooped a few of the eggs into a jar, which she placed in her pocket. She scurried off over the rock, her black cloak billowing behind her.

The waves were so large that they splashed her no matter how she tried to avoid them, and Mite almost lost her nerve. She kept close to the cliff and pretended that Noa was with her.

It was low tide, and a little beach of black basalt was exposed beneath the sea cliffs. This was where one of the mages said he had seen the spider.

Mite shivered with excitement. She had never seen a braided spider before—they were almost extinct in Florean. People had trapped them and hunted them until they were gone, because they were poisonous. Mite didn't think this was fair. Spiders only bit when they were scared, which was something Mite could understand—after all, when she was scared, she exploded. So when she heard Julian order the mage to set traps along the cliffs, she knew she needed to go on a rescue mission.

"Hello! Coming through!" she called to warn the beach fleas to get out of the way. After a while, her stomach began to rumble, and she thought longingly of the licorice cakes back at the castle. She wondered if Anna, the cook, would let her have another before dinner. She'd only had five today.

Finally, she found the traps. After examining two empty ones and a third that held only a confused gray spider, which she set free, Mite's luck turned.

Hunched in the back of the fourth trap over the body of a dead mouse, the braided spider was bigger than any spider Mite had ever seen, so big she wasn't sure it would fit into the other jar she had brought with her. Fortunately, she had also brought along bait in the form of dead flies, and the spider darted into the jar to feast on them, neatly folding its legs inside. Mite twisted the lid on.

Now that she had found the spider, though, she wasn't sure what to do with it. A storm was coming, and she didn't have time to take it to the other side of the island where the mages wouldn't find it. She would have to keep it in her room for now. The spider ran one long leg slowly along the glass, as if testing for weaknesses.

Mite's stomach gave another grumble. She tucked the jar in her bag, then scrambled back the way she had come, her thoughts full of licorice cakes.

Mite didn't get her cake. By the time she got back to the castle, someone had noticed she was missing and told Julian. She met some mages who had been sent out to find her, and behind them was Julian, frowning and serious, and she had almost cried. But he just drew her into a hug and told her not to wander off again without telling him.

That night, Mite waited in bed, her stomach in knots. Was Julian mad at her? Would he not want to read her a story? She couldn't sleep if he didn't. He had read to her every night since Momma died. Mite's memories about her death were jumbled—she had only been five, after all, which was practically a baby. But she did remember that Julian had read her a story that night, because Momma always did, and that he kept turning away to wipe his eyes.

She leaned over to check on the spider under the bed. Once she'd made it back to her room, she had transferred the spider into a larger jar, which hadn't been easy. As soon as the spider tasted fresh air, it made a getaway, its many legs ping-pinging against the glass. But Mite knew how spiders thought, and had the other jar ready, so the spider merely ran from one prison into another.

"I'm sorry I can't let you out," Mite said regretfully. She usually let her spiders roam free, but given the braided spider's size, she suspected it would eat the others. "But you're my honored guest, so I'm going to take care of you for as long as you're here."

Mite didn't know what *honored* meant, but it sounded welcoming. The spider hulked against the back of the jar, perfectly still. Now that she was able to look at it properly, Mite was impressed by the spider's beauty. It had a red spot on its back, which gazed up at Mite like another eye.

"We'll have to think of a name for you," Mite said. She always named her pets, though given that she had so many, she sometimes forgot what their names were. "How about Patience? That's the name of the dog in my favorite story."

When finally Mite heard Julian's footsteps outside her door, she felt a surge of relief. She shoved Patience back under the bed.

Reckoner came in first, snuffling at the floor. Being nearly blind, he made his way mostly by smell. He flopped onto his usual spot on the woven rug, where every night he left a patch of dragon drool. Mite scratched his head. She liked Reckoner. She was glad Julian hadn't chosen a scary dragon for his familiar. There had been other dragons on the island where he'd found Reckoner, bigger and healthier and much more impressive pets for a future king, but Julian had felt sorry for old Reckoner, and wouldn't hear of leaving him behind.

Julian entered the room, carefully stepping over the dragon's twitching tail. Mite eyed the tray he carried, which held a glass of milk and something wrapped in cloth. "What's that?"

"This?" Julian settled on the edge of her bed, his face serious, but this time Mite knew he was only pretend serious, and she started to smile. "I heard from a reliable source that a certain princess didn't get her cake this afternoon. Would there be any truth to that rumor?"

He unwrapped the cloth, revealing a perfect golden cake,

studded with licorice and lightly steaming, as if fresh from the oven.

"I warmed it for you," Julian said as Mite let out a cry of delight and lunged at the tray.

"Thank you," she managed around a mouthful. Cake *and* a story was almost too good to be true, especially after worrying that she wouldn't get either. She was glad Julian had forgotten about what she'd done.

But as if reading her mind, he said, "Don't think you're off the hook, Maita. You know you're not supposed to go off without me or Noa—or Kell, if she's free. Tomorrow you'll stay in the tower with me and practice your writing. I should be making you do that more often, anyway. If only that last teacher I found for you two hadn't panicked and run off . . ."

Mite nodded. She wasn't worried anymore.

"Where did you go, anyway?" Julian said, flicking through one of the storybooks.

Mite hated lying, especially to Julian. But she knew he wouldn't allow her to keep a poisonous spider in her room, no matter how pretty it was. Julian didn't like any of her pets, though he tolerated them as long as they didn't land in his hair or crawl up his leg. The last time that had happened, he had let out a stream of words Mite had never heard before, then dashed out of the room quicker than she'd ever seen him move. He had finished reading her story through the door.

But Mite knew she had to lie. Because sometimes, spiders

needed someone to protect them, just like people did. "I was looking for woodbugs," she said quietly.

Julian gave her a long look, but he didn't ask any more questions. Mite let out her breath. Under the bed, Patience went *tap-tap* against her glass cage, but fortunately the noise was covered by the nighttime scuffling of the stinging beetles that lived in Mite's closet.

"All right, Mighty Mite," Julian said. "What would you like to hear this evening?"

8

Noa Attends Her First Meeting of the Council

"*Let me get* this straight," Tomas said. "You want me to bake cakes for a sea serpent? One who spends her spare time plotting to kill us all?"

"She especially likes lemon-lime," Noa said. "Just tell your father they're for Julian. He won't ask questions."

"He might if he notices they're the size of a seal."

They were sitting in the shade of a lime tree in the village square, which, in typical Florean style, had a large garden at its center filled with trees and flowering bushes. Noa was happily flaunting her cloak pin—a sapphire-studded *JM*, overlapping so that the letters looked like a dragon in flight—which was worn only by royal councillors.

"What is this for, anyway?" Tomas said. "Don't tell me the king's trying to turn that thing into a pet."

"Not exactly," Noa said. "I need information about that myth I told you about. The Lost Words. I think Beauty might be able to help—if I give her a good reason."

The idea had come to Noa in the night—her best ideas usually did. Beauty had been around for a long time, tangling with kings and queens and their mages, none of whom had been able to best her. No one knew exactly how old she was, but Noa thought there was a good chance the sea serpent would know whether there had once been mages with powers that didn't exist anymore. At the very least, Beauty had probably eaten a few of them.

One of the villagers looked Noa's way, and she puffed out her chest to show off the pin.

"You look like a peacock," Tomas said.

Noa deflated a bit. "Will you help? Nobody else can know. Julian always tells me to stay away from Beauty. He won't like that we're eating cake together now."

"Doesn't that go against your family motto or something?" Tomas said. "*Marchenas are always first?*"

"Our motto is about helping each other," Noa said. "Not being honest all the time. Who could manage that? Please, Tomas?"

"Of course I'll help you," he said. "I always do. That's why whenever you get one of your mad ideas, you come to me."

He sounded cranky, but Noa figured that was because he wasn't quite as floury as usual—it was Sunday, and his father's assistants were cleaning the ovens.

"Did you finish repairing the bakery?" Noa asked.

Tomas nodded. The bakery had been scorched by the fire that had swept through the village, which had been started by a corrupted mage. Julian had sent soldiers and mages to help with the repairs, but the cobbler's and the mustard shop were still shuttered and blackened. It was unusual that a village the size of Astrae would have a shop just for mustard, but the island had long been famous for it. Noa hoped it was more famous for dark magic now, though she supposed a place could be famous for dark magic *and* mustard.

"Oh, great," Noa muttered. Striding toward them was the green-eyed sentry who'd been making eyes at Julian in the tower. She walked self-importantly down the middle of the road, which required the villagers to get out of her way. Julian probably wanted to lecture Noa for leaving the castle without waiting for Mite to wake up.

The sentry bowed to Noa. "Princess, the king sent me to summon you for a meeting of the council."

Noa leaped to her feet. "Really?" Several villagers looked her way, and Noa lowered her voice to a more stately pitch. "Yes, of course. Thank you." She said a quick goodbye to Tomas, whose only response was a long-suffering sigh.

The sentry led her along the winding village thoroughfare and turned onto the road paved in black lavastone that went to the castle. It took much longer than cutting across the hillside did, and Noa wanted to break into a run. She forced herself to maintain a dignified pace, which made her irritable.

"So," the sentry said. "Is your brother seeing anyone?"

You don't waste any time, Noa thought. She widened her eyes and blinked slowly. "Julian sees fine. He only needs glasses when he reads."

The sentry looked suspicious, which meant she was clever—most people fell for Noa's innocent little sister act. "I mean, is he dating anyone? One of the other mages told me he hasn't since Gabriela."

Noa hopped over a lizard in her path, silently seething. After the events of the past week, she didn't want to hear Gabriela's name ever again, and certainly not thrown around casually by someone who'd been on the island for all of five minutes. Noa hated to admit it, but she was still impressed by Gabriela's dramatic escape off the sea cliff. Gabriela did everything with flair, even betrayal.

"I know he dated Lord Henry back at court," the sentry went on. "And wasn't there another mage before Gabriela— Florence something or other? And of course, everyone knows about him and Antony Farseer—that was a scandal for your mother, wasn't it? The future king dating the son of a convicted pirate? But then, Julian doesn't mind associating with pirates, does he?"

At this point, Noa would have paid the sentry to be quiet. Being subjected to a narrative summary of Julian's love life was beyond the pale. "Oh," she said, pretending to be embarrassed. "I thought everyone knew about him and Leo. But I guess you're new, after all."

The sentry's eyebrows shot up. "Leo?"

"Yes." Noa was trying to smother her laughter. Leo was Julian's most trusted scout, and Kell's second mate. It was a good thing he was a scout and spent most of his time in a rowboat far away from everyone else, because he smelled like a catch of herring left out in the sun. He had lost half his teeth in a series of drunken brawls, and wasn't exactly Julian's type, but he was as far as you could get from the type presented by the prim sentry, who looked like she measured her bangs with a ruler.

The sentry looked disappointed, but also thoughtful. Noa realized, too late, that she probably should have picked someone other than Leo—the sentry looked as if she were sizing up her chances against that particular competitor, and liking them just fine.

They followed the lavastone path back to the castle, entering through the gatehouse at the back. The council room, which was also the throne room, was at the end of a long hallway, and here the sentry bowed to Noa and left. The guards held the huge doors open for her, and Noa felt a prickle of happiness. She had never been welcomed into a council meeting before.

Julian lounged on his throne, his legs dangling over the

arm and his eyes fixed absently on the orb he was hovering over his open palm. The other royal councillors milled about the recessed aisle at the center of the room, some muttering in small clusters, others gazing at the papers piled on the council table. Renne murmured something in Julian's ear as Noa came in.

"Glad you could join us, Noabell," Julian said, extinguishing the orb with a murmured word and a flick of his wrist. "I'm happy to see that you know where the door is, in addition to the windows."

Noa strode down the aisle with a bounce in her step. Julian's quips weren't going to dim her excitement. She was a royal councillor!

The throne room was grand, anchored by pillars of dark basalt and framed with windows of colorful sea glass, through which the sunlight poured and splashed the floor with squares of gold. On either side of the aisle rose tiered benches like seats in an amphitheater. The throne at the far end, made from fantastically shaped driftwood and jagged spears of obsidian, commanded immediate attention.

Julian rose and went to the table, and the councillors fell silent. There were eleven in total—five of Julian's most trusted mages, as well as an ambassador from each of the six Florean islands he had conquered so far.

"Let's begin," he said. Murmuring something in Hum, Julian summoned a larger orb, which rose above the table to the height of a lamp before shattering into a hundred tiny glints to illuminate the scattered papers. "You'll notice that we have a new councillor. I trust you'll give her ideas your full consideration."

A few of the councillors, including Renne and Asha, a wizened mage who had also served their parents, smiled at Noa. Others, including most of the ambassadors from the islands Julian had captured, watched her with varying degrees of curiosity and disapproval. Noa gave them her best imperious stare, which didn't achieve much except to make some of them smile condescendingly. She decided that she would start practicing in front of a mirror.

"First, the reports," Renne said.

Each of the ambassadors described the state of their islands, including their defenses and the taxes they had raised for Julian's treasury. Julian looked distracted. At one point, he summoned another orb and began tossing it lazily from hand to hand. Reckoner awoke, sniffed around for Julian, then snuffled against his hand for chin scratches. Once he got them, he flopped back down under the table. He repeated this process five minutes later. Reckoner had a short memory.

The ambassadors droned on. Renne broke in occasionally to do some droning of his own, though his was flustered and occasionally confusing. Renne wasn't any better at public speaking than he was at magic or strategy, and Noa wished for the thousandth time that Julian hadn't appointed him second-in-command, which made him head of the council. Noa had tried to talk him out of it, but Julian wouldn't hear a word against his childhood friend. She'd also tried to get him to replace Ellabeth, a mage so ancient she could barely do magic anymore, and whose only contributions to council meetings were to loudly demand that the councillors repeat themselves and occasionally snap at Julian to stand up straight. There were plenty of other capable mages on the island to take her place, but Julian refused to sack her, for Ellabeth had been Mom's councillor since before he was born. Noa had grudgingly come to accept that this sort of impractical loyalty was one of Julian's weaknesses that she was never going to change.

There wasn't much new information since the last meeting, and Noa began tapping her foot impatiently. Julian eyed her with amusement. When the last ambassador fell silent, he said, "Perhaps we should come to our main order of business."

"Yes," Asha said. "I've been waiting to hear more about these mysterious magics you hinted at yesterday."

Julian told them what he'd told Noa, recounting the myth of the Lost Words and what he'd learned from the captured mage. Noa watched the faces of the councillors as he spoke. The ambassadors looked puzzled, if not skeptical. But the mages' eyes sparkled with excitement. It was clear that the myth of the Lost Words was well known among them.

"Forgive me, Your Highness," said one of the ambassadors, a man with yellow hair and a very red nose. "But this strikes me as a fool's errand. We have plenty of magic at our disposal—what we don't have is territory. We should focus on capturing more islands, not chasing after long-lost grimoires. You can be sure that Gabriela isn't so easily distracted."

Julian's expression didn't change, but Noa saw him stiffen ever so slightly, as he always did when Gabriela's name was mentioned. His mages knew this and avoided bringing her up whenever possible, but this ambassador was new and clueless.

"You don't get it," Noa said before Julian could respond. "This isn't just about finding new spells—it's about stopping Xavier from getting them."

The ambassador looked down his red nose at her. "And if he does? Are we not led by the most powerful dark magician in Florean?"

"Julian can't protect us against magics he's never seen, let alone used himself," Noa said. "If Xavier finds the Lost Words, it could be the end of us."

Several of the mages were nodding. The ambassador huffed. "We don't even know they exist."

"Precisely," another ambassador said. "Could this be some elaborate scheme of Xavier's to send us on a wild-goose chase? His mage may have been lying."

"He wasn't," Julian said. "But perhaps you'd like to hear it from him?"

A shadow seemed to fall across the council. Renne was regarding Julian with an uneasy look that made Noa frown.

Renne was Julian's oldest friend—when had he started being afraid of Julian?

Julian motioned to the guard at the door, who vanished into the antechamber. Seconds later, he was back, and behind him were two more guards, each supporting the arm of the man between them.

"Here we are," Julian said pleasantly. "Say hello to the council, Thadeus."

The man, who wore the red-and-gold cloak of Xavier's mages, looked up. Noa recoiled, and several of the councillors gasped. The man's eyes were shadow. A strange, swirling shadow that ran from lid to lid. His face was pale, his mouth slack. He barely seemed alive.

"Tell them how long Xavier has been searching for the Lost Words, Thadeus," Julian said.

"Since the spring harvest," the man intoned in a voice that wasn't his own. It was Julian's voice, Noa realized with horror, only twisted and wrong, as if Julian had stepped inside the man's head and was pulling out information like papers from a cabinet. "He sent out his spy ships last month."

"You see?" Julian said with a cold smile that Noa didn't like one bit. "He'll tell you anything."

"What's happened to him?" Asha said, her hand over her throat.

"I don't exactly know," Julian admitted. "I wanted more information from him than he was giving to Renne. So I decided to experiment with a truth spell I've been working on."

"You experimented on him?" Noa repeated. *This* was how Julian had learned about the Lost Words?

Julian nodded, perfectly calm. "After that, he was very cooperative."

"Well, sure," Noa spat. "You turned him into a zombie."

Julian blinked. "How else was I supposed to get him to tell me Xavier's plans?"

"Oh, I don't know," Noa said. "Offer him gold? Charm him into joining our side? I can think of a few ways, and so could you if you bothered to think at all, instead of just throwing magic at things you don't like."

A little silence followed this speech. The councillors shuffled their feet and tossed nervous glances at Julian. He blinked, and Noa thought she saw a flash of hurt in his eyes, followed quickly by annoyance. "I had to be sure I was getting the truth. Thadeus gave me a lot of information about Xavier's plans, some of which we already knew from our spies. I have no reason to disbelieve the rest, including everything he told me about the Lost Words."

Asha stepped forward and waved her hand in front of the mage's face. Her initial, horrified reaction seemed to be changing to fascination. "I've never seen a truth spell produce such a powerful effect. They're usually too easy to throw off to be of much use."

Noa's heart thudded. "Will he get better?"

"Let's hope not. I like seeing Xavier's mages this way," said a tall, auburn-haired woman with an unpleasant smile. It was Esmalda, Julian's least savory councillor, one of several criminals who had joined him over the last year. She'd been their mother's councillor once, until she'd been thrown into prison for working as an assassin. Esmalda said she'd been falsely accused, and maybe that was true, but something about the weather mage made Noa's skin crawl. Also, Esmalda often encouraged Julian's worst instincts.

"He's cooperative, is he?" she added, prodding the man's shoulder. "Why not make him dance?"

"I think you've made your point," Renne said. He alone among the councillors looked squeamish; the others were regarding Julian with varying degrees of bewilderment and awe.

"You have me convinced," said the red-nosed ambassador. He looked awed, too, but also like he wished he was far away from the shadow-eyed mage. "But what if we spend months searching for these magics, only to come up empty-handed?"

"I can put your mind at ease," Julian said. "There are two places where Xavier is looking for the Lost Words—one is an island called Evert. We can reach it in a few days."

"This sort of spell will be enormously useful," said a blood mage, peering into Thadeus's vacant face. "Tell me, did you base it off Pizarro's Theorem?"

Julian launched into a complicated account of the truth spell, but Noa didn't hear any of it. She couldn't stop staring at Thadeus. He could have been staring back at her, as they faced each other across the table, but Noa knew he couldn't see any of them. He was gone, an empty shell. It was worse than being dead.

Noa didn't offer any more opinions for the rest of the meeting, and Julian didn't ask her to.

9

Noa Doesn't Figure Things Out

Noa hugged her knees to her chest, savoring the salty breeze on her face. The stars peeked through windows in the clouds, which framed the crescent moon like white curtains. The mast flapped cheerfully, as if it was enjoying the night, too.

Fortunately, the iguanas were asleep, so Noa didn't have to worry about having her toes tickled during her shift at the prow. She listened to the lava crickets singing peacefully along the basalt shoreline and nibbled at the cake she had brought with her—plum, with an oozy jam filling that turned her fingers the color of twilight. The cakes were still flooding into the castle, to the dismay of the servants, who had taken to storing them on windowsills and rafters and using the less popular flavors, like spiced nettle and toasted seaweed, as doorstops.

Usually Noa loved taking a shift at the prow. But tonight she was too distracted to appreciate it. She hadn't spoken to Julian since the council meeting that morning—he hadn't come to dinner, as he'd been too busy meeting with his scouts and with Kell and her mates. Noa didn't know if he had come to say good night, because she had left to go to the prow before then, even though her shift wasn't scheduled to start for another hour.

She didn't know what to do. On one hand, the council meeting had been a success. She'd helped Julian get the councillors on his side, and now they were searching for the Lost Words, which was what Noa had wanted. On the other hand, Julian had never seemed more like a dark mage than he had at that meeting—the kind of dark mage that parents throughout Florean told stories about to frighten their children into behaving. Noa could still see the man's shadow eyes staring at nothing.

Well, you're still on the council, she reminded herself. After pestering Julian about it for so long, it was a victory. So why didn't it feel like one?

"You've changed course," said a voice behind her. Kell limped up to the prow, cursing as she lifted her wooden leg over one of the sleeping iguanas, who were difficult to see among the bracken.

"Only slightly," Noa said. "I thought we could approach the coordinates from the west. It'll lengthen the journey by a few hours, but we'll avoid the most dangerous pirate islands, and we can use the northwest current to speed us up."

Kell thought it over. "Good plan," she said. "Why didn't I

think of that? You know, you could really be the brains behind King Julian's operation, little miss, if he'd only let you be."

"He is letting me," Noa said, feeling a ghost of pride at the memory. "Didn't you hear? I'm on the council now."

"Are you? Well, that's the first practical thing King Julian's done in a while, possibly ever." Kell eyed her. "Is that what you wanted?"

Noa frowned. "It's exactly what I wanted."

"Exactly what she wanted! Thirteen's a shade young to know exactly what you want," Kell said. "Come to think of it, even seventy-three and a half is a shade young to know exactly what you want! Ha!"

"I want to do whatever I can to help Julian defeat Xavier." Noa's jaw tightened, and her hand drifted unconsciously to her charm bracelet. "He killed my mom."

Kell's grizzled face softened. "I know, little miss," she said. "I just meant that I thought you'd be keen to do something other than play King Julian's spider, at least some of the time."

Noa's eyes narrowed. "His what?"

"You know. The brain behind the throne. The person who sits in the shadows and spins webs to trap his enemies and hatches schemes to keep him in power, while he smiles that wicked smile of his and charms the world with his magic tricks and his pretty face. Every ruler who's ever lived has had a spider. Sometimes it's a family member. Sometimes it's just an advisor. But they all have them."

"I—" Noa sputtered. "They do?"

"Oh, sure. The people who serve Julian would follow him over a cliff. Problem is, without a brain like yours to guide him right, that's exactly where he'd lead them. He needs someone like you. They all do."

Noa's face was hot. "I'm not Julian's *spider.*"

Kell shrugged. "All right. So when that brother of yours wins control of Florean, what then?"

"Then . . . then I become one of his royal councillors, for real," Noa said slowly. "Maybe even a minister."

"Minister of what?"

"I don't know," Noa snapped. "What does it matter? He's not king yet."

Kell laughed. "All right. I don't mean to put a stingray in your bathtub. I'm just saying that with your smarts, you could do anything you want. You don't have to help King Julian rule Florean just because he's your brother."

"That *is* what I want."

"Sure it is. But it doesn't have to be *all* you want, is my point."

Noa felt an odd twinge of uncertainty. She never really thought about what would happen after she and Julian defeated Xavier and took Florean back—partly because she didn't know if they ever would. They were trying to take back a kingdom, after all. When she imagined life as Princess Noa, sister of King Julian and second in line to the throne of Florean, all she saw was a blurry space, like open waters shrouded by morning fog.

"I'm not sure how much help I am to Julian, anyway," she said. "He barely listens to me."

Kell raised her eyebrows. "No? Whose idea was it to reassign one of my sailors to guard that wretched snake? Who convinced the king to send a spy to Xavier's court a few months back? I think he listens to you more often than you realize."

Noa shrugged, though Kell's words made her feel a little better. "I want to be Julian's advisor. Besides, I don't know what else I would do."

"Ah, that's all right if you don't know yet. Black seas, I was sixty-two and two months before I figured out what I wanted to do with my life! Do you know, I raised eight children all by myself? Husband was no help—that old lout wouldn't lift a finger, not even to put his shoes away. Oh, I cooked and cleaned for him for years, worked my fingers to the bones. Then, one morning, I opened my eyes and said, 'Wait a minute. There's a door right there. I could walk out.' And that's what I did. You should have seen the look on his face. Ha!"

Noa knew the rest of the story, but it was a good one, so she listened to Kell tell it anyway. Kell had become one of the most feared pirates in all the thirteen seas. After a decade spent terrorizing merchant ships and royal vessels alike, she had been hurt by cannon fire, losing her leg and the hearing in her right ear. She probably would have kept pirating if it had just been that, but she was also plagued with headaches and sudden dizzy spells that forced her to lie down wherever she happened to be, which was somewhat dangerous if, for example, you happened to be captaining a pirate ship being boarded by the king's navy. So she had come to Julian, offering her navigational skills and knowledge of the pirate seas, and he had taken her on in spite of the fact that quite a few of the ships she had robbed had belonged to their parents.

"Your shift's long over, little miss," Kell said after she had run out of stories. "Don't you want to head off to bed?"

Noa idly traced a pattern in the sandy soil. "I'd rather stay here, if that's all right."

"Suit yourself." Kell pulled out a battered deck of cards and began assembling a complicated game of Poison Apple. The windy night grew quiet, broken only by the occasional muttered "Ha!"

"Kell," Noa said. "Do you think that Julian's . . . well, bad?"

Kell turned over another card. "Bad at what?"

"No, I mean . . . do you think he's *gone* bad?"

Kell considered. "I can't say. You need to be good to know if a person is bad. Isn't that how it works? I went bad long ago. Ha!"

"I don't think that matters," Noa said.

"Oh. Then I'd have to say that I've never thought much about it. The king is the king, and I can't see he's changed much since I signed up to captain this mad island. But if he had, it wouldn't bother me."

"It might if he decided to feed you to Beauty."

"Good point." Kell seemed remarkably unperturbed by this prospect.

"It's just—" Noa stopped. "That mage Julian captured. Thadeus. I've—I've never seen anything like that."

"Wasn't a pretty sight, was it?" Kell added another card the stack. "But as he's one of the mages Xavier sent to snatch you two girls away, I'm not surprised the king didn't treat him kindly. . . ."

Noa froze. "To snatch us away?"

"Of course. Perfect opportunity to do it—mages gone mad, chaos everywhere. Good thing those soldiers you met didn't recognize you. Probably expecting you to be all decked out in gold and jewels and all that, not barefoot and running wild the way you do. . . ."

Noa's heart beat a slow drumroll. "But Xavier attacked us because he thought we were getting close to the Lost Words."

"Oh, sure. He wanted to kill the king, or capture him. But failing that, he ordered all his mages to get their hands on at least one of you two and bring you to Queen's Step. After all, that'd be just as good as capturing the king, and a lot easier, to boot. . . ." Kell trailed off suddenly. "Oh, black seas. I wasn't to speak of this to you, child. The king didn't want to frighten you."

"Then Xavier . . . He's been plotting to kidnap me and Mite for a while?"

"That's what Thadeus said. King Julian suspected it

already, of course. It's the first order he gave me when I got here—to watch over you two. He knew Xavier would try something like this eventually. Probably he's tried before, but this is the first time he's gotten close. Xavier knows the king would surrender in a heartbeat if he captured either of you."

Noa's breath felt cold in her chest. It made sense, of course. Xavier was as ruthless as he was clever. Why hadn't Noa realized he might try to get to her and Mite?

Probably because, Noa realized, she was used to seeing the war for Florean as a war between Julian and Xavier, and herself as a figure in the background, pulling as many strings as she could. But Julian knew it wasn't just about him, and when he fought Xavier, he fought as much for Mite and Noa as he did for himself. Probably more, knowing Julian.

Kell threw another card down and let out a whoop. "Another win! Either my luck is improving, or I'm cheating much more effectively."

Noa got up. She felt cold and shaky, and she wanted the comfort of her familiar room, and Willow. "Good night, Kell."

"Eh? Oh, wait. I thought of an answer to your question before." She turned, her silver hair glowing like the moonlit clouds. "The witch and the whale hunter!"

"What?"

"You ever heard that story?"

"No." Noa frowned. Witches were a silly myth, creatures

who lived in trees or volcanoes and cast spells without words or grimoires. Nobody believed in them, except little kids.

"You need to read more books, girl. Lot of wisdom there, more than in your maps and charts." Kell cleared her throat. "So the whale hunter's a poor man, see? He's out hunting in dangerous seas, near an island piled with shipwrecks like broken bones. He pulls up on the beach for lunch, and out of nowhere, there comes this old lady. She asks for passage back to town, and he doesn't want to take her, 'cause even though she's little, the seas are so bad now that any extra weight could tip the boat. But she's standing there, shivering, so he gives in. As they go sailing back to town, a great wave rises up, but it doesn't capsize them. It picks them up on its back and carries them into the harbor like a gentle mare. When the whale hunter turns around, he finds the old woman is gone, and in her place is a witch, fresh and beautiful as a field of crocuses. And what's more, caught in his net is the fattest whale he's ever seen. The witch gives him this odd smile, and then she's gone. And he realizes that all those shipwrecks must have belonged to the whale hunters who turned the witch down and refused to give her passage." She grinned as if expecting Noa to grin back.

Noa was unimpressed. "I don't understand what that has to do with—"

"Waifs and strays, girl," Kell said. "Waifs and strays.

Witches are wise. You judge a person by how they treat the lost, those with nowhere to go and no one to help them. You want to know if the king's bad—well, he took me on when nobody else would have. You ever seen him do different?" She turned back to the cards and began setting up another game. "Never heard of the witch and the whale hunter! Do you good to spend a little more time in the library, and a little less hunched over that notebook and compass. Life's more than numbers and maps."

Noa left Kell muttering to herself and walked back to the castle, turning her thoughts over and over.

PART II

Evert

10

Beauty
Accepts a Bribe

The island of Evert jutted out of the water, an oddly misshapen lump that reminded Noa of a potato. She stood on the beach, eyeing it across the waves with Julian, Kell, Renne, and several other councillors. Mite was back on the dry sand, looking for shells. Behind them, keeping a respectful distance, a crowd of villagers had gathered to gawp at the strange sight.

The strangest thing about the island—besides the fact that it wasn't shown on any map, and that the only way to find it was by sailing backward toward its coordinates, a tricky feat for most ships, but not for Astrae—was that it seemed to be sweating. Mist rose off its black rocks, which were completely barren of trees and grass and even penguins, who tended to like strange places.

Noa folded her arms and glared at the island as if squaring off against an opponent. Xavier's mage had said that the king's ships had come here looking for the Lost Words, and then gone away again empty-handed. Could Noa and Julian succeed where Xavier had failed? Or was Evert a dead end?

"Let's try circling it once, Captain," Julian said. His brow was so furrowed that his dragon tattoo looked to be in danger of falling into his eye. "Perhaps we'll find a harbor where we can put a boat in."

"Aye, Your Highness," Kell said, and limped off.

Renne raised his eyebrows. "Seems an odd place to hide anything, let alone the Lost Words."

"Maybe that's the point," Noa said.

Julian didn't say anything. The shadows under his eyes were darker—he'd barely slept during the four-day voyage, poring over books of myths and legends until late into the night. Finally, he said, "Tell the sailors to prepare the longboat. We'll launch as soon as Kell finds a suitable harbor."

Noa noticed Tomas standing up on the path, waving to her. She gave Julian and Renne an excuse and hurried over to him.

"Do you have it?"

Tomas nodded. He glanced over his shoulder to see if anyone was nearby. Then he carefully lifted up the corner of the blanket laid over his wagon. Beneath it was the biggest cake Noa had ever seen, puffy and golden and still lightly steaming. It took up half the wagon.

"It's cinnamon raisin," he said. "We ran out of lemons. I hope that's all right."

"What happened to the other one?" Noa said. They had gone looking for Beauty yesterday with a lemon-lime cake in tow, but hadn't found her. One of the scouts had told Noa that she had dived *beneath* the island, which she'd been doing a lot lately. It struck Noa as suspicious behavior, but then, Noa couldn't recall Beauty ever engaging in *un*suspicious behavior.

"It's day-old," Tomas said in an affronted tone.

They walked along the beach until they came to the sheltered cove where Noa had made her bargain with Beauty. There was nobody there, sea serpents included.

A familiar figure jumped out from behind a rock. "What are you doing?" Mite asked. Of course she'd been following them. Her pockets were stuffed with shells, which she liked giving to her pet bugs so that they could hide in them.

"Tomas baked Beauty a cake," Noa said. "We're going to give it to her."

"Is it her birthday?" Mite looked excited. "Are we having a party? Do we all get cake? How will Beauty fit in a party hat—"

"It's not a birthday cake," Noa said. "I'm going to go talk to her, and you can only stay and watch if you promise not to tell Julian. If you can't keep it secret, you have to go back to the castle."

Mite chewed her lip, weighing the choice between lying to Julian and being left out of something. "I won't tell," she said, her voice glum.

Noa pulled the blanket back so that the scent of the cake could waft down the beach. It smelled delicious, built in layers spread thickly with cinnamon and brown sugar, with fat raisins soaked in butter pressed into the top. Mite looked as if she was about to start drooling. She scuttled closer to the cake, her gaze darting to Noa, clearly plotting to steal a piece when she wasn't looking.

"Mite—" Noa warned.

A huge shape lunged out of the water, and there came a sound like two dozen swords unsheathing. Mite screamed and toppled over. Then, as quickly as Beauty had appeared, she was gone, and the wagon of cake was empty but for a few raisins.

Noa brushed the water from her eyes. They were all drenched. Tomas looked too stunned to move. Water dripped down his long nose like a fountain.

Noa marched to the water's edge. "Beauty!"

A long stream of bubbles erupted on the surface of the water. Then Beauty's head surfaced, still chewing. "Ah," she mumbled around the cake. "That is the most wonderful thing I've ever eaten. What is that delicious aftertaste?"

Tomas blushed. "Orange peel."

"Really?" Beauty gulped, her black eyes widening. "How inspired!"

Noa didn't think she'd ever seen Tomas look so pleased. "Well, you have to caramelize it first—"

"Can you two trade recipes some other time?" Noa said. "Beauty, I have a business proposition for you."

"A business proposition? How dreary. Is there any more cake?"

"That's the business proposition." Noa steeled herself and waded into the shallows, stopping only feet away from Beauty's huge shadow. "Tomas bakes the best cakes you'll find anywhere in the thirteen seas. I'm prepared to offer you a regular supply."

"I see." Beauty's expression didn't change, but at the word *cakes* her tongue slashed out to lick her lips. "And how will I thank you for such generosity?"

Noa folded her arms. "As you reminded me, you've been around for a while. I'm sure you've seen a lot of the world."

"More than your brother's royal advisors and all his books combined could tell you," Beauty agreed. Her voice was free of arrogance, as if she were merely stating a fact.

"I bet you even know things that could be helpful to Julian," Noa said. "If you could answer a few questions, I'd be very grateful. It wouldn't take up much of your time."

Beauty thought it over, eyeing Noa with her wet black eyes. "Why do you think I'd be truthful?" she said at last.

"Because you're a lady of honor, of course," Noa said, raising her eyebrows as if surprised. The serpent might be bloodthirsty, but she had observed that insulting Beauty's honor riled her more than anything else.

Beauty smiled appreciatively. "What a clever flatterer you are, little Marchena. Very well—I accept. I will answer one question for one cake."

Noa mulled it over. One question wasn't much, especially given how long it took Tomas to prepare a serpent-sized cake. But Beauty likely knew more about the Lost Words than anyone living, so maybe it was worth it.

"Very well," she said. "My question—"

"Oh." Beauty pouted. "I'll need a cake first, dear."

Noa gritted her teeth. "You just *had* one."

"That was before I agreed to anything." Beauty's voice was sinuous.

And so Noa and Tomas had to go back to the bakery to fetch the day-old lemon-lime cake. Tomas muttered mutinously the whole way about moisture and crumb quality, but in the end, Beauty seemed just as delighted with the second cake as she had been with the first.

"I believe you owe me an answer to one question," Noa said. "Unless you have a complaint about the cake?"

"It would be impossible to complain about such a delicacy," the serpent said, narrowing her eyes at Tomas in what Noa could have sworn was a smile.

Noa rubbed her eyes. "*Good.* Now, tell me everything you know about Evert."

"That isn't a question, dear. Have you forgotten our bargain?"

Noa shrugged. It had been worth a try. "I'm assuming you've seen this island before."

"Yes. Well, that was easy."

"That wasn't a question, either," Noa said. "I think you're the one who's forgotten our bargain."

"Your remarkably talented friend has put me in a good mood," Beauty said. "But not that good. Do get to the point, dear."

"Fine." Noa crossed her arms. "Here's my question: What secrets is the island hiding?"

Beauty blinked. "How do you know it has secrets?"

"You can only find it by sailing backward," Noa said. "Plus, it's really funny-looking. It obviously has secrets."

"That's a rather broad question."

"Well, it was a rather large cake."

Beauty let out a slow hiss. "Very well, clever little Marchena. I know that, long ago, something was hidden here. I don't know what, but I know that the mages hid it well—they made the island difficult to find, and they changed its shape to conceal their secret. It used to be called something else, too—Orchid Island. After the mages enchanted it, they called it Evert."

Noa's heart leaped. So the Lost Words *were* hidden here! "How did they change its shape? You have to answer that, Beauty. It's part of the question."

"I can't tell you what I don't know." Beauty slid back into

the water. "If you have any more questions, little Marchena—and I do hope you will—you know where to find me."

Noa hopped from the boat onto the beach, which wasn't easy. Evert's barren rock was weirdly slippery, as if it had been greased. There was no seaweed anywhere, nor any barnacles or mussels.

Julian marched up the shore as soon as his boots touched ground, forcing everyone else—all the mages on the council, plus several scouts—to hurry after him, slipping and sliding. Noa remained behind on the beach, which wasn't much of a beach, except in the sense that it was where the sea met the island. There was no sand. No stray pebbles. Only that strange, smooth rock, which had a reddish undertone, as if the island had been flayed.

"Evert," Noa muttered to herself. "Evert." She walked along the shore and over a little rise, beyond which was more featureless stone. She was looking for a place to sit, but there wasn't any, really, so in the end she squatted on the uncomfortable stone, which sweated and steamed and made the back of her trousers wet.

She was certain the island's name was important. The mages had changed it after they enchanted it, after all. She opened the encyclopedia she had snatched from the library. Encyclopedias weren't magical texts, so of course they were covered with dust, because Julian never bothered looking at them.

Evert meant a lot of things, it turned out. It was the name of an ancient goddess, and a species of crab with a bad temper, even for crabs, and also an ice cream dish eaten on Caraway Island. But Noa's eyes zeroed in on one definition.

"Julian!" she shouted. No reply. He was too far away. She shoved the encyclopedia into her pack—it barely fit next to the Chronicle—and sprinted up the shore. Evert was not an island made for sprinting—the rock was so wet and slimy that after a few falls, Noa abandoned the idea and settled for fast marching.

Julian stood on a rounded hilltop, obscured by a swirl of magic. Little stars of light opened and closed, and a strange breeze lifted the ocean spray and spun it around him. Beneath his feet, unlikely spears of grass and flowers sprouted from solid rock, and daisy petals rose in the air to join the vortex. He held a piece of rock from the island that glowed and crackled; as Noa watched, it became lava and dripped slowly through his unscathed fingers. His eyes were narrowed in concentration as he muttered words in the nine languages, strange words that sparked like fire or glinted like gold.

"Julian!" Noa called again. She pushed through the others, who were clustered below the hill, muttering and darting glances at him. She had to stop outside the vortex, which was now flecked with fire. "Julian!"

The vortex sputtered and died. "What?" Julian said irritably, brushing ash from his hands. "Noa, can't you see I'm in the middle of something? The mages cast some sort of spell on this island to hide the Lost Words—"

"It's inside out!" she interrupted. "Julian, the mages turned the island inside out!"

He looked at her as if she'd barked at him. "What?"

"Evert!" She didn't seem to be able to stop yelling. "It means 'inside out.'"

"I thought it meant ice cream."

She made a frustrated sound and flipped opened the encyclopedia. "'Evert: noun. To reverse, to turn inside out.'"

He looked exasperated. "I'm sure it means a lot of things. It's also a name. Augustine Evert, fourth-century fire mage, known for—"

Noa slammed the book shut. "Beauty told me the mages renamed the island after they enchanted it. They obviously meant for it to be some sort of clue—maybe they wanted the Lost Words to be found again one day."

"Beauty told you? What does she know about any of this?"

Noa felt like strangling him. "Julian, just once in your life, will you pay attention! Look at this place! If this isn't an island that's been turned inside out, I don't know what is."

She watched Julian pause, watched him actually consider what she was saying. "But how?"

"*I* don't know," she snapped. "You're the high and mighty Dark Lord—can't you guess?"

She hadn't meant to say that. It just came out, like a hiccup. After all, Julian had been distant since the council meeting, buried in his books, and he'd barely listened to the lecture she'd given him about not turning people into shadow-eyed ghouls. She couldn't help being frustrated.

Julian's brow furrowed. "'High and mighty'?"

"Look, how many hundreds of grimoires have you read?" Noa rushed on. "Surely there are spells to turn things inside out."

"What would be the point of turning things inside out? I mean, I suppose there are laundry spells in Salt that help—"

"There you go!" Noa said. "Think of the island as a big inside-out sweater. A sweater with a lot of pockets. You can't find the Lost Words, because they're in one of those pockets. You have to turn the sweater right side out first before you can get at them. Does that help?"

"Yes, Noa. Imagine the island as a sweater. Your magical advice is always appreciated."

"Well, the magic bit is your job," she huffed. "I just figure things out."

Julian pressed his hand against his eyes. She thought at first that he was overcome with frustration, but when he took his hand away, he was smiling. Not the detached, cruel smile he sometimes wore when dealing with his underlings, but an actual grin. Noa's heart gave a happy skip. She had always loved Julian's smile—it filled his eyes with mischief and made him look younger, more like the Julian who used to read with her late at night after their mother thought they were asleep, while the palace cats snored at the foot of the bed and a fire crackled in the hearth.

"Noabell," he said, "you are an absolute genius."

11

Julian Scares Everyone

Julian stayed on Evert for the rest of the day, pacing and muttering strange spells and generally unnerving everybody. Left to their own devices, his mages wandered around like headless chickens, some trailing after him with ideas that he either ignored or viciously shot down, others flitting back and forth between the two islands with books and papers he demanded and then tossed aside unread when they were handed to him.

Shortly before sunset, he ordered everyone back to Astrae. Then he gathered up all the earth mages and had sailors row them to Evert, stopping a distance from shore at evenly spaced intervals around the island. They all chanted the spell Julian had given them, and Evert rattled and shook horribly and sent huge waves crashing against Astrae. But it didn't change at all.

Julian spent the night there, along with a handful of his poor mages, who were fetched in the morning looking bedraggled and wild-eyed. Whatever strange spells Julian had been testing in the dead of night on that barren rock seemed to have satisfied him, for he ordered the earth mages back into boats, along with an equal number of fire mages. They ringed the island once again and began chanting something that sounded like the crackle and clamor of a blacksmith's shop. Evert began to shake so hard that even Astrae was rocked by the waves, and Noa had to sit down on the beach to avoid falling over. Then Julian summoned a cloud in Squall, and stepped on top of it. It lifted him high above Evert, so high Noa felt herself grow dizzy. There came a boom of thunder, and then a strange glowing substance that looked like mist made of fire reached down and wrapped around the island.

And then, with a *pop*, Evert turned right side out.

It was the worst *pop* Noa had ever heard, a *pop* that echoed off the breakers and rattled her teeth, like a billion balloons exploding at once. But once the echoes died, and Noa and everybody else were able to unplug their ears and pull themselves to their feet, they found themselves looking at an entirely new island.

It was still roughly the same shape, though lumpy in new places and flat in others. It must have been forested before the mages turned it inside out, but now the trees lay in crushed heaps, as if a horde of giants had stamped all over them. A cloud of pollen steamed off the island, and the waves around it were strewn with bits of trees and flowers and other rubble. Once the sea had calmed, Noa waded out and retrieved several flattened orchids that had been blasted all the way to Astrae. She felt a little sorry for Evert, which had the look of a mangy dog that had grown used to mistreatment.

Julian returned to Astrae that afternoon with a stormy look on his face and a book tucked under his arm. It wasn't a book Noa had ever seen before—it was twice the size of a normal book, with a plain black cover. Julian held it carefully, for the book was old and falling apart. Noa didn't get more than a glimpse of it before he stomped past her and into the castle, but there was something about the book she didn't like. Looking at it made her throat feel scratchy, as if she was coming down with a cold.

"Is that it?" she demanded of Renne, who was just stepping out of the boat Julian had abandoned. "Is that the Lost Words?"

"Probably," Renne said. "One of them, anyway. We discovered the book in a cave. It was easy to find, but I suppose the mages didn't need to bother coming up with a good hiding spot given that they were planning to turn the island inside out."

"How do you know it's got one of the lost languages in it?" Noa asked.

"Well, it's written in a magical language that Julian isn't able to speak."

"But—oh." Noa swallowed.

Julian could speak all nine magical languages. That is, he could speak all nine *known* magical languages.

"So it's true," Noa murmured. Lost magical languages did exist, and they'd found one of them before Xavier had. It was an enormous victory. And yet . . .

"But Julian—" Where magic was concerned, Julian could do anything. It made Noa feel anxious and unsteady to imagine a world where he couldn't. "He must be able to speak it. If he can speak all nine known magical languages, surely he can speak the unknown ones, too. Maybe there's a spell on the book to protect it from being read."

Renne gave her a weary look. "You sound just like your brother. Julian is convinced that he'll be able to find a way to read it. You can guess what that means."

Noa bit her lip. "We're going to sit here until he figures it out."

"Exactly," Renne said. "Or drives himself insane, I suppose. Which, given the mood he's in, I'm slightly more worried about now than I have been in the past."

Noa waited a few hours, then pounded on the door to Julian's tower. He didn't let her in until she'd been at it for at least five minutes. By then, her fist was sore, and she was in a thoroughly bad mood.

"Was I not loud enough?" she snarled as the door swung open, revealing a pale and unkempt Julian, his hair sticking up and his shirt untucked.

"I believe we've discussed this," he said. "When the door is locked, it's because I'm working on something important. You can open it yourself if it's an emergency."

Noa knew this, of course, but she hated overriding Julian's lock, which only she and Mite could do. You had to stick your finger into the lock like a key so that the lock could sense if you had Marchena blood. It didn't hurt or anything, but Noa couldn't shake the impression that something inside the door-knob was *sniffing* her.

Noa marched past Julian, then stopped in her tracks. Mite sat at the table, swinging her legs, in the middle of devouring a sandwich. Her mouth was smeared with cheese grease and tomato sauce.

Noa whirled. "So you'll let her in, but not me?"

"She is considerably quieter than you," Julian said pointedly.

Noa huffed. She wasn't really upset about Mite, who had been hysterical when she had learned that Julian was going to be spending the night on Evert and would not be there to tell her a bedtime story. Or at least, she had been hysterical in the way Mite became hysterical, running from one end of the castle to another like a silent whirlwind, with Noa and half the castle staff trying to catch her before she fell down the stairs and broke her neck or got herself so wound up that she blew up another wing. As it turned out, Julian hadn't forgotten after all, and had returned to tell her a story at the usual time before sailing back to Evert. But that hour of uncertainty had not been pleasant for anyone involved.

"Renne's worried about you," Noa said. "He thinks you're going to drive yourself mad."

Julian waved a hand dismissively. "Renne worries too much."

"Well, if you are going to go mad, I'd prefer it if you could wait until after you're king of Florean." Noa hesitated, then went over to the book sitting on the table. She poked at it, half expecting it to burst into flame or something. "For an enchanted book, it doesn't look like much, does it?"

"I don't like it," Mite said through a mouthful of sandwich. "It smells funny."

Noa agreed. But in addition to smelling funny, the book made her feel strange. When she touched it, she got that scratchy-throat feeling again, as well as a weird sense of antic- ipation, like a sneeze. A strange murmuring filled the tower, like the hushed voices in a library. And also—

"What was that?" She spun around, her heart pounding.

Mite gave her a funny look. "What?"

Noa scanned the tower. She could have sworn she had seen someone out of the corner of her eye, a tall figure in a gray robe. There was something strange about his face, but the apparition was gone before she could pinpoint it.

She rubbed her eyes. She hadn't slept well last night. What- ever Julian had been doing over on Evert had made a warbly, sonorous sound, like a thunderstorm with a cold.

She flipped open the book, and found herself staring at a

lot of gibberish. Unlike most magical gibberish, though, the words swam strangely when she looked at them.

She slammed it shut. "This thing is giving me a headache."

"You're not the only one." Julian tossed the book he had been staring at across the tower and pressed his fingers into his eyes. He had flopped down on the floor against one of the bookshelves with his long legs stretched out.

Noa sat beside him. "You really can't read it?"

"No—it's like the words fall out of my head as soon as I look at them. It's incredibly frustrating."

Noa bit back a retort. That was how she felt when she looked at *any* magical language. "You don't say."

Julian reached for another book. "It's clearly enchanted. The mages would have wanted to protect it from being read."

"They put it in an inside-out island," Noa pointed out. "Julian, have you considered that . . . well, maybe you just can't read it? Maybe you can't use whatever power is in that book."

"Yes, Noa," he said irritably. "I've considered it. Contrary to what my mages say about me behind my back, I don't think I'm all-powerful. But I have to try."

"Why don't we look for the other lost language?" Noa pressed. "Didn't Xavier find two sets of coordinates? That mage you wrecked said so, didn't he?"

"Oh!" Julian's eyebrows disappeared beneath his hair. "So now you're interested in what Thadeus has to say? I understood from your lecture the other day that you thought I'd done something heinous in getting that information from him."

Noa glared right back. "I didn't think you were listening to that."

"It's hard not to listen to someone at that volume. I've never had a worse headache."

Noa silently counted to five. Did Julian really believe that he hadn't, even in the smallest way, deserved to be yelled at? Sometimes Noa wondered if her secret mission hadn't already failed.

"Also," Julian said distractedly, reaching for another book, "what's this about me and Leo? Shelby told me yesterday that you said we were an item."

It took Noa a moment to remember that she had in fact said this, and to understand that Shelby must be the green-eyed sentry who'd summoned her to the council meeting. "What? You and Leo?"

Julian wasn't fooled. "You shouldn't spread rumors like that, Noa. Were you making fun of him? Just because someone could use a bath doesn't mean they deserve—"

"I wasn't making fun," she said through gritted teeth, thinking how rich it was for Julian to lecture her about mocking someone's hygiene when he went around turning people into zombies and feeding them to sea serpents. There were moments when she wanted to strangle him, and others when she wondered why she hadn't already.

She looked at the book, and again felt that scratchy feeling.

Was it her imagination, or were there more shadows in Julian's tower than usual? "What power do you think that book has?"

"I don't know." He rubbed his head, making more of his hair stick up. "The ancient mages didn't provide any clues. Well—except for this, I suppose. It was marking one of the pages."

He pulled something out of his pocket and handed it to her. It was a strip of hide from some sort of animal. The fur was brownish and soft. As she stroked it, some of the fibers crumbled. Like the book, the hide was very old.

"What if it's something bad?" Noa said.

"There are no 'bad' magics," Julian said, and Noa finished for him quickly, before he could go off on one of his soliloquys, "Only magics that people are afraid of. I know, I know." She tapped her fingers on her knee. "Have you had the other mages look at it?"

"Yes. None of them can read it, either."

"Maybe nobody can. Maybe magic dies if it's locked away too long."

"Maybe." Julian sighed. Absently, he reached out and plucked leaves from Noa's hair that she must have accumulated during her morning survey. He didn't look irritated anymore, only tired. "So what should we do?"

Noa's eyebrows shot up into her scalp. Julian smiled. "I'm not sure I deserve that look. It's not as if I never ask for your advice."

You used to. But Noa didn't want to start an argument now. In fact, with Julian sitting there smiling at her with his old smile, she just wanted to forgive him for everything.

"We might not be able to speak whatever language is in that book," she said. "But we stopped Xavier from getting it. So you should congratulate your mages, and the sailors, too, especially after scaring them half to death yesterday. Where else has Xavier been looking for the Lost Words?"

"The southern reaches of the Ayora Sea. Greenwash Strait. Thadeus doesn't know if Xavier has ships there now, or if they've come and gone. That's the extent of his knowledge—we'd have to capture another one of Xavier's mages to get more recent information."

Noa fixed him with her iciest stare. "And if we do capture one?"

Julian pressed his hand against his face with a groan. "We'll tickle their toes until they talk. I don't care—you're in charge of prisoners from now on, Noabell. I can't take any more harassment from you. I still have a headache, you know."

"Serves you right," Noa said loftily, but inside she was exulting. True, refraining from doing a bad thing because you didn't like being lectured wasn't quite the same as having morals about it, but she chose to see it as progress nevertheless.

"We should set sail for Greenwash Strait today," she said. "Hopefully the king hasn't sent his entire navy there. You can obsess over that old book on the way."

"Fine." His gaze drifted, and he lost his Old Julian look, which was replaced with what Noa thought of as his Dark Lord Julian look. "I wouldn't mind if the king's navy was there. I have a few ideas for how to repay Xavier for those mangoes."

Noa stood up. "Well, you don't need my help with that."

"I can give you advice, Julian," Mite piped up.

Julian rose. "I'm sure you can, Maita. Would this advice be pertaining to cakes, by chance? I'm afraid you have to eat your salad before we discuss that subject."

"It's not about cakes!" Mite said. "It's about the cats. I have an idea for how we can stop them catching birds."

"And bugs, too, I suppose."

As Mite launched to a complicated description of a cat warning system involving magical bells and light beams, Noa slipped away. Before the tower door closed behind her, she glanced over her shoulder. It seemed for a moment as if a shadow hung in the air above Julian, stretching dark tendrils out as if to embrace him. But then she blinked, and the apparition vanished.

That afternoon, Noa tried to write in her Chronicle, but her thoughts kept drifting back to the book from Evert and those strange, swimmy words. She didn't know why she was so fascinated by some moldy old magical book that was probably useless, but for some reason, part of her wanted to look at it again.

She paced through the castle, along the beach, then back up to the castle (there were still cakes in the kitchen, and she tucked two chocolate creams into the pockets of her cloak). Eventually, her wandering feet took her to the throne room.

It was empty, except for Asha and another mage, who sat on one of the benches with their heads bent together in conversation. Asha smiled at her when she came in.

Noa plopped down on the throne. Sometimes she came here when she wanted to think—sitting on the throne felt like being at the prow with the wind in her hair. Her feet didn't quite touch the floor, but that was okay.

What were they going to do if they got to Greenwash Strait and it was bristling with the king's warships? What if they got there and found not only warships, but a strange new magic at the command of Xavier's mages? She opened the Chronicle and unfolded the map of Florean she had glued into the inside of the cover. But even as she tried to focus on strategy— usually her favorite subject—her thoughts kept returning to the book.

Her gaze fell on a strange statue that had appeared beside the council table. It was a woman, carved from bronze, her mouth open in a silent scream. Something about the statue made Noa's skin ripple with goose bumps.

She hopped off the throne and walked over to it, peering into the statue's face. Then she recoiled.

It was Esmalda.

"Doesn't much improve her, does it?" a voice said.

Noa started back with a cry, and nearly tripped over Asha, who put out an arm to steady her.

"J-Julian did this?" she said.

"Who else?" Asha looked grim. "I wasn't here to witness it. But I hear it wasn't pretty."

Noa forced herself to look away from Esmalda's horrified face. "Why?"

Asha blinked. "Didn't he tell you? Renne caught her writing a letter to Xavier, offering to turn spy for him—for a price."

Noa's mouth fell open. "*Esmalda?*"

Asha nodded. "You're not the only one who was surprised. It seemed like she worshipped the ground King Julian walked on. But I've found that when it comes to spies, it's always the person you least suspect."

Noa's thoughts whirled. Julian had once turned one of the king's soldiers into a tree. That had been different, though—the man had snuck onto the island and stabbed a villager. Esmalda was one of his own mages, and a councillor. As much as Noa disliked her, she was one of them.

"When did he do this?" Her mouth felt dry.

"This morning. You saw the mood he was in when he returned from Evert. I suspect Esmalda could have fared worse."

Noa didn't see how. Her hand shaking, she reached out

and brushed her fingers against Esmalda's wrist. It was cold as stone, and horribly smooth. Noa imagined that cold metal creeping up her legs, freezing her stomach and stopping her heart—

"Why did he leave her here?" she asked.

"He said it would be a warning." Noa had never heard Asha criticize Julian, and there was no criticism in her voice now. But she didn't look happy. "In case anyone else is tempted to betray him."

Noa couldn't sleep.

She stared up at the ceiling of her bedroom. It was a nice bedroom, in her opinion. At first, she had missed her room in the royal palace in Florean City, and had tried to make this one look as similar as possible. But even after the mages moved the walls around, and even with all the furniture in the right spots, it would never look like her old bedroom. Her old room had overlooked a manicured garden full of daisies, miconia, and lanternflowers; her new bedroom looked out over a rocky shore often populated by smelly sea lions. Her old bedroom had a floor of polished black marble; the new one was uneven with missing tesserae that formed a simple blue-and-white pattern. Eventually, though, she had come to like the new bedroom just as well, with its shell-shaped balcony and stone walls that kept it cool even on hot days. Over time, she had filled it with blue whales—they were woven into the rug, and painted onto the walls, and lined the windowsill in the form of ceramic figurines. Julian had even placed little whale-shaped lights in the ceiling that came on after sunset.

Noa pressed Willow to her chest. Her thoughts kept returning to the book. She knew with a bone-deep certainty that there was something *wrong* about the power it held. She didn't know how she knew, but that didn't make her any less convinced. Julian might believe that magic couldn't be bad, but Noa wasn't so sure. Maybe there was a good reason why the mages had bound that old language and hidden the book away. And maybe Julian shouldn't have the power it contained. Maybe it would only make him stronger, and crueler, and less like the old Julian.

All these fears mixed together with her strange desire to look at the book again, to hold it in her hands and stare at those mysterious words. She had never felt that way about any magical object before, and it made her even more convinced that something about the book was wrong.

Finally, after tossing and turning for an eternity, Noa flung back the covers and hopped out of bed, pausing only to tuck Willow back in. She picked up a lavastick, blowing on the end to stoke the ember, then padded past Mite's room and up the stairs that led to Julian's tower. The door was still locked.

Grimacing, Noa stuck her finger into the lock. There was

a small scraping sound, which was disturbing, and then something that felt like a tiny creature breathing on her fingernail, which was worse, and then the lock clicked and Noa pushed the door open.

She gazed into darkness. A strange, shifting darkness. Setting her jaw, she stepped inside.

The moon hadn't risen yet, but starlight shone through the tower windows, and the lava slumbered in its cauldron, dark but for a few gleaming fissures. She didn't see the book anywhere, so she quietly climbed the spiral staircase up to Julian's loft. This held only a bed and a carved wooden wardrobe that Julian had owned since he was a boy. Piled around the bed were more books, seemingly at random. Julian himself was sprawled across the bed on his stomach, fast asleep. His arm dangled over the side, as if reaching for the plain black book that lay just beyond his fingertips.

Noa shook her head. It was just like Julian to fall asleep with a book, even if he couldn't read it. She pulled the blankets over him. He didn't stir, and she doubted he would if she yelled in his ear. The spell he'd used to turn Evert right side out had been big, and he'd take a few days to recover.

The book also did nothing strange when Noa picked it up, nor when she carried it downstairs to the lavaplace. Reckoner, slumbering beside the dying glow, let out a growl when she settled into Julian's chair, but he went back to sleep after she let him smell her hand. Julian's cats ignored her completely, except for one who invisibly pounced on her slipper. Noa abandoned the slipper to its fate, and it hopped onto the windowsill, where it began to molt like a strange purple bird.

Her hands shook. Perhaps it was only her imagination, but it seemed like the tower had grown darker since she had picked up the book, as if the stars gleaming through the windows had dimmed.

She ran her fingers along the spine. She didn't know why, but holding it felt good. Right.

She opened the book.

Inside the cover was a mess of words, just as illegible as any magical language. And yet, as Noa stared at them, the words began to dance. It was as if the letters were rearranging themselves. Noa flicked to the first page, and then, slowly, dreamily, through the rest of the chapter. Whoever had written it had a fine hand, though in places—perhaps because they had been in a hurry—some words were marred with blots of ink. Noa was so intent on the book that she didn't hear the murmuring begin again.

Now that she actually focused on it, she found that the book was not, in fact, divided into chapters, but letters— it was indeed a dictionary, filled with words that rolled strangely off Noa's tongue. That was when she realized two things at once:

One, she was reading a magical language.

And two, the man in the gray robe was standing in front of her.

He towered over her, blocking out the light, and his face was in shadow. But it was the same man she had glimpsed before. Reckoner's snout was practically resting on the man's bare foot, yet the dragon gave no sign he could see him.

"W-who are you?" Noa said.

The man gave no reply. The lavalight outlined his body—there was something terribly wrong with it. His outline was smudged and frayed, with little drifting tendrils of gray, as if he were made of fog. In places he was entirely translucent. He reminded Noa of a bit of cloth left outside in the sun and rain, worn threadbare by the elements.

The man eyed Noa with a greedy interest. Shaking, she slid off the chair and backed away. But she walked into something cold and unyielding as a stone wall. She spun, and found herself staring at a woman. She was also clad in a gray robe, and in her eyes was the same hunger. She gripped Noa by the shoulder, and her fingers were cold as snow.

"Julian!" Noa screamed. She tried to wrench away, but another pair of icy hands rose out of nowhere and gripped her other arm. "Julian!"

The tower was now full of threadbare figures. Some had tendrils for arms and legs, while others were mere smudges of gray. Her screaming woke Reckoner, who gave an indignant snort. But that was the last thing she heard. A shadow rose above her that was like the shadow she had seen before, rising over Julian. It reminded her of a curtain fluttering in the breeze. It terrified and fascinated her—she wanted to reach out a hand and push it aside, to see what was behind it. But before she could do anything, the cold hands thrust her into the air, and through the darkness.

12

Noa Finds a Door under a Shadow

Noa screamed, squeezing her eyes shut. Behind the shadow, the world was cold and dark. She stumbled forward, choking. The air was thick and tasted of ash.

She opened her eyes. She was no longer in the castle. And she knew with a bone-deep certainty that she wasn't on Astrae. All around her was a hazy darkness. Strange ruins reared up: a tower lying on its side; a cracked marble fountain; a stone archway leading to nothing.

The threadbare people shoved her along, murmuring all the while. Their voices were as frayed as the rest of them, and she could make out only the occasional word. Noa tripped over a bit of rubble. She didn't fall normally, but drifted slowly to the ground like an autumn leaf. When she lifted her hands, they were dark with ash.

The man reached out to pull her to her feet. She let herself go limp, and then, when his grip loosened, she wrenched her arm free.

She lowered her head and ran right into the woman who was in her way. She was so frayed and translucent that she didn't have a face. When Noa rammed into her, she drifted several yards before falling into a heap on the ground.

Noa ran.

Running wasn't the same in this strange place, either. It was slower, and every step sent her gliding several paces through the air before her foot touched ground again. Beyond her stretched hills of shadowy sand and valleys so dark she couldn't see the bottom, covered with ruins: houses and palaces and amphitheaters, all jumbled together as if a child had scooped them up and then smashed them onto the ground. The architecture wasn't at all the same; some of the ruins looked Florean, while others looked foreign or impossibly ancient. Noa whirled to see if the threadbare people were following her. They were, but they didn't seem able to move as fast as she could. After a few minutes, she left them behind. She didn't stop running, though.

Finally, she could go no farther. She fell to the ground, her lungs burning, coughing from the smoky air. She was in a little circle of standing stones, in the shadow of something that looked like the broken hull of a ship, half-buried in sand. Noa crept deeper into the shadow and drew her knees up, shaking all over. Would the threadbare people find her here? She could see nothing but ruins and hills of sand. This place was horribly silent. Her knee was bleeding—she must have skinned it when she tripped.

Tears trickled down her cheeks. She wanted Julian. She wanted *Mom*. She clutched at her charm bracelet, pressing the blue whales into her skin.

"Noa?"

"Julian!" Noa sprang to her feet. She didn't see him, though she looked in every possible direction. "Where are you? Where am *I*?"

"Noa, listen to me." Julian's voice was muffled, as if he were speaking from behind a wall. "You need to go back to the place where you fell through."

"Where I fell through?"

"Yes. Do you remember?"

"I don't know. I ran for a long time. There were people . . . *things* chasing me. Can you come get me?" Her voice sounded high and shaky, like a little girl's, but she was too frightened to care.

"No," he said. "I'm sorry, Noabell."

"Why not? Where am I?"

There was a slight pause. "Let's just focus on getting you out," Julian said, and Noa realized that wherever she was, it must be terrible, if Julian was afraid to tell her the truth. "Try following the sound of my voice."

A tear trickled down her cheek. "But I can hardly hear you!"

There was a pause, and then something drifted toward her. A tiny glowing orb, like the lights Julian had put in her ceiling.

"Can you see that?" Julian said.

Noa's heart leaped. "Yes!"

The orb gave a little bob, and then it began to retreat through the shadow, wavering like a lighthouse beam through fog. Noa raced after it. She saw several gray figures moving in the distance, but they didn't catch sight of her. In her haste, she tripped over a block of stone carved with unfamiliar runes, wrenching her ankle. Her eyes watered from the pain but she forced herself to her feet and limped on.

Finally, Noa saw a hill looming up in front of her, which was crowned with the crumbling tower that looked like a fist. "I recognize this!" she cried. "I think this is where I came through!"

"Good." Julian's voice was a little louder here. "Now, do you see a door?"

"A door?" Noa blinked. "No—there's just a lot of rubble."

"Keep looking." The orb bobbed reassuringly. "It's there."

Noa gritted her teeth. "Julian, I'm telling you, there's nothing here!" Panic rose in her throat. Would she be stuck in this horrible place forever?

"How about a mirror?"

"A mirror?" Despite herself, Noa almost laughed. "Where do you think I am, a bathroom? I just told you—"

"All right, all right. How about a fountain? Or perhaps a small pond?"

Noa reminded herself that Julian was trying to help her, and was not deliberately trying to drive her mad. "No."

"Hmm." She could practically see him running a hand through his dark hair. "Try the shadows, then."

"The sha—" Noa stopped. She saw the shadow rising above Julian's head. She saw the creatures thrusting her through a cloud of darkness. "The shadows are a door?"

"Possibly. I'm going off myths and legends here, Noa. Just try one."

"What if it doesn't work?" Her voice was high and shaky again.

"Then we'll try something else. I'm not going anywhere, I promise."

That's all well and good, Noa thought. *At least you know where you are.*

Still, Julian had found her, even if she couldn't see him, so she knew everything would be all right. Julian could rescue her from whatever this place was, just like he'd rescued her that time she fell asleep in a rowboat and drifted out to sea with the tide.

"There's one by this tower," she said. She didn't like the look of the tower—it seemed as if it could come down on her head at any moment—but there was a big, dark shadow beneath it, like the one she had seen in the castle.

She stepped up to it, and again she felt that odd sensation, as though the shadow was a curtain she could push aside. Something moved at the edge of her vision. She jumped, throwing her hands up in front of her, certain it was another gray, threadbare figure ready to drag her away.

An otter stared back at her, its dark eyes wide. It was an ordinary sea otter, its dark fur shiny, as if it had just hopped out of the water. In its mouth it held a fish, still twitching. Noa couldn't imagine how it had found a fish in this lifeless place. But then, she couldn't understand how she had found an otter there, either.

"Who are you?" she said stupidly. Surely this was some sort of magical otter, despite its ordinary appearance. The otter rose onto its hind legs, which didn't make it much taller.

"What is it?" Julian's voice said.

"I—I don't know. But it's not like those things that brought me here."

"Well, if it tries anything, tell it to leave you alone. You speak their language—they'll listen to you."

Noa froze. "I *what*?"

She thought of how she had felt drawn to the book from Evert. How the words had begun to make sense the longer she stared at them.

She could speak the lost magical language, which meant

she was a magician. Like Julian, and Mite, and Mom, and every Marchena before them.

Her head swam, and for a moment she thought she would faint. *I'm a magician*, she thought numbly. The words bounced around in her head, but she couldn't make sense of them. It was impossible that she could be a magician after wanting it for so long; Julian may as well have told her she could fly if she flapped her arms hard enough.

"W-what language is it?" she asked.

He paused, longer than before. "It's death."

"Death!" she shrieked. "Is that what I am? A *death* mage?"

"I think so," he said.

"Then I'm in *Death*? And those things that dragged me here were ghosts?"

"Noa, we can talk about this later. Just get yourself back."

Noa was shaking down to her slipper. She was a magician. She had been attacked by ghosts. She was in *Death*. Her logical mind clanked and whirred itself into exhaustion, and could make no sense of it.

The otter was still staring at her. Then it moved between her and the shadow, its nostrils twitching.

Noa's heart thudded. The otter looked young and healthy, which meant it was only as big as a small dog. But that didn't mean it couldn't hurt her. Was it some sort of Death guardian? Did it want to stop her from leaving?

Julian had said that it would listen to her if she spoke to it.

"Please move," she said, her voice faint. "I need to get back to the castle."

The otter didn't move an inch.

"You're speaking Florean," Julian said in the carefully patient voice he used with Mite when she was in danger of exploding.

"Of course I am!" Noa wished that Julian were there so that she could strangle him. "How am I supposed to say anything in a language I just learned I could speak tonight?"

"You've known how to speak it your whole life. You just didn't know you knew, because the spell the mages put on the Words made you forget the knowledge that you were—"

"Oh, black seas!" Noa was cold, and frightened, and something inside her snapped. She scooped up a rock the size of her fist and hurled it at the otter.

Well, not quite at it. It was still an otter, or at least it looked like one, and a person would have to have a heart full of stale bread crumbs to hurt an otter. But the otter didn't know she'd missed on purpose, and it darted aside with an angry growl. The fish fell onto the ground and flopped about, getting itself covered in the ashy grime that seemed to cover everything.

Noa lunged forward, toward the shadow that now seemed like only a shadow, but when she imagined it as she had seen it before, like a curtain, that was what it became. Sharp claws slashed at her leg, and she yelped in pain. She kicked out and managed to shake the otter off. Maybe it thought her leg would substitute for the lost fish, or maybe it was just out for revenge. Noa didn't intend to find out.

She grabbed a handful of shadow. It was light and thin as gossamer, but oddly sticky, like putting your hand into a spiderweb. Beneath the shadow was a hole. It was oval and pointed like a staring eye. On the other side of the hole, through a filmy sort of darkness, was a familiar wall and a familiar bookshelf.

She was looking into Julian's tower!

Before she could think too hard about the impossibility of picking up a shadow like a curtain, or the wisdom of jumping into mysterious holes in Death, Noa flung herself through.

13

Noa Recovers from Death

Noa stretched and yawned. She had been awake for a while, but it felt nice to just lie there under the blankets with a cat warming her feet.

She didn't remember much of what had happened after she returned from Death—she must have fainted on the way back. When she awoke, she was on the floor of the tower, and Julian was muttering a blood spell over her. She didn't feel any pain, but part of her knew she must have been hurt worse than she thought, for Julian's face was pale. She closed her eyes, and when she had opened them again it was morning, and she was curled up in Julian's bed with sunlight streaming through the tower windows.

She turned her head to watch the whitecapped sea glide past the island. She knew she should be terrified by what had happened, but she was too full of excitement to have room for anything else. The events of last night had resolved into one heart-stopping revelation:

She was a magician.

Noa wanted to dance around the tower. So she could speak the language of death, which was more than a little creepy and would not have been her first choice of magical powers, but she was still a magician. She wasn't the only Marchena in generations to be born without any magic. She could speak a long-lost magical language, which made her a lot like Julian, powerful in a unique way that set her apart from everybody else. She was definitely more unique than Mite.

And surely there was a way that she could use her magic to defeat Xavier. She imagined herself standing before Julian and his council and demonstrating her powers to exclamations of awe. She saw herself waving her hands and capturing the islands of Florean one by one. (Her imagination was fuzzy on how this would work, but it did a fair job of supplying the intimidating, windswept black cloak that she would be wearing.) She saw Julian seated on the throne of Florean, turning to smile his old smile at her, his eyes bright with happiness and gratitude.

She was a magician!

She lay there in a giddy state until she happened to glance down at the foot of her bed and found a small freckled face staring back at her.

Noa bolted upright with a scream in her throat, dislodging

the cat. "Mite! How long have you been there?"

"Not long," Mite said. She jumped up from where she'd been crouching with her chin propped on the bed. "Since you woke up and started grinning and rubbing your hands together. What's so funny?"

Noa's heart was still thudding. "Oh . . . I was thinking about all the ghosts I just met," she said. "I told them that I had a little sister, and they said they would drop by to visit you one night. Isn't that thoughtful?"

Mite paled. "They didn't say that."

"Not all of them," Noa agreed. "Though there was one ghost who seemed particularly interested. . . . The shadows are like doors for them, you know. He said he'd use the shadow under your bed. He wore a big black hood, so I couldn't see his face, but I think it looked a little like this." She put two fingers in her mouth and stretched it wide while bugging her eyes out.

Mite made a strangled sound and went thundering down the staircase. "Julian!"

Noa fell back against the cushions, chortling. A moment later, Julian came up the stairs, an exasperated look on his face. "What's this about you threatening your sister with ghosts?"

"I wouldn't say *threatening*—"

"You don't use your powers to frighten people." Julian swept his cloak out of the way and sat on the edge of her bed. "That's one of the cardinal rules of magic."

This was the most hypocritical thing Noa had heard in her

life. "You frighten people all the time!"

He frowned. "Only people who deserve it."

"Mite deserves it. She's a sneak." Noa faltered, though, as she remembered Esmalda. She shoved that thought away. She didn't want to worry about anything right now.

She was a magician!

"So the cardinal rules of magic." She sat up and pushed the covers back. "What are they? I have to know now, since I'm a magician and all."

Julian gently but firmly pushed her back against the pillows. "Before you run off and inhale every grimoire I own, we need to make sure you're all right."

"I'm fine."

"I'll be the judge of that. You were pretty badly scratched up. What was it that attacked you?"

"I don't know," Noa lied, because it didn't sound very impressive to admit that she'd gotten into a fight with an otter, even if it had been a magical one. "But it was big."

Julian stretched his hand over her, murmuring a few words in Marrow. "Well, you seem healed. A little tired, but that's normal after you use a lot of magic."

"I didn't use any magic," Noa said. "A bunch of ghosts came along and grabbed me, and dragged me back to the Beyond with them!" She lashed her arms out dramatically in a grabbing motion.

Julian looked thoughtful. "There are stories about ancient mages who traveled to the land of the dead. I always thought they were just stories, but perhaps those mages were able to speak to ghosts, like you. Your power may be different than the others. . . . Perhaps ghosts are drawn to it, even without you speaking their language. As soon as you released your power by reading that book, they came to you."

Noa's exhilaration was wilting at the edges. "Can we . . . stop them from doing that?"

"I expect so. There are methods you can use to control your power. And once you grow more confident in speaking their language, you should be able to command the ghosts, just as a fire mage commands flame. I'll teach you."

"You will?"

"Of course. We should start as soon as possible. Tomorrow, if you're up for it."

Her excitement blossomed again. She was going to have magic lessons with Julian! Normally, magician children went to Northwind Island, which was home to a magic school where they lived for a year, or until they mastered basic enchantments. Noa had often fantasized about Northwind Island, but this was just as good. "We should start now!"

"Not so fast, Noabell. You need to eat something. I've already sent for lunch."

"Lunch?" Noa looked at the position of the sun and

realized he was right—she *must* have been tired. "How did you know I was in Death? You seemed to have it all figured out last night."

"Not exactly," he said. "I knew something bad had happened. Reckoner practically dragged me out of bed, howling his head off. I found the book by the lavaplace, and I guessed that you had been there. I went to your room, but you were gone. So I used a blood spell to track your location—that sort of magic is difficult, and I wasn't sure I could do it, given how much magic I spent on Evert. The spell told me you were in another world. It also told me you were dead."

Noa felt cold. "That I was dead?"

"Yes." Julian rubbed his face, which was very pale. "I panicked. If I hadn't, maybe I would have found you sooner. What the spell told me was a contradiction—that you were alive somewhere, but also dead. So I invented a new spell—"

"Invented a spell?" Noa repeated. "Just like that?" She was used to Julian's slapdash flair for magic, but sometimes he still managed to surprise her.

"Yes. A spell that would use our shared bloodline to allow me to communicate with you, wherever you were. If you had truly been dead, I wouldn't have been able to do that—I soon realized that the first spell had actually been telling me that you were in the land of the dead, not dead yourself. I guessed the rest based on the myths and legends I've been reading about the ancient mages."

"Are you going to explode, Noa?" Mite said, her head popping up from the stairwell.

"No, Mite," Noa said. "Not all magicians are as dramatic as you."

"I'm not dramatic!" Mite seemed to consider. "Or if I am, I can't help it."

Noa turned back to Julian. "We need to start making plans. We have one of the Lost Words! How shall we use it to get rid of Xavier?"

"You need to learn about your magic before we think about any of that," Julian said. "Even then . . ."

Noa stared at him. "What are you talking about? What was the point of looking for the Lost Words if we don't use them?"

"The point? The point was to find a weapon that I could use against Xavier. Not to turn my little sister into one."

Noa's fantasies crumbled and toppled like sandcastles. She had just found out she was a magician, and Julian was acting as if it was nothing. As if she was still just his little sister, still the same girl who'd done nothing but cry and run away the night Xavier stole the throne from the Marchenas. She wasn't that girl anymore. She was strong. She was a magician! "So it's all right for you to risk your life, but not me?"

"Yes," he said, in a voice that stopped his mages in their tracks. But it didn't daunt Noa.

"That's not fair." She wanted to sound as cold as him, but her voice had a tremor in it. "I want him gone as much as you do."

Julian blinked, then took her hand. She knew that, like her, he was thinking of those terrible hours in the fishing boat. The sloshing of the waves; the dark all around. The palace disappearing into the sea like a sinking ship.

"We're still on course for Greenwash Strait," he said in a placating voice. "We're going to keep searching for the Lost Words. If there's another book, we have to keep it out of Xavier's hands."

But Noa wasn't about to give up. "Julian, why did we sail all the way to Evert? Just so you could turn an island right side out? We found one of the lost languages of magic! Let's use it. Let's get rid of Xavier once and for all."

Julian didn't answer for a moment. "I'll think about it," he said finally. He didn't look like he was going to think about it. If anything, he looked gray at the idea of Noa tangling with Xavier. But that didn't matter.

Noa settled back into her pillows, strangely calm. Her anger cooled into something dark and unyielding as basalt, glittering with anticipation.

She was a magician now. And she was going to do whatever she could to make Julian king of Florean—whether he liked it or not.

14

Noa Has Her First Magic Lesson

Noa paced back and forth, each step thudding in a satisfying way against the flagstones. She had decided to wear her black boots today instead of her usual sandals. They were more magician-like, in her opinion, though warm for the weather. Her sweaty feet made small squishing sounds as she walked.

She was in the expansive courtyard at the back of the castle, waiting for Julian to come and start her lesson. Mite was playing in the fountain, even though Noa had told her not to. But as Mite was now soaked from head to foot, Noa didn't see the point of dragging her out—she wasn't going to get any wetter.

The salty wind rustled through the ivy that wreathed the courtyard. Astrae was chugging along at a nice pace toward Greenwash Strait, and hopefully another lost language, which should have felt satisfying, but Noa found that becoming a magician had temporarily driven many of her plots and schemes out of her head. She was filled with fantasies about the wondrous feats she would surely be able to perform soon. She wondered how magicians got anything done.

A number of Julian's mages were standing about or sitting on shaded benches. They had all heard about Noa's new power, of course, and had come to see it for themselves. Noa was glad she had worn the boots, though she did wish they would squish a little more quietly.

When Julian finally arrived, he was carrying a single book. Noa was unimpressed. She had expected him to come to their first magic lesson with stacks of books, as well as rare magical objects—she didn't know what kind, but certainly rare ones.

"What, am I just supposed to read this?" she said when he placed the book in her hands with an elaborate flourish. It was the dictionary from Evert. "That's not much of a lesson."

"You're going to read it aloud," Julian said.

"Oh, well, that's something I couldn't have thought of myself."

Julian gave her a look. He seemed a little more well-rested, though his eyes were still shadowed. "A part of you already knows every word in this book, but you need to get comfortable with the language. Maita Marchena," he added, turning, "get out of that fountain. If you ruin another cloak, Petrik will tear out what's left of his hair."

"I don't see the point of this," Noa said. She was still tetchy from yesterday. "You don't want me using my magic to fight Xavier."

"There *are* other uses for magic besides getting rid of traitorous, murdering kings," Julian said. "We're going full steam ahead to Greenwash Strait, Noa, but we won't arrive for a few days. We may as well figure out what you can do."

Yes, Noa thought. *Let's figure out how I can get rid of a traitorous, murdering king.* "What if the ghosts come again?"

"They shouldn't unless you summon them," Julian said. "That's how magical languages work—speaking random words in Briar, for example, wouldn't cause that vine to flower. I have to command the vine to do my will. That's all spells are—commands, precisely phrased."

"I know," Noa said impatiently. "But the ghosts came before without me summoning them."

"Yes. If that happens again, I'm going to anchor you."

"Oh, good." Noa let out a sigh of relief. That was what Julian did when he and Mite practiced magic, to keep her from blowing things up. A mage could anchor another mage, or keep them from losing control of their power, if they had the opposite power.

"What's the opposite of death magic?" Noa said.

"Blood magic." Julian smiled. "Yet another reason why I knew the Lost Words weren't a myth. Marrow has no opposite, yet all the other languages do. They aren't in perfect oppositional harmony—at least, given what I've seen so far. But then, a lot of mages make the same point about Salt and Spark, or Worm and—"

"Uh-huh, right." Noa wasn't in the mood for Julian's tangents, or rather, she was further away from the mood than usual. "So what's the language of death called, anyway?"

He raised his eyebrows. "You tell me. You're the only one who can speak it."

"Oh!" She got to name a language! She tapped her chin. Most of the magical languages were named for what they reminded people of—Worm, for example, the language of earth and stone, was a moist, slippery, undulating language. Briar, the language of plants, sounded sharp and unpleasant. She remembered the words slithering across the page of the book, and how they had chilled her.

"Shiver," she said quietly.

Julian accepted this with a nod. "All right. Let's hear a few words."

Noa hesitated, then opened the book. As before, she understood at once that she was looking at a dictionary, that the strange symbols on the page were arranged into lists of words. An odd sense of calm washed over her, and she no longer felt afraid.

"Flower," she read. "Flicker. Florean Archipelago. These are just normal words! There's nothing magical about them. This really is just a dictionary."

She looked up and found Julian's blue eyes narrowed in a wince. Mite, who sat dripping in the leafy shade, had her hands over her ears. "I don't like that," she said with finality.

Noa blinked. "Was I speaking Shiver?"

"Yes, you were." Julian seemed to make an effort to relax his face.

"What did it sound like?"

"Awful," Mite said.

"I don't really know how to describe it," Julian said, after a moment. "Sort of . . . dry. And crunchy. Like walking on dead leaves."

"Leaves don't sound like that," Mite muttered.

"It's normal to slip into a magical language without realizing it," Julian said. "At least at first."

Noa nodded. After all, some of her earliest memories were of gazing out from her crib at a dark-haired boy babbling nonsensically at her.

"I find that thinking about the element can help," Julian said. "When I say something in Spark, I picture fire. Try picturing the ghosts, or something else you saw in Death."

Noa would rather not picture the things that had dragged her from the castle. She tried thinking of the otter, and imagined she was speaking to it. She waved her hands about as she had sometimes seen Julian do. "I command you to leave me alone!"

She knew she had spoken in Shiver, now that she was

paying attention. But she was also aware that something was off. It was like trying to speak a foreign language—her mouth couldn't form all the words properly, and she had to guess how some things sounded.

"Good," Julian said. "What did you say?"

Noa told him, and he nodded. "As you already know, or I hope you know, whether a spell is successful or not depends on a mage's fluency in the language they're using. All mages are born able to speak at least one language of magic, but that isn't the same as speaking fluently. Do you understand?"

"Yes," Noa said slowly, for she had always been a little fuzzy on that point. "But I don't understand why some mages are more fluent than others."

"No one does," Julian said. "Some people are just born with a talent for magic, I suppose in the same way that certain people are born with a gift for music or speaking. However, even if you aren't naturally gifted, you can improve with practice, just as a poor orator can. Take Asha, for example. She's one of the most powerful light mages in Florean, but when she was a child, she could barely speak Hum. She had to work hard at it."

"She's still not as good as you," Noa said. She wasn't trying to flatter him; it was just a fact.

He shrugged. "Like I said, no one knows exactly how it works. But you shouldn't be discouraged if it takes a while before you can cast effective spells in Shiver."

"What kind of spells? Can I kill people? Or summon the ghosts of the ancient mages?" She asked the question that had haunted her since she found out about her magic. "Could I . . . could I talk to Mom?"

Julian's face softened. "I don't know."

Noa was frustrated. Julian was supposed to know everything about magic. "Why not?"

"The records relating to Shiver—or whatever it was called in ancient times—were destroyed. It's anyone's guess what your powers entail. We'll have to work it out as we go. One thing we do know is that you can cross great distances quickly in Death. When I looked for you that night, the blood spell told me that you were somewhere in the Ferral Sea."

Noa's jaw dropped. "That's hundreds of miles away!"

"Yes. It makes sense, though—in the stories, ghosts pop up wherever they feel like it."

Noa liked this. It was a little like having a magical doorway that could take her anywhere in the thirteen seas. "What about the shadows? Is every shadow a doorway to Death? Or out of Death?"

"I suspect so," Julian said. "I guess they're all connected somehow, even if Death is more compact than the living world."

This was convenient, if creepy. So Noa could use any shadow to get into Death, if she wanted. "So what are we going to do?"

Julian scanned the courtyard. He motioned to a passion flower vine dangling from a trellis. "Let's try to answer your first question."

Nervously, Noa approached the vine. "You want me to kill it?"

"Start smaller. Try just one flower."

Noa focused on a large bloom at eye level. It was a rich orange with delicate yellow stamen. It was hard to think about the flower and the otter at the same time. She ended up picturing an orange otter. "Ah, all right," she stammered in Shiver. "Die. Please?"

The flower did nothing. A bee alighted among the petals and dug around hungrily. Noa considered trying to kill the bee, but she knew Mite was watching.

"No, no," Julian said. "You're asking a question. You have to tell it what you want it to do. Here." He let out a stream of words in Briar that snagged at Noa's ears like thorns. The vine sprouted dozens of new flowers and coiled along the stones.

"What did you say?" Noa demanded. "That was more than just one command."

"I told the vine to grow. But I also told it how—where to point its leaves to gather the most sun, which stones to grasp hold of. Plants often need instructions."

Noa thought this over. She looked back at the flower. She told it to stop taking water from the vine, to brown and wither and go to sleep. She tried saying it a dozen different ways, but still the flower was unchanged. The bee fluttered around her head, as if in mockery.

"The words don't feel right," she said, frustrated. "It's like trying to speak backward or something."

"Come here." Julian led her over to the fountain. He showed her several Salt spells, ordering the water to churn, to freeze, to slosh over the side in waves. He even made a wave form itself into an eerie, lurching figure with foam for hair.

"I invented that one," he said, after the water creature dissolved. "Mages used to think you couldn't use Salt to make the sea take on unnatural shapes, but I found that if you command it to assume a state between water and ice—which requires fluency to keep it there—you can then shape it into whatever form you wish."

Noa was still staring at the place where the figure had disappeared. "How did you work that out?"

"Patience. That's the only way to master your powers."

That only made Noa more frustrated, though she wasn't sure if she was annoyed with herself or with Julian. It felt worse to fail at magic when he stood there making success look so easy.

"Make a dolphin, Julian!" Mite said, leaning over the fountain. She let out a cry of delight when Julian slashed his hand out dramatically, rings flashing, and summoned a watery dolphin. It sailed over their heads and shattered against the courtyard.

Noa's gaze was drawn to a weed poking up between the flagstones, where there was now a dolphin-shaped puddle of water. The weed was brown and clearly dead. She knelt beside it.

"Could you—" She stopped. No asking questions, Julian had said. "Drink the water," she said. "Open your leaves to the sunlight. Live again."

She knew that it was impossible, and indeed, the weed did nothing. But she felt, somehow, that something was listening to her. Not the weed, exactly. But *something.*

"All right," she said, "how about you move this leaf here? Just a little bit."

The leaf twitched.

Noa leaped back, her heart pounding. "Did you see that?"

"Yes, good!" Julian knelt beside her. "Try it again, my Noabell."

She did. The dead plant didn't always move when she asked it to—it seemed to depend on how she pronounced the words in Shiver, and the words weren't easy to pronounce. It felt a little like trying to roll shards of ice around in her mouth while singing in perfect tune.

Julian made her practice over and over again until she had made every brown leaf move. Noa's head began to pound, but she forced herself to focus. Next, Julian brought out one of the fish Anna was planning to cook for supper, still alive and swimming in a bowl. She had just as much success with that as she had with the flower. She thought the fish looked even more energetic than before.

"Interesting," Julian said. The sun was overhead now, filling the courtyard with sunlight. Most of the mages had left, having realized that Noa wasn't going to open a gaping portal into the Beyond or summon an army of ghosts, or anything else entertaining. A bead of sweat kept trickling into Noa's eyes. She was beyond regretting her boots; she wanted to throw them into the sea, then herself after them.

"Perhaps death magic doesn't give one the power to kill," Julian went on in a musing voice. He was looking past her, his thoughts somewhere else. "If so, it may not be in opposition to blood magic at all. I'll have to do more research. . . ."

"I'll help," Noa said, standing up. She welcomed the idea of spending time in the cool library. "It's my magic, after all "

"Your Highness," Renne said, appearing from one of the castle doors. "The scouts' reports are ready."

Julian nodded. He turned back to Noa, but his attention seemed far away. "Thank you, but it will be quicker if I work alone."

"But—"

"We'll continue your lessons tomorrow," he said, following Renne. When Mite made to go, too, he said, "Not now, Maita. Stay with your sister. I'll see you at supper." Mite's face fell, and he winked and murmured something to the fountain. A cloud of droplets rose into the air, humming like bees. Mite squealed and set to chasing them around the courtyard.

Noa stared at Julian's retreating back, a flush rising in her cheeks. For a moment, she wondered if he was disappointed in her for not being better at Shiver, and felt an awful, prickly shame rise inside her. But no, it wasn't that. As usual, Julian just wasn't thinking about her.

Noa didn't understand. She had always wanted to be a magician, even before Xavier, before Astrae. Now that she was one, why wasn't she happy?

She turned and fled the courtyard.

15

Tomas's Biggest
Fan Strikes Again

Noa rose before the sun. She dressed quickly in the darkness, then slipped out of the castle through an unguarded back corridor, pausing only to grab a cake (caramel apple) and a piece of dried fish.

Julian thought they were going to have another lesson that morning. But Noa had no intention of being there. When Julian came looking for her, she would be far, far away. Her lesson yesterday had given her an idea, one that Julian wouldn't like one bit.

Tomas was waiting for her by the cove where they'd met Beauty, just as he'd promised when she went to see him yesterday. He had the wagon again, covered with a blanket. When he saw Noa, he started.

"You look like you've seen a ghost," Noa said with a snort.

"Have I?" Tomas's gaze darted left and right. "Have you brought one with you?"

"Why would I bring a ghost? They're not dogs."

Tomas rubbed his face. He gave her a look that Noa recognized—it was how he looked at Julian.

"What, are you afraid of me now?" Noa asked, pleased.

"Well, yes," Tomas said. "People in the village are saying you can summon ghosts just by whistling, and kill a man by tossing your hair over your shoulder."

Noa liked the sound of that, but she shook her head. "So far, I only know how to get attacked by ghosts and make weeds jiggle." She added, "You don't have to tell anyone that."

Tomas sighed. He drew back the blanket, revealing another huge cake, lemon-lime again. "I hope I don't have to tell you how difficult it is to keep my father from guessing who these cakes are for. I've tried saying they're for the king's dragon, but—" The rest of the sentence was overtaken by a scream as Beauty lunged from the water and snatched up the cake, nearly taking Tomas's arm with it.

Noa marched up to the water's edge. "Beauty! You have to stop doing that."

The sound of gnashing teeth and a horrible snort was her only reply.

"I have another question," Noa said.

"Mmm. I'm all ears, dear," replied the serpent's voice from the darkness. Noa could barely make out her enormous silhouette against the predawn sky. "You've earned it. Or, rather,

– 188 –

your talented friend has. He outdid himself this time."

Tomas was blushing. Before they could get into baking techniques, Noa said, "I want to know about death mages. Tell me how they moved through the Beyond."

"Do I look like a mage?" Beauty spoke around the mouthful of cake, though she covered her mouth politely with her tail. "That's a question for dear Julian."

"No," Noa said. "All the books about death mages were destroyed. Nobody knows what their powers are, or how they use them. But you said you were alive when Evert was turned inside out. That means you were alive when there were still death mages. And I'm willing to bet you know a thing or two about their powers, given how much you love spying on people."

Beauty let out a low chuckle and crooned, "Clever, clever little Marchena."

"Well?"

"Perhaps I do know something about death magic. Perhaps I know about other magics, too, lost magics that dear Julian couldn't even imagine. . . ."

Noa's interest was piqued. "Like what?"

Beauty blinked slowly. "Is that another question? I don't see another cake. . . ."

Noa gritted her teeth. "Let's just stick to death magic, then."

"I don't know how the mages moved through Death,"

Beauty said. "I know only that they used guides."

Noa frowned. "What kind of guides?"

"I don't know. Creatures of some sort who inhabit the Beyond."

Creatures. Noa swallowed.

"That's all I need to know. Thank you, Beauty." She turned and marched back up the beach. Tomas trailed after her.

"What are you going to do?" His voice was panicked. "You're not going to—to summon a ghost, are you?"

"No," Noa said. "I'm going to go to them." She paused under a tree, its leaves like black lace against the stars. It didn't cast much of a shadow, given the early hour, but there was a slightly darker darkness than everywhere else. And it felt right, somehow. Noa's fingers itched to catch hold of it and pull.

"Does the king know you're doing this?" Tomas demanded.

"Not exactly. And you're not going to tell him. Well, you'll need to tell him if I don't come back."

Tomas's face was red. He looked torn between shouting and bursting into tears. "Noa, I know you're a Marchena, and coming up with mad magical plots is probably in your blood or something, but I'm your friend. That's why you have to listen when I say this is completely—"

"Tomas, trust me, I have a plan," Noa said. "Look, I'm a magician, all right? I can handle myself. If you could bake Beauty another cake while I'm gone, that would be great. I'll have more questions for her about the Lost Words when I get back." Then she picked up the shadow as if it were a rug hiding a trapdoor, and leaped.

Jumping into Death wasn't as difficult as it should have been. After falling for a few feet, not very quickly, she hit sand with a soft *whump*.

She tried to smother the cough that rose in her throat. Death looked just as it had when she left it, and it smelled the same, too. She was instantly on the alert, scanning the sandy hills for ghosts. Oddly, she hadn't encountered any since that night in Julian's tower, and she didn't see any now.

Her hands shaking, she reached into her pack and pulled out the fish. She tore it into pieces and scattered it across the sand. She sat down, leaned her back against a broken bit of staircase, and waited.

It was a long wait, and soon she was shivering. She had remembered to put on a sweater under her black cloak, and she was again wearing her heavy boots, but it wasn't enough. The cold seeped through the fabric like water.

Finally, she saw the otter. It seemed to slither out of a crack in a ruined wall. Otters had always reminded Noa of snakes; they had an oily, undulating grace regardless of whether they were swimming or walking. It nudged the fish with its nose, but didn't eat.

Noa's heart thudded. She remembered those strong claws

slicing across her leg. This couldn't be an ordinary otter, despite its appearance—it was in Death, after all. She had intended to use the fish to distract the creature if it attacked her, and here she was luring it to her. Still, she'd made the decision to come here. She wasn't going back now.

"I command you, Death guardian," she said in Shiver, "to lead me to the palace of King Xavier in Florean City."

16

Noa Flatters
an Otter

The otter watched her, motionless, its back arched like a wave.

All right, then. Noa reached into her pack and broke off a piece of cake. She tossed it to the otter. It sniffed it, then hesitantly nibbled. Noa gave a silent prayer of thanks for Tomas and his cakes, which were proving increasingly useful as all-purpose monster treats.

She decided she might as well act as if she knew what she was doing. "Well? Will you be my guide?"

The otter finished the cake. "You're a weird sort of ghost," it said.

Noa nearly jumped out of her skin. "You—you talk."

"You're surprised." The otter was speaking Shiver in a quiet voice that sounded a bit like a young boy's. "Why did you speak to me, if you didn't think I could understand? You're not very bright, are you?"

Noa ignored that. "I'm not a ghost, I'm a magician. What are you?"

"What am I? Are you blind as well as thickheaded? I don't feel like talking to you. But I may change my mind if you give me more of that." It edged forward, eyeing the cake.

Noa tossed another piece, mainly to stop it—and its claws—from getting any closer. She decided to try a different approach. "I'm sorry I threw a stone at you."

"You didn't," the otter said, munching. "That must have been someone else."

Noa blinked. "There are more of you?"

"All otters can move in and out of Death," it said. "It's a useful place if you want to avoid a shark. Or hide a nice salmon."

"All otters?" Noa stared at the unremarkable brown creature before her. "You're saying you're not some sort of—I don't know, special otter? You don't have any powers?"

The otter stared at her. "Are you saying I'm not special?"

"No, no," Noa said. "I mean, you're certainly very . . ." She trailed off, for the otter was the most ordinary-looking otter she had ever seen. "Handsome."

The otter swiped a paw over its face. "Am I?"

It seemed so pleased that Noa hurried on. "Oh, yes. In fact, um, that's why I thought you had magical powers. I thought maybe you put a spell on yourself."

The otter preened. "Nope."

"Are otters the only creatures who know how to get into Death?"

"For the most part," the otter said. "Cats find their way in sometimes. Ravens . . . crows. But they usually can't get out again. We're the only ones clever enough to use the shadow doors."

Noa's surprise was fading. She'd often observed that otters were among the slipperiest of creatures, and they seemed equally agile in two worlds, land and sea, while most beings—people included—preferred sticking to one. She didn't see any reason why they shouldn't be just as adept at navigating Death.

"How impressive." Noa was beginning to realize that the otter had a bottomless appetite for compliments. "And you seem like you must be the cleverest of them. So clever that I bet you could find any door in the world. Even one that leads to the palace in Florean City."

"The palace? That's easy." The otter dashed off. Noa had to run to keep up with it, and even then, she would have lost the mercurial creature had it not waited for her to catch up. Eventually, it stopped by a broken stone house. Noa leaned against it, coughing from the smoky air.

"Is that it? We didn't go very far."

"Nothing is far here," the otter said smugly.

Noa examined the shadow that lay beneath the wall. "And this goes to the palace?"

"Somewhere in the palace," the otter agreed.

"Somewhere?"

"The doors aren't exact. Sometimes they move."

"Great," Noa muttered. She reminded herself that she was lucky to have a guide at all; she would never have been able to find a door to the palace on her own. A thought occurred to her.

"Otter," she said, her heart thudding, "Can you talk to the ghosts?"

"Sure," it said. "But we don't. They're boring. All they do is mope."

Noa swallowed. "Could you find someone for me?"

"Who?"

"Queen Tamora," she said. "I don't know if she's here. But could you—could you spread the word that I'm looking for her? Tell the other otters, and any ghosts you see."

"I like hide-and-seek," the otter said. "I win almost every time. All right. But she's probably not here. Most ghosts that come here only stay a little while, then they go somewhere not even otters can find a door to."

Noa balled her hands to stop them from shaking. She had been afraid of an answer like that. Still, she had to try. She felt that familiar ache, and wished she'd brought Willow.

But that was silly. She was a mage on a serious mission, not a little girl missing her toy. She swallowed her tears and stood up straight. "Would you mind waiting until I get back?"

The otter looked dubious. Noa added, "I mean, I've heard that otters are very patient creatures. But if that's not true—"

"Oh, it is true." The otter stood up straighter. "We're more patient than anybody." Noa gave it the rest of the cake, and it flopped down on its back with the treat balanced on its chest, looking extremely pleased with its situation.

Steeling herself, Noa picked up the shadow, and leaped.

Light flooded her eyes, and her boots hit the ground hard. She stumbled and fell against a marble floor polished to such a sheen it hurt, especially after the darkness of Death.

When she looked up, she choked on a yelp. She was crouched behind a column in the palace throne room. The space was enormous, a glittering sea of white and black marble. And there on a dais beneath a row of windows streaming with pearly dawn light was a golden throne, with two guards standing motionless behind it.

Noa couldn't move. This had been her home. Her mother had sat on that throne, receiving noble guests and ambassadors. For a moment, Noa could hear her mother's laughter ringing out through the hall.

"Are you lost?"

Noa spun, and found herself facing a palace guard. The woman had a kind face, and was smiling at Noa.

"Um—" She frantically blinked the tears back, trying to remember the story she had rehearsed. "Yes, sorry. I'm one of the new pages. The palace is so big!"

"That's all right." The woman patted her shoulder, clearly assuming Noa was upset about being lost. "It takes a while to get the hang of things. Where's your uniform?"

Noa looked up as if startled. "Oh no! I knew I forgot something. Papa will be so angry—"

"No, he won't," the woman said gruffly. "Come along. I'll find you a spare. Just mind you remember it next time, all right?"

Noa nodded, brushing away a tear.

The guard shook her head. "I don't know what your papa was thinking, buying you that cloak. Black cloaks are banned in Florean City. You'll have people thinking your family are Marchenans."

"Marchenans?" Noa said, turning wide eyes of innocence on the guard.

"You know. Supporters of the Dark Lord. Come on, don't dally. I'm supposed to be on duty."

This was interesting. Did Julian have supporters in Florean City? Noa knew she couldn't ask questions without arousing suspicion, so she filed the information away.

Twenty minutes later, she was striding purposefully along one of the servants' corridors, her new red cloak billowing behind her and her old clothes stuffed into her pack.

She had no intention of attacking Xavier or anything like that. No, she was here to gather information about his plans, particularly how they concerned the Lost Words. She would find out if he'd recovered any magical languages himself, and if so, what they were and how he planned to use them against Astrae. Then, Noa thought smugly, she would take that information to Julian, and show him just how valuable her newfound powers were.

She spent the morning wandering the palace, eavesdropping. She knew that nobody paid much attention to pages, most of whom were the second or third children of unimportant nobles, and that as long as she acted as if she knew where she was going, people would leave her alone. She knew every room and hallway, and she knew which parts of the palace to avoid in order not to arouse suspicion. Sometimes she recognized a guard or ambassador who had served under her mother, but none of them recognized her. Noa wasn't surprised—she had been barely eleven when they'd fled, and she looked different now, being a head taller and skinny rather than round-faced and plump. Her freckles had faded and been replaced by a smattering of pimples, which she had never been grateful for until now. Grown-ups didn't seem to change much in two years, she noticed, apart from sometimes getting fatter.

A strange sense of unease hung over the palace. Noa often found herself eavesdropping on conversations held in hushed whispers in shadowy corners. If anyone saw her listening, she hurried up to them and nervously asked for directions somewhere, as if she had been waiting for them to notice her.

After a few hours of this, one thing had become clear:

people were almost as afraid of Xavier as they were of Julian. They whispered about the executions of dark mages, and even about the new king going too far. Noa didn't understand it— most people disliked dark mages. Why would they be so upset about Xavier killing them? Then she glanced out a window.

Queen's Step didn't have any beaches, just a stretch of rocky shore that disappeared at high tide. Down on that shore was a row of skeletons chained to the rock. At least, they were skeletons now, the bones picked so clean they gleamed in the sunlight. It was low tide, and crabs scurried hither and thither. It took Noa a moment to put those two things together, and to realize that everyone in the palace—all Xavier's mages, servants, and soldiers—would have been able to watch as the crabs devoured the dark mages.

Noa drew back from the window. She had to sit down for a while after that, because her knees had turned into pudding. She had seen animal skeletons—dead whales and seals sometimes washed up on Astrae—but never people. A servant asked if she was all right, and she forced herself to answer normally, concealing her clenched fists beneath her skirt.

After another hour of spying, she knew that she couldn't stay in the palace much longer—she was beginning to attract frowning looks from some of the guards she had walked past more than once. Yet she couldn't leave without finding out more about the Lost Words.

She rubbed her clammy hands against the red cloak and

took a deep breath. Then she set out for the royal wing of the palace.

Noa hadn't wanted to go there. Partly because pages weren't normally allowed in that part of the palace. But also because the royal wing had been her home.

Her heart thudded in her ears. She felt like a ghost herself, retracing the path she had often taken all those years ago—past the councillors' offices, up the black marble staircase, past the courtyard with its flowering vines. She worried briefly that the finches would recognize her and raise a fuss. There was the banister she and Julian used to slide down. She forgot all about being mad at him. She just wished he were with her.

She lost her nerve at the sight of the guards standing at either side of the huge doors. Her old bedroom was beyond those doors. What would it look like now? Was it still a bedroom, or had Xavier turned it into something else? She doubled back and slipped into a small garden, folding herself onto a bench between two trellises crowded with climbing roses.

She brushed away her tears. She hadn't realized how hard it would be to come back to the home that had been stolen from her. Last night, she had tried to think of everything that could go wrong, but she hadn't thought about this. She hadn't come up with a contingency plan for her own memories.

Voices murmured behind her. Several people were approaching. Noa tried to press herself into the trellis, but the roses were prickly. Her thoughts were too jumbled to remember any of the excuses she had invented for her presence in the royal wing. She jumped to her feet, but before she could dart away, three people rounded the corner.

Two of them were councillors—Noa could tell by their fine clothes and elaborate cloak pins, which were just like Gabriela's. They blinked at her, their expressions only slightly surprised, as you might be upon finding an iguana in your boot.

The third was King Xavier.

The current king wasn't an old man—he was only five or six years older than Julian. But he looked like one, with his pale, colorless hair, heavy glasses, and skinny, frail frame. Even the layers of red and bronze velvet that made up his cloak couldn't conceal the stoop in his shoulders from a childhood spent hunched over books in libraries. People said that Xavier was a strategic genius—that was how he had built up a rebellion against Noa's mother. Not because people liked him better, or because he was a great hero or warrior, but because he had known exactly what rumors to spread, what false promises to make, and how to bribe the generals and the greedy nobles who felt ignored in the queen's court to take his side.

Noa's breath died in her throat as Xavier's eyes met hers. He had been one of her mother's councillors. She had spoken to him several times; he had even attended her tenth birthday party—

"Get out, girl," Xavier snapped. His voice was just like the rest of him, thin and reedy. But his pale blue eyes were sharp with intelligence, though they barely rested on Noa before he turned to one of the councillors. "I thought I ordered this area cleared."

Noa bowed, shaking with fury. She tried to disguise it by making her face a mask of fear. She ran from the courtyard and down the corridor. But rather than turning and going down the stairs, she went straight through a series of servants' halls until she came to another entrance to the courtyard. She slunk toward the ivied nook where she had left the king and his advisors, keeping to the shadows.

"—have to take precautions," the king was saying. "We need more information from him. Otherwise what good is he?"

Noa peered through the greenery. The king was pacing, his eyes like shards of glass, while his councillors hovered nervously.

"The Dark Lord's movements have become increasingly erratic, Your Highness," said the older of the two councillors, a woman with a Ferralian accent.

"But we're certain he's nearing the Gabriolan Islands?" Xavier said. The councillor nodded.

Noa frowned. How did Xavier know where Astrae was? The island was invisible if viewed from behind, so he couldn't have spies following them. And the stretch of sea between Astrae and the Gabriolans was empty of islands to station sentries.

The councillor said something that Noa couldn't hear. They had moved behind a canyonweed bush, and its fat yellow flowers obscured the woman's face. Noa's toes went numb with fear at the sound of her own name.

Xavier shook his head. "Maria, if I ever manage to get my hands on just one of those brats, I could have Julian Marchena eating out of the palm of my hand. He'd cut his own head off to spare his sisters any pain—and after he did, we could quietly execute them both and finally have done with the whole rotten Marchena line. One day."

If Noa's toes had been numb before, now her whole legs were, and at least half her stomach. She barely dared to breathe. It was one thing to hear secondhand that Xavier wanted her and Mite. It was quite another to hear it from his own lips, while his pale fingers absently plucked petals from the climbing roses.

"Your Highness, perhaps we should focus on the plan," the younger councillor said.

The king made a thoughtful sound. "We'll wait until he reaches the Devorian Rocks. That's the perfect place for an ambush. And then, after I take it from him, we'll watch his defenses crumble. We may not be able to get our hands on his sisters—yet—but we can have the next best thing."

Take what? Noa's thoughts were racing. What did Julian value more than anything else, apart from her and Mite? Had Xavier figured out that they'd found one of the Lost Words?

She silently prayed for the councillors to ask questions, but clearly they knew exactly what the king meant.

"What if he guesses our plan?" Maria said. "What if he's protected it with magics that we haven't anticipated?"

Xavier let out a humorless laugh. "You're giving Julian more credit than he deserves. That boy hasn't had a strategic thought in his life. His mother was just the same . . . it's why she never suspected me. No, Maria. For all his terrifying magical gifts, Julian Marchena will fall—and it will be because of his own lack of cunning."

17

The Castle
Is Haunted

Noa barely remembered the journey back to Astrae. She knew she had fled through the shadow of a tree fern just as the king and his councillors turned to leave, and that the otter had led her back through Death, but everything else was a blur. A shapeless fear had seized hold of her mind, crowding out everything else.

King Xavier was going to kill Julian. He was going to kill Julian just like he had killed Mom.

For some reason—maybe because, as the otter had warned, the shadow doors moved around—she fell out of Death into waist-deep water on the shore of Astrae, through the shadow of a boulder. She waded to the beach, where one of the mages found her and marched her back to the castle. She was deposited in the empty throne room, dripping all over the marble.

Noa sat on the throne and drew her legs to her chest. It was a warm day, but she was shaking. She fiddled with her charm bracelet, and the little glass whales clinked soothingly. Slowly, far too slowly, her fear ebbed, and she was able to think more clearly. King Xavier wasn't going to kill Julian—not if she remained calm and remembered everything she had overheard. She pulled the Chronicle out of her pack—which, obviously, was waterproof, because who didn't think to wear a waterproof pack?—and began scribbling frantically.

The door to the throne room slammed open, and Noa jumped. Julian strode in, cloak billowing and hair sticking out every which way. He looked angrier than she had ever seen him.

"What on earth were you thinking?" he demanded before he even reached her. "Sneaking into the palace like that. If Xavier had seen you—if *anyone* recognized your face—not to mention you barely know how to use your magic, and here you are leaping in and out of the afterlife as if it's a swimming pool—"

"So you figured out where I went," Noa said. "Good. That saves time."

Julian looked as if she'd thrown a handful of ice in his face. He wasn't used to being interrupted, Noa knew, but they didn't have time to wait until he calmed down.

"Julian." She closed the Chronicle for emphasis. "I went to the palace undercover to figure out if Xavier's found the other lost language. And it's a good thing I did, because I found out that he's planning to attack Astrae again. He's going to send someone to steal something from you. Something important."

"What?"

She shook her head. "My guess is that he knows we found one of the lost languages. Maybe his mages went back to Evert and noticed that you turned it right side out. We have to avoid the Devorian Rocks—he's planning to ambush us there. I don't know how he knows we're going that way."

Now Julian was staring at her as if she'd dumped a bucket of ice on his head. For a moment, the only sound was that of the waves drifting in through the open windows.

"How do you know all this?" he said finally.

"I heard it from Xavier," she said. "I eavesdropped on him and his councillors."

Julian blinked a few more times. Then he strode up to the throne, knelt, and pulled Noa into his arms.

She rested her head on his shoulder, and some of the tears she'd been holding back in the palace spilled out. She wanted to tell him about all the familiar places she had visited, and how wrong it had felt. Their mother's throne, now guarded by soldiers in Xavier's colors, and Xavier himself, striding around as if he owned the palace and always had. But there wasn't time.

Julian drew back. His blue eyes were serious. "Noa, I realize that I can't stop you from using your magic. But promise that you'll tell me before you do something like this again. At least give me a chance to talk you out of it."

Noa wanted to point out that if he had talked her out of it, they never would have learned about the king's trap. She also wanted to point out that he hadn't given her many chances to talk to him lately. But she just looked away and nodded.

Julian's brow furrowed. "What are you wearing?"

"I was undercover," Noa said, exasperated. "Obviously."

Julian sighed. "You have a lot of explaining to do, my Noa-bell. But I suppose we don't have time for that now, do we?"

"No, you have to go tell Kell to change course," Noa said. "And double the sentries."

Julian rose. "All right. Go get dried off and have something to eat. We'll talk more about this later."

Noa wondered if that was true. She watched Julian sweep out of the throne room, then headed for the door to the main hall. She paused by the statue that had been Esmalda. She had been lurking there in the shadows this whole time, and Julian hadn't even looked at her.

"I'm sorry," she said quietly, because she felt like someone should be. Then she left, trying not to imagine the statue's eyes boring into her back.

"Noa, look!"

Noa looked up just in time to see the lava leap up in the cauldron, then collapse with a hiss.

Mite frowned. She said something else in Spark, but all the lava did was spit out a cloud of ash. It was beginning to harden, a dark crust spreading across the surface.

"I don't know what happened," she said, chewing her lip.

Noa sighed and picked up the poker. Julian's spell kept the lava in a liquid state, provided you stirred it occasionally. "Mite, you don't need to teach me magic. And leave the lava alone. It's cold out."

A storm had rolled in that afternoon, pelting Astrae with chilly rain. The wind howled and the waves crashed so high that the castle foyer was now two inches deep in seawater. They were perfectly dry in Julian's tower, of course, but the wind kept finding crevices in the walls to squeeze through. The cats had come up with a new game in which one of them, invisible, would grab at the end of Noa's blanket and yank it around, while another would pretend the writhing blanket was a mouse and pounce on it. At least every five minutes the blanket would be yanked off her lap. Noa was used to the inconvenience of invisible cats, but this was a bit much.

She settled herself before the lava again, shivering. She didn't like this storm. While it was perfectly normal to encounter squalls in Malaspina Pass, caught as it was between two towering volcanoes, this one had come out of nowhere. She was glad that Julian had ordered the sentries to stay on duty.

There came the sound of metal scraping against wood as Mite dragged a bucket of earth across the floor. She scooped out two handfuls and placed them on the rug. "It's important to be loud when you do magic," she said, her face serious.

"Sometimes I'm too quiet, and the dirt just ignores me. Julian said it's okay to be quiet most of the time, but not when you're casting a spell." She babbled something in Worm, and the pile of earth rose into the air. Mite grinned.

Noa smothered a sigh. "Thank you. That's good advice."

"You try it." Mite looked around. "Are there any ghosts here? You could try bossing one around. Not a scary one," she added quickly.

Noa didn't reply. There were ghosts in the tower—that was the problem. None of them had tried to grab her (yet); they just hung around at the edges of her sight in a woebegone sort of way, as if they really were dogs that were used to being ignored. If she turned her head quickly enough, she could sometimes glimpse a pallid face or a tendril arm, but as soon as she did, the ghost would fade into the shadows. Why was Julian's tower the only place she saw ghosts?

She wondered if the otters had started looking for Mom yet. She'd been trying not to wonder that all day, because she didn't want to hope. The otter had said ghosts didn't linger, but clearly, some ghosts did.

What if Mom was one of them?

The table was set for dinner—the servants had come and gone some time ago, and the food was rapidly getting cold, but Julian hadn't arrived yet. Noa thought it was probably going to be one of those nights where Julian didn't come to dinner at all, and she and Mite ended up eating by themselves, sending a full plate back to the kitchen for the servants to heat up again whenever Julian was ready for it.

Noa was just opening her mouth to tell Mite that they should probably start eating when Julian strode in, bringing half the storm with him. He was sopping wet, his hair plastered to his head. He paused on the threshold and sneezed three times.

"Well, the island's battened down," he said, removing his boots and setting them by the lavaplace, where they began to hiss. "Kell thinks the storm's heading south, so we're going to wait it out until it passes rather than moving with it. Not now, Miss Claudia," he said to the cat trying to rub up against him. He padded up to his loft, sending a small waterfall cascading down the stairs as he went, which effectively discouraged the cats from following. When he came back down, he had changed into dry clothes, and his towel-dried hair was sticking out every which way.

"You should have eaten," he said, flopping down in a chair. Reckoner, having woken at the sound of his voice, happily fell over on top of his feet.

"You said you'd be here," Noa said.

There was a knock at the door, and one of the kitchen servants came in. "Hello, Marsha," Julian said, tossing her a dazzling smile, the wattage only slightly dimmed by his dampness.

The woman curtsied, blushing furiously. The servants

loved Julian—he was far kinder to them than he was to his mages, and he spoiled them, paying them twice what even the palace servants in Florean made and ignoring any bad behavior on their part. He had once commented when the head cook had caught one of the maids stealing silverware that anyone who thought they needed to steal something as meager as forks and spoons should be allowed to keep them. "Just came to see if you'd be needing anything else, Your Highness," Marsha said.

"No, thank you," Julian said, even as Noa opened her mouth to ask for the soup to be warmed up. "Everything looks delicious."

Noa sighed. "Can the sentries see at all in this weather?"

"As well as can be expected. I wouldn't worry about it."

"There's a surprise," Noa muttered. She didn't like herself when she was this snappish, but her stomach was growling and the cats had stolen her blanket again, and it was impossible to be pleasant when you were cold and hungry. Besides, she wanted to be angry at Julian for almost forgetting about dinner again, especially after he'd promised they would talk.

Julian sighed. "Noabell, I'm not in the mood to argue. If you have any suggestions for turning night into day, or fog into moonlight, I'm all ears."

He sneezed again, and Noa relented. She helped herself to smoked salmon and sea broccoli, then passed the plate to Julian. "Did you put any sentries up on the Nose?"

"Yes. It's all taken care of." He set down his cup and gave

her a meaningful look. "I believe we have something else to discuss. That is, you sneaking off this morning and putting your life in danger."

"I don't remember any sneaking," Noa said. "I remember a daring undercover mission to the palace." She folded her arms. If Julian thought he was going to lecture her now, he had another think coming.

He rolled his eyes theatrically. "I know that look. All right, we'll take that point up another time, when you're not in a mood."

"I'm always in a mood. So is everybody. No one is ever not in a mood."

"When you're in a different mood, less like Reckoner's when I try to give him a bath. Now, what is it that you overheard? Apart from what you told me earlier?"

Noa swallowed a mouthful of cassava soup. A ghost hovered at the edge of her vision, but she ignored it this time. She opened the Chronicle to the notes she had taken while eavesdropping in the palace. "Xavier has been executing nobles who he thinks are loyal to you. At least, people think they've been executed—mostly it's just a bunch of mysterious disappearances."

Julian's spoon froze on its way to his mouth. He set it down. "Which nobles?"

Noa consulted her notes and read him the names she had heard. There were more than ten of them. When she was done,

Julian's eyebrows were drawn so close together, they were almost touching.

"I know most of those names. They're all nobles who were part of Mother's court." He let out his breath. "It sounds like we may have more supporters in Florean City than I thought. Xavier hasn't convinced them all that Mother was a monster, and me a worse one."

"We don't have supporters if the king kills them all," Noa pointed out. "Although some people think a few of them ran off before Xavier could get to them."

Julian clicked his rings together. "Whether they fled or were executed, it can't be good for morale. Xavier's going to make people just as afraid of him as they are of me."

Noa thought that through strategically, as she knew Xavier would have done. "As long as he's only getting rid of unpopular people, his court will probably stay loyal to him. But I think he may have gone too far—I heard one of his councillors say he was planning to retire, just to get away from the king. And the mages aren't happy. Apparently Xavier wants to ban certain kinds of magic from Florean City."

"He'd ban them all if he could."

"And he's still killing dark mages," Noa said. She glanced at Mite, thinking of the skeletons and all those scurrying crabs. Instead of saying it out loud, she passed her notes to Julian.

He read the part about the dark mages, but he didn't look surprised. Noa wondered if he'd already known the gruesome details. "At this rate, Mite and I will be the only dark mages left in Florean before I retake the throne," he said grimly.

Noa opened her mouth to reply, but at that moment, another ghost drifted into view. He hovered just behind Julian, and then, when he noticed Noa watching, slunk back into the shadows. There was something familiar about him, but Noa couldn't place it.

Something smashed behind them. Noa whirled to see a different ghost standing over Julian's desk. He had knocked over a half-empty glass, spilling water across several books. Half his face was worn away, but his eyes were full of such bitterness and malice that Noa was filled with cold terror. The ghost held her gaze for a second before fading away.

"What was that?" Mite said around a mouthful of octopus. She had been eating steadily, watching their conversation with an avid gaze.

"The wind, I guess," Julian said with a sigh. "I'll clean it up later."

Noa's heart thudded. Julian's tower was drafty and inhabited by, on average, half a dozen invisible cats. It was perhaps unsurprising that things were often being knocked over, lost, or moved around. Once, Noa had watched an odd breeze float one of Julian's papers into the cauldron, an important document containing spells he'd been working on for a month. Another time, a lavastick had suddenly overturned next to him, setting the sleeve of his cloak on fire. That had been particularly strange, because most of the cats were afraid of flame.

Noa hadn't always been able to see ghosts, but that didn't mean they weren't there. She'd just never given them much thought, the way you tended not to think about things you couldn't see.

Had Julian's tower been haunted all along?

"—but if they did flee, perhaps they'll come to us," Julian was saying. He was leaning his chair on its back legs, his hands clasped behind his head. "It would be useful to have the nobility on our side. . . ."

The oddly familiar ghost flitted into view again. Noa choked on her water. Mite pounded on her back as she coughed.

"What is it?" Julian said.

Noa felt light-headed, and not from the coughing. She knew who the ghost was—or rather, she knew who it had been. It was one of the not-fishermen they had stumbled across when Astrae ran into the fake island.

One of the men Julian had killed.

"You look like you've . . . ," Julian began. "Oh! *Have* you seen a ghost?"

Noa swallowed. The ghost of a woman drifted into view. She held a sword at her side, and was dressed in red and gold, Xavier's colors. It was one of the soldiers Noa and Mite had met during the mango attack. The one who had let them go. She and her companions hadn't made it off Astrae.

Julian's tower was haunted by the people he had killed.

"Oh no," she whispered. She felt all wobbly, and gripped the table so hard her hand went white.

"Noa." Julian put his hand over hers. "What's wrong? Are they threatening you?"

"No, they..." Her voice was a croak. The soldier had faded into the shadows, but something told Noa she would be back. Something told Noa she never left.

She stared at Julian. How did you tell someone something so awful? She prayed that Julian wouldn't do anything reckless. He watched her with narrowed eyes, as if prepared at any moment to leap to her defense with some spell.

"I think your tower is haunted," she whispered so that Mite wouldn't hear. "Not by just anyone. By people you killed."

Julian blinked. "Are they trying to hurt you?"

Noa shook her head.

"Oh." His gaze drifted for a moment. "All right, then."

And he went back to his dinner.

Noa stared at him. Mite's gaze darted between him and Noa.

"Is that all you have to say?" she said. "'All right'?"

"Is there anything I can do about this?"

"I don't think so."

"Then yes. That's all I have to say."

"But I just told you—" Noa couldn't understand it. How was Julian not as distressed as she was? He didn't seem to feel anything at all—he just sat there calmly cutting up his broccoli, as if she'd told him he was being haunted by a family of tortoises. "How can you be so heartless?"

He looked surprised. "What does being heartless have to do with it? I'm fighting a war. People die in wars. How they choose to spend their time afterward isn't my concern."

Noa's mouth fell open. Her pulse was throbbing in her ears. She pointed at the ghost across the room. "Standing right there is one of the fishermen you tossed to Beauty a few days ago. Don't you want to say anything to him? Don't you feel the least bit sorry?"

Julian's eyes narrowed. "Why would I feel sorry? Those men were part of Xavier's plot. Am I supposed to regret disposing of his servants, given that they would have happily taken me captive if they'd had the chance, and ki—" He stopped, glancing at Mite. "And hurt the two of you?"

"I'm not saying you should regret it," Noa said. "I'm saying you should feel sorry. That's different. Just because you have to do a terrible thing doesn't mean you should feel good about it. You're not that selfish."

"Selfish?" Julian's face grew cold, and a shiver ran up Noa's back. "Believe me, I'd love to have the time to be selfish once in a while. But I don't, and I haven't since Mother died. All I have time for is this." He gestured at the tower filled with grimoires and experiments. "And if I happen to enjoy giving Xavier's followers what they deserve, why is that so wrong?" He laughed. "If I am being haunted by the ghosts of Xavier's loyal subjects, then I say: good. I hope they enjoy watching me send their companions to join them in the Beyond."

Noa didn't know what to say. Julian had never looked less like the old Julian, his eyes hard and glittering, and the amusement in his face turned into something dark and ominous as distant thunder.

Mite ducked under the table with a whimper. Julian let out a long breath. "Maita, it's all right." He helped her out. "Noa, please pass your sister the bread. How about we practice making toast? Do you remember the spell for that?"

Noa passed the bread, trying not to let her hand shake. What she had seen in Julian's eyes frightened her more than any ghost. What was she going to do? She was convinced more than ever that her secret mission was in shambles.

There came a pounding on the door. Julian stalked over and wrenched it open, revealing a sodden Renne.

"What happened?" Julian said sharply. For it was clear that something had—Renne was pale and wild-eyed, and seaweed clung to the hem of his cloak.

"It's Beauty," he said without preamble. "She's in a frenzy, and none of us can calm her down. She's claiming someone stole her child."

18

Noa Goes Hunting

When they got to the low cliff overlooking the water, all they could see was a whirlpool bubbling amid the crashing waves.

"Beauty!" Julian called. He dashed his wet hair from his face. He hadn't bothered to don his already sodden cloak, and he looked tall and sharp-angled framed against the storm. "Show yourself."

The bubbles grew larger. Then Beauty surfaced, or rather her tail did—it struck the cliffside, causing Renne to topple into the water.

Julian lashed out his arm, calling out a spell in Salt, and a wave lifted Renne back onto the cliff, fortunately with all his limbs.

"Do that again and I'll see that you regret it," Julian said in a voice like a knife's edge. He murmured something in Marrow and Salt, the two languages he had used to bind Beauty to the island. Before he could finish, though, Beauty's head surfaced.

Her eyes were so wide there was a ring of white around the black, and her body shook. She was so large that the sea itself seemed to tremble.

"Foolish, evil boy," she spat in a voice that was nothing like her usual dulcet tones. "You're responsible for this. You took my freedom, and now—" She let out a horrible roar and lunged forward with her jaws snapping a foot from Julian's head. He put his hands out and forced her back down with a lash of magic that made the ground tremble, his body braced as if against a fierce wind.

"Noa, go back to the castle," Julian barked over his shoulder. Noa glared at him. She slunk back a few feet, but no farther.

"Beauty," he said, "control yourself, or I'll do it for you. I've been generous enough not to keep you on a chain, my monster. That will change if you don't behave."

"Oh, yes," Beauty hissed. "Yes, that's next. Go ahead, black-hearted child. Chain me, torture me, I care not. Nothing compares to the loss of my daughter."

Noa started forward. "You have a daughter?" She ignored Julian's thunderous look and stepped to the edge of the cliff. "Why have we never seen her?"

Beauty snarled. "She was born only days ago. I planned to tell no one, certainly not any of you Marchenas. The wicked king would have her on a leash alongside her mother. No, I planned to raise her until she was old enough to escape."

"That's why you've been hiding under the island," Noa

murmured. "Then—then it's not because you're plotting against Julian?"

Beauty struck the cliffside, hurling her entire body against it this time. Noa stumbled and would have fallen if Julian hadn't caught her.

"What do I care about the lives of human kings?" she snarled. "My daughter . . . They stole my daughter. . . ."

After I take it from him, we'll watch his defenses crumble. Noa drew a sharp breath. Xavier hadn't been planning to steal the Lost Words.

He had meant Beauty's child.

"Who took her?" Noa shouted over the waves churned up by Beauty and the storm.

"One of his enemies." Beauty shot Julian a look of pure hatred. "That raven haired witch. He's turned my child into a pawn in his wicked schemes. Oh, my daughter, my daughter . . ."

Dread settled in Noa's stomach. She felt Julian freeze, his hand tightening painfully on her arm.

"Gabriela." Her voice was hoarse. "How did she take your daughter?"

"I know not. I only saw her leave, heading north. She took my child and sailed beyond the edge of my tether, and I couldn't follow."

"Get every able-bodied sailor into a boat with a salt mage," Julian snapped at Renne. His face was white and his gaze was as cold as it had been in the tower. "Gabriela can't have gone far in this weather."

"There's a slight problem," Renne said. "We don't know which boat is hers. We spotted six of them, each heading in a different direction—as they retreated from the island, they turned their fog lights on. They wanted us to know they were there, and that they were using decoys."

Julian cursed. Then he said, "It doesn't matter. I'll sink them all."

"*No*," Noa said. "Julian, you can't. Those boats will be full of sailors who are just following orders. You can't—"

"Noa, go back to the castle. Now." Then he was gone, striding into the storm with Renne at his heels.

Noa dashed the water from her eyes and made to go after him. She froze as a horrible chuckle rose from Beauty's throat.

"He's vulnerable now," she crooned. Her eyes were so wide that Noa wondered if she'd gone mad. "That's some comfort, at least. . . ."

"What are you talking about?" Noa said.

"My daughter and I are bound together," Beauty murmured. "Until she's old enough to care for herself. That's how it is for my kind. If my child dies, I die. And then Julian will be without his fearsome guard dog. I wonder how long Xavier will wait to attack him after that?"

Still chuckling, she sank beneath the waves.

"Where's Julian?" Mite hovered at Noa's elbow, her eyes wide. "Is he okay?"

"He's fine." Noa tossed aside the chest she had overturned, spilling Julian's socks all over the place. She was in the tower loft, rifling through his things. "He'll be back soon. He hasn't forgotten your story."

"What are you doing?"

Noa threw open a chest, but found it stuffed with useless books. Her hands shook, and her thoughts wheeled like panicked birds. "I'm going on a rescue mission."

Gabriela had kidnapped Beauty's daughter. Noa didn't understand how she knew that Beauty had a daughter, or that sea serpents died when their children were taken from them. She also didn't understand how Xavier had known that Astrae had changed course. But none of that mattered right now. What mattered was that Gabriela and Xavier wanted Beauty dead, because it would weaken Julian. The part of Noa's mind that loved strategy above anything guessed that Xavier was planning a one-two punch: eliminate Astrae's strongest defense, and then attack them with the Lost Words. Perhaps that meant he was close to finding the other lost language.

Noa wasn't particularly worried about Julian being weakened, and as for Beauty, good riddance. What worried her more was the thought of Julian killing all the sailors in the Ayora Sea in his single-minded pursuit of Gabriela.

Noa thought of the ice in Julian's gaze. She didn't know

if she'd lost him or not—if he'd been entirely replaced by the ruthless Dark Lord who ordinary Floreans had nightmares about. But if she let him drown dozens of sailors whose only crime was being unlucky enough to get tangled up in one of Gabriela's plots? She was certain it would push him over the edge. Well, Noa wasn't going to give up on her secret mission—on Julian—even if he turned Astrae into a sea monster zoo or made necklaces out of their enemies' teeth while cackling at the moon. It was *Julian*. She would rescue Beauty's daughter and be back in five minutes, in time to call him back to Astrae before he did anything stupid.

Mite looked over her shoulder. "What about the ghosts?"

"They won't hurt you," Noa assured her distractedly. "They only care about Julian."

"They want to hurt Julian?"

"Mite, I'm sorry, but I don't have time for this," Noa said. "Why don't you go to bed?"

Mite's hands twisted around each other. "Will you come with me?"

"No. I can't waste a moment. Rescue mission, remember?"

She dug around at the back of Julian's wardrobe. Her fingers gripped the edge of an old chest, and she pulled it out. When she opened it, she found it empty save for a long rectangle of green fabric.

Noa drew the scarf free. She knew it well—Gabriela often wore scarves, and it still smelled like her perfume, a sort of nighttime forest scent. Julian didn't realize Noa knew that he'd kept it, nor that he had a letter Gabriela had written him hidden inside a particularly musty book, but then he'd always been terrible at keeping secrets from her. As much as Julian pretended to hate Gabriela, Noa knew otherwise.

Mite had gone pale at the sight of the scarf. "Don't leave, Noa. Julian got mad when you went to the palace—"

"This is more important than the palace." Noa's voice was grim. "I have to do some hunting of my own. I'm going to get Beauty's daughter back before Julian tracks them down. In the mood he's in, he probably won't even bother to rescue her—he'll just throw magic at those ships until they vaporize."

Which, Noa thought, Gabriela had probably realized. That was why she'd included so many decoys in her plot. And even if Julian did find her, she probably had some clever escape planned. After all, Gabriela had always relied more on her brains than her magic. Well, if she thought she was cleverer than Julian, she was probably right, but if she thought she was cleverer than Noa, she had another thing coming.

Noa lifted the nearest shadow and leaped into Death.

19

Noa's Rescue
Mission Ends Badly

Ten minutes later, Noa fell through a shadow and onto the deck of a moving ship.

She lay there for a moment, disoriented. She hadn't been sure her plan would work. The otter had been silent for a long moment after she asked it to lead her to Gabriela's ship. Then it had said that it was difficult to pass from Death onto moving vessels, that those were the most unpredictable doorways of all. It was possible, the otter warned, that Noa would fall out of Death and into the middle of the ocean, with no rescue in sight. Then Noa had shown it Gabriela's scarf, and the otter had nodded once and led her to a shadow without further argument.

Something inside Noa had known that the scarf would help the otter find a shadow door to Gabriela. Part of her noted that she was getting better at using her magic, but she pushed her pride away. She could gloat later—now she had to focus.

The deck she had fallen onto was wet with rain, but the clouds were only spitting now. Gabriela must have sailed through the worst of the storm. The ship was a modest size, but well built, with a single lurid red sail. A lantern swung on a hook, illuminating the deck with flickering light. Noa was lying in the shadow cast by the ship's figurehead, a fanged mermaid clutching a sword. Two mages stood only a few yards from her, their red cloaks the only vivid thing in the dimness, but fortunately they weren't looking in her direction. She drew her black hood over her head and tucked herself deeper into the shadow until they walked away.

Noa crept toward the staircase leading belowdecks, keeping to the shadows as much as possible. She guessed that Gabriela would have brought along only a skeleton crew to keep the ship light and speedy, and she hoped that meant she wouldn't run into any mages.

Noa paused and drew a shaky breath. She wasn't going to run into Gabriela. Her mission was all about speed. She would find Beauty's daughter, free her, and then leap through the nearest shadow.

A sailor stomped up the stairs toward her. Rather than running in the other direction, Noa swallowed her panic and drew her hood farther forward as she continued down the stairs. As they passed, she said gruffly, "What a night, eh?"

The sailor snorted. His face was lowered against the weather, and he barely glanced at her. "This mission can't end soon enough. That thing's still screeching."

Noa snorted back and kept going, her heart a wild thing in her chest. She waited for the sailor to turn, to call for her to stop, but he didn't.

People were good at explaining away inexplicable things, Noa had often noticed. The man wouldn't have thought it possible for an intruder, let alone Julian Marchena's sister, to appear out of nowhere on their ship in the middle of a storm, so he just told himself she was one of the crew. She was almost the height of a grown woman, after all, and in the darkness her hooded face was impossible to make out.

Noa found a narrow corridor at the bottom of the stairs. To the left was an open hatch with a ladder leading down into the hold. The ladder disappeared into shadow, and from the shadow rose a horrible wailing.

Noa's hands flew instinctively to her ears. The sound was like a child's cry mixed up with a kitten's mewl and a snake's hiss, baleful and uncanny. The last thing Noa wanted to do was go down into that hold.

She set her jaw and stepped onto the ladder.

"Hey!"

Noa looked up, and found herself facing another sailor who had stepped out of one of the rooms off the corridor. The woman's eyes were wide as she stared at Noa, who realized belatedly that her hood had fallen back.

Noa scrambled down the ladder, reaching up to swing

the hatch shut. The sailor thundered toward her, but Noa was quick: she fumbled for a lock, found one, and slid it into place. She heard the woman cursing as she wrenched at the handle on the other side.

Filled with nervous panic, Noa half fell the rest of the way down the ladder. The hold was completely dark. The wailing was horribly loud and echoing, and Noa couldn't pinpoint where it was coming from.

She ran her shaking hands along the wall, and hit a lantern suspended from a hook. Her pulse racing, she switched it on. She knew she had only moments, possibly seconds, before the sailor told Gabriela she was there.

The light revealed a low-ceilinged space, narrow and long. And at the far end, in a dirty corner that smelled of old blubber, was Beauty's daughter.

The serpent hissed at Noa, but the sound died in an odd sort of gasp. She was perhaps as long as Noa was tall, and several times as thick as an ordinary snake. Her head and tail were cruelly bound with metal rings that dug into her skin. Her eyes were as black as Beauty's, but she was toothless: when she hissed, Noa saw only pink gums like a human baby's.

Noa ran forward. The serpent was shaking—someone had wrapped her in wet towels to keep her skin moist, but most of them had fallen away.

Noa had no love for Beauty, and she suspected that her daughter would grow into a similarly terrifying monster, but she nevertheless felt a surge of fury at Gabriela for treating the infant serpent like this. It hadn't harmed anybody. Not yet, anyway.

Noa pulled on the chains, and the serpent let out another wail. Fortunately, the chains weren't locked with a key—they just needed to be unlatched, which the serpent wouldn't have been able to do, lacking hands. Noa supposed that Gabriela wasn't particularly worried about anyone on the crew trying to unchain a sea serpent, toothless or not.

Unfortunately, once the chains fell away, the baby serpent sprang at Noa, knocking her over. The creature slithered across the floor, wailing and throwing herself against the walls.

Noa drew herself up onto her knees, holding her head, which had struck the floor hard. Gritting her teeth against the pain, she forced herself to stand and throw open the only window, a high porthole that was just barely above the water. A wave sloshed through, splashing Noa in the face and startling her so much she breathed in a gasp of it.

"Here—hurry—" she managed between coughs. The serpent, though, had already seen the sloshing water, smelled the salt. She lunged for the porthole, ramming into Noa and sending her sprawling again. This time Noa's cheek scraped against the wall as she fell, and her elbow jarred against a table, sending a shock of pain up her arm. The serpent couldn't quite reach the porthole, though, so Noa, head spinning and blood trickling down her face, was forced to hoist her up to it. Of course, the baby serpent didn't understand that she was being set free, and she struck Noa with her tail over and over again, wailing so loudly that Noa thought her eardrums would burst. A part of her noted that she hadn't thoroughly thought through this part of the rescue mission. Finally, bruised and wheezing, Noa managed to grab hold of the slippery creature and shove her ungently through the porthole. There was a splash, followed by the sort of wonderful, balm-like silence that follows every earsplitting racket.

Noa slid to the ground, her forehead pressed against the wall. She knew she needed to escape through the nearest shadow, but she wasn't certain she could stand up. Her vision swam. She crouched on her hands and knees, focused only on not throwing up.

She hoped Beauty's daughter would be able to find her way back to her mother. She hoped that she had rescued her in time, that Beauty was still alive. She needed to get back to Astrae to make sure. As she drew a slow, deep breath, she became aware of a loud thump behind her, not unlike boots hitting floor, followed by a second thump. She turned.

Gabriela stood at the bottom of the ladder, rising from a crouch, next to a sailor who raised her bow and arrow and pointed it at Noa's chest.

"So—you're a magician now, are you?" Gabriela said in that familiar raspy voice. She took a step forward, her bright gaze sweeping Noa. "It's all right. I'm going to heal your injuries, but you'll need to stay still—and don't even think about casting any spells. I don't want to have to order Jessa to shoot."

The throbbing of Noa's head was joined by a strange roaring sound. She opened her mouth, but before she could get a word out, darkness closed over her like a wave.

20

Gabriela Gets a New Captive

Noa woke slowly. She seemed to be lying in a bed, her head propped up by a pillow. Someone had healed her cuts and bruises from wrestling with the sea serpent, and her mind was clear. The only thing wrong was that she was tied up.

She didn't open her eyes, or move, though her pulse quickened with panic. She flexed her muscles imperceptibly. There was some sort of strap around her midsection, holding her to the bed, as well as ropes binding her wrists. She was still on a ship, and every time it swayed in the waves, she felt how taut the ropes were. She doubted she could move more than an inch or two.

From all this, Noa deduced two things: that Gabriela was holding her captive, and that her situation was bleak. She couldn't very well jump through a shadow if she couldn't move. Which meant she had to figure out a way to get untied.

Now that she had made sense of her situation, Noa opened her eyes to deal with it.

She was in a sparsely furnished cabin, probably in the middle of the ship, for there was no porthole. Gabriela sat with one polished boot propped against Noa's bed, balancing her chair on its back legs. Her raven-blue hair cascaded down her back, and she looked long and lean and nimble, like a deer pressed and stretched into a new shape—until you looked at her eyes, which were large and ferociously intent, like a wildcat poised to pounce.

Noa felt the same fury rise up inside her that she had felt at the prow of Astrae, gazing at Gabriela from across the sea cliffs. She tried to keep it from her face.

"How are you feeling?" Gabriela said in a kind voice that made Noa want to shove her out the nearest porthole. "You had a bump on your head. If it's still bothering you, I can try another healing spell."

"It still hurts," Noa lied, because it was always best for your enemies to think you were weak. "But I'd rather have headaches for the rest of my life than be healed by a lying traitor like you."

Gabriela rubbed her eyes. "I guess I deserve that, don't I? Noa, I'm sorry I had to lie to you and your sister while I was on Astrae. I hated that to protect Florean from Julian, I had to hurt you two. You're so young. . . ." There was a pleading look in her violet eyes. "How many times do I have to apologize before you believe I'm sorry?"

Noa stared at her in disbelief. "You've lied to me since the day I met you. Why should I believe a word you say? Besides, if you feel so guilty, why have you tied me up?"

"I wish I didn't have to," Gabriela said, and she did sound genuinely sorry, which only made Noa hate her more. "But I'm not sure how your powers work, and until I am, I thought it would be safer this way. I didn't gag you—though I'll have to if you start casting a spell."

Noa could think of no better response than a murderous glare.

"I don't know of any magical gift that would allow you to step out of the sea and onto my ship," Gabriela said. "I suppose this means Julian found one of the Lost Words, didn't he? I suppose I should congratulate you."

Noa deepened the glare until her eyes hurt.

Gabriela sighed. She looked like a tired martyr, weighed down by Noa's anger. She ran the green scarf through her fingers. "Thanks for returning this. I didn't think you'd keep anything of mine."

"I didn't," Noa spat. "I'd've burned it. I found it in Julian's room."

Something flickered in Gabriela's gaze. But then it was gone, and she said, "Julian always was sentimental. I find most murderers are."

"You're one to talk about murderers." Noa was trembling. "Your precious king killed my mother."

Gabriela's face softened. Noa could practically hear the

thoughts running through her head. *Poor little orphan. She can't help what her family is. Julian poisoned her mind.*

Noa knew this because Gabriela had said something like it on Astrae, the day before Julian discovered she was a spy. *I care about your brother,* she had lied, *but he isn't a good person, Noa. You see him as a hero, but he's not. He's the villain.*

Gabriela lowered her chair with a *thunk.* She stalked gracefully over to a low table and poured a glass of water. "I thought my plan was foolproof, yet you've managed to wreck it. Summon a storm to force Julian to bring that ridiculous island to a stop, after which we'd be able to locate it. Distract his sea monster by throwing cakes over the side of the boat, then swim beneath the island and steal the child."

Part of Noa's brain thought, *How did she know Beauty liked cakes?* Another part guessed that Gabriela had managed to steal Beauty's daughter by inventing some spell in Salt that allowed her to breathe underwater. She filed the first question away— something told her it was important. "How did you do it?" she asked, to give Gabriela a chance to brag about her cleverness. Noa wanted to make her feel clever, certainly cleverer than Julian's poor gullible little sister.

Gabriela smiled. "I came up with a spell that allowed me to breathe underwater. Julian's not the only inventor in Florean."

Duh. Noa made her eyes wide and surprised. "But how did you know Beauty had a daughter? Have you been spying on her?"

"No, but we've had salt mages spying on her, er—husband," Gabriela said. "That's what the creature calls himself, anyway. He visits her whenever Astrae crosses deep water. He told another one of the beasts that she was expecting, and when."

Noa didn't have to fake surprise that time. She'd had no idea that Beauty was married—whatever that meant in sea serpent terms. She wondered briefly what a sea serpent wedding looked like, then wished she hadn't. She doubted the guests would be served cakes. Or if they were, you wouldn't want to know the ingredients.

"Why didn't you just kill her?" Noa said. "She would have died anyway if she stayed away from her mother."

"Eventually," Gabriela agreed. "But the king wanted to use her as a bargaining chip. He thought Julian would be persuaded to abandon some of the territory he's stolen if it meant saving the life of his creature."

Noa shook her head. Julian probably would have done that, too, which wouldn't have been particularly clever *or* villainous of him, but she didn't see the value in pointing that out to Gabriela. She doubted King Xavier would have given Beauty's daughter back. No, he would have tricked Julian into retreating, then killed her.

Gabriela crossed the room and held the glass to Noa's lips. Noa just looked at her.

Gabriela gave another one of her sad sighs. "Noa, you have to drink. Please."

"I will," Noa said. "But not with you."

Gabriela set the glass down. "I'll release you as soon as I'm able. Please be patient."

Noa blinked. "You're going to release me?"

"Of course. Do you think I would hold a child hostage?" The look on Noa's face made Gabriela sigh. "Well, I wouldn't. Not even if it ended this war."

"Right," Noa said. "So you tied me up for my health?"

Anger flickered in Gabriela's eyes before it was replaced by that annoying sadness. "I don't know what powers you have, Noa. Do you think I would risk you lashing out at me or my servants?"

"Oh, I see," Noa said. "You'll hold me prisoner until you figure out exactly what I can do, so you can tell Xavier about it. You don't actually mind holding children hostage, as long as it's temporary."

Gabriela's jaw tightened. "If you promise to conduct yourself honorably, perhaps—"

"Honorably!" Noa said. "You know all about honor, do you? Is lying to someone honorable? Is spying honorable?"

"I was doing what my king commanded." Gabriela's face was red.

"Ugh," Noa said. Gabriela was such a goody-goody. Still, it was clear that Noa had gotten under her skin. She made a mental note to add "morals" to the list of Gabriela's weaknesses that she kept in the Chronicle.

"I'm only doing what's best for Florean," Gabriela said. "Julian is tearing it apart."

"Xavier is the one who—" Noa began hotly, but Gabriela talked over her. "He's surrounded himself with criminals. He's willing to kill anyone who gets in his way. Does that sound like someone who's cut out to be king? What do you think he'll do if he takes the throne?" She leaned forward. "You were probably too young to know this, Noa, but your mother was a lot like Julian. Whenever an island rebelled against her, she sent in mages to burn their villages to the ground. She put pirates and thieves on her council. All dark mages are the same."

"You're wrong," Noa spat. "All those things—that's just what Xavier wants you to think. He spread all kinds of rumors about Mom to get people to hate her."

"Noa, I know she had criminals on her council. So does your brother, for that matter. Kell Brown is the most wanted pirate in Florean. She's the captain of Astrae! How could Julian trust someone like that if he wasn't just as bad as her?"

"That's not . . ." Noa didn't know how to finish. She didn't know how to convince Gabriela that when Julian had hired Kell, it had been the right thing to do, even if it sounded wrong on the surface. That was how Xavier had made everyone hate Mom—he had taken all the things about her that sounded bad and mixed them up with lies until he'd created a twisted mirror image of the queen that most people couldn't tell from the real one.

"You know those villages your mother burned?" Gabriela's hand briefly tightened on her knee. "Mine was one of them. Why do you think my family lived on our fishing boat? We had nowhere else to go. She left us with nothing."

Noa stared at her. It couldn't be true—could it? Growing up, she'd sometimes heard her mother speaking to her advisors of rebellions. They were over quickly, and Noa had always had the impression that her mother didn't see them as important. She'd never really thought about what it meant to quell a rebellion. About the children who might end up without a home.

Gabriela touched her arm. "Noa, I know that Xavier—well, he's not perfect. But he's a better king than Julian. Anyone is better than a dark mage."

Noa shoved her doubts away. Gabriela wanted her to doubt, and she wasn't going to play her game. "He's not perfect?" Noa repeated. "He's killing mages. Not just dark mages—people like you. He wants to wipe out magic in Florean completely."

Gabriela didn't look at all surprised by this news. Her gaze grew distant. "I don't expect you to understand, Noa. Maybe one day . . ." She let out her breath. "The thing is, I don't believe in heroes. There were no heroes to save my village when it burned, and there will be none to prevent Julian from filling Florean's waters with sea serpents and Florean's government with criminals as bloodthirsty as him. The truth is that most of the time, the only thing that can defeat a monster is another monster."

Noa watched her for a long moment. Her heart thudded, and she felt vaguely sick. Gabriela watched her in turn, waiting.

"I'll tell you how many times you should apologize," Noa said finally. "Until you choke on it."

Gabriela's expression darkened. She stood to go, but paused at the door and motioned to someone Noa couldn't see. "I'm sorry you're not willing to listen. We'll talk later, and I hope you'll think about what I said. I still consider you my friend."

Noa opened her mouth, but another mage had appeared at Gabriela's shoulder, murmuring a spell in Marrow, and she found she couldn't speak. Her voice was gone. Gabriela gave her another sad look, as if someone else had tied up her dear friend Noa, and there was absolutely nothing she could do about it. She swept from the room.

Noa spent the next hour wrestling with the ropes binding her hands. All she got out of it, though, was chafed wrists. She even pushed off her boots and tried to undo the knots with her toes, but toes, it turned out, were little more than useless lumps stuck on the ends of your feet. Noa supposed it was her own fault for not doing regular toe exercises to strengthen them in case something like this ever happened, and resolved to start if she ever got back to Astrae.

Noa's next idea was to try to grab the shadow of the bed cast by the lavastick, part of which lay on the wall by her head.

She couldn't reach it with her fingers, so she tried to grab on to the edge with her teeth.

She strained her neck, stretching as far as she could. Unfortunately, this wasn't far, and she just missed the shadow. Gritting her teeth and sucking in her stomach so that the rope slackened slightly around her torso, she stretched another precious inch. She nipped at the shadow and managed to drag it toward her. It tasted sweet and slightly sticky, like sap, nothing like what she'd expected (not that she'd given much thought to the flavor of shadows). She flicked it over her head like a blanket and shoved her face through the hole underneath.

Success! She was looking into Death. It was like looking through a window several feet off the ground. She seemed to be in the shadow cast by a hill.

"Otter?" she called, and then she started. Her voice was back! Clearly, blood spells lost their hold in Death. That was lucky—or creepy, depending on how you looked at it. "Otter!"

One of the creatures flowed into view, licking fish off its face. "Oh!" Noa said. "Are you the same otter who was helping me before?"

"Do I look like the same otter?" the otter said haughtily.

"Er," Noa said. "Sorry. I hit my head, and I'm a little confused. You're far handsomer than the other otter."

The otter puffed out its chest. "Really?"

"Oh, yes. The handsomest otter I've ever seen," Noa said, wondering if she was laying it on a little thick. With otters, though, it seemed like the thicker, the better. "Look, I know you're probably busy with . . . ah, otter business, but do you think you could help me with something?"

"Do you want me to look for someone?" the otter said. "We've all been looking for the queen, like you asked. It's fun, but we haven't found her yet."

"Thank you," Noa said. "But right now, I need to get untied."

The otter crept up to the edge of the window Noa was looking through. "You're caught in a trap." It sounded sympathetic. "Does someone want to skin you?"

"Something like that," Noa said darkly. She thought fast. "Your teeth look sharp."

The otter bared them. "The sharpest teeth you'll ever see."

"Sharp enough to gnaw these ropes?"

The other made a disdainful sound. It shook its fur and leaped out of Death.

Noa drew her head back, blinking away the brightness of the cabin. The shadow drifted back to its original spot with a sort of wet snap, like lips smacking together. The otter was sitting on her chest. It scampered over to her left wrist and began to bite at the ropes.

"Ow!" Noa said, or rather mouthed, for her voice was gone again.

The otter gave her a sly look, then went back to gnawing. It didn't say anything. Noa guessed that otters could only talk while they were in Death, given that she'd never heard them do it in her world.

Footsteps sounded in the corridor. "Someone's coming!" Noa mouthed desperately. "Hide!"

The otter ignored her. It grabbed the rope in its teeth and yanked. The rope tore, and Noa was free—part of her, anyway. She grabbed the blanket, which had been covering her arms before, and yanked it back into place. A quarter second before the door opened, the otter slither-slunk into what seemed like little more than a crevice in the wall, and vanished.

Gabriela entered the room with a servant. "Just leave it there, please, Mona," she said. "Thank you."

The servant placed the tray of food down on the table and bowed herself out, but not after darting a curious, wide-eyed look at Noa.

Gabriela sighed after she left. "I'm afraid the rumor that I've captured Julian Marchena's sister has spread fast. Everybody wants to get a look at you. Are you hungry?"

Noa mouthed a bad word. Gabriela said, "What was that? Oh, sorry. I forgot." She spoke in Marrow, and Noa felt her voice return.

She repeated the bad word.

Gabriela frowned. "I see you haven't thought over what I said."

"Being tied up isn't good for thinking," Noa said.

Gabriela made no reply to that. She looked distracted.

She picked up the bowl the servant had brought in and sat down on the edge of Noa's bed. The bowl was full of onion soup, and Noa felt her mouth water. As much as she wanted to refuse anything from Gabriela, she was too hungry. Gabriela patiently fed her soup until the spoon scraped the bottom of the bowl.

"Better?" she said.

Noa's thoughts raced. She needed to give Gabriela a reason to leave. "I'm still hungry. Is there any more soup?"

Gabriela nodded, her thoughts clearly elsewhere. "I'll get you some in a minute." To Noa's dismay, she settled on the edge of the bed. Her weight made the blanket shift, almost revealing the torn ropes. Noa's heart thudded.

"I've heard from the king," Gabriela said slowly. "I sent him a report with one of the wind mages, informing him that you snuck onto the ship—"

"You what?" Noa nearly shouted.

Gabriela didn't meet her gaze. "He's ordered me to bring you to Florean City immediately."

Noa fought against the panic rising inside her. "Of course he did. He wants to use me to hurt Julian."

Gabriela looked uncomfortable. "He says he's making arrangements to ensure that you're happy in the palace. You don't have to be afraid."

Noa fell back against her pillow. "I don't know why I always thought you were smart."

Gabriela pressed her hand against Noa's bound one. "Noa, you're too important to the king. Yes, he will probably send word to Julian about this, to encourage him to surrender. But even if Julian refuses, you'll be taken care of. I promise." She sounded as if she was speaking as much to herself as to Noa.

The boat suddenly rocked to one side. Gabriela caught herself on one of Noa's legs, dislodging the blanket more. Noa's heart skipped a beat, but Gabriela didn't look down.

"The wind must be picking up," she said, frowning. "I'm going to check in with the captain." And with that, she was gone.

The moment she was through the door, Noa flung the blanket back. She scrabbled at the ropes binding her right hand, taking longer to untie them than she would have if she'd been calm.

The king's voice floated back to her, just as clear as it had been in the palace courtyard. *If I ever manage to get my hands on just one of those brats, I could have Julian Marchena eating out of the palm of my hand....*

... We could quietly execute them both and finally have done with the whole rotten Marchena line....

Noa's palms were sweaty. She managed to wriggle out of the rope wrapped around her torso. She rolled off the bed, her palms thudding against the floor.

The shadow. Get to the shadow, any shadow.

The closest one was beneath the table that held the empty

soup bowl and the fading lavastick. Noa lunged at it.

"How did you do that?" asked a voice behind her. Noa whirled.

Gabriela stood in the doorway with her mouth open. Behind her were two mages, also openmouthed. Noa lifted the shadow and prepared to leap, but one of the mages gave a sharp command in Marrow, and she froze—literally. Her muscles seized up in an awful full-body cramp, and she couldn't move. She was crouched on her knees, the shadow gripped in her hand and the safety of Death beckoning underneath it. But it might as well have been a mile away.

"Black seas, Noa." Gabriela dismissed the mages with a gesture and strode forward, her face white with anger. "Clearly I have to assign someone to guard you at all times. Your powers are more dangerous than I guessed." She hooked her arms under Noa's immobile ones, and began to drag her back across the floor. "Let's get you tied up again, and then—"

The boat rocked, violently this time, and Gabriela fell over and rolled across the floor. Noa rolled, too, ending up on her back with her limbs stuck in the same ridiculous posture, her legs bent and one hand stretched out as if she was in the middle of some weird dance routine.

"What in the thirteen—" Gabriela began, and then something exploded.

Gabriela cried out, her hands going to her head. A long, gaping hole had appeared in the ceiling, as if several boards in the deck had been peeled away. Green vines writhed through the gap like snakes, wrapping around more boards and wrenching them back. People were screaming, and feet pounded along the corridor and across the deck. Thunder crashed and a bolt of lightning illuminated the sky, setting off a new wave of screams. Then a familiar voice called, "Noa?"

Noa's heart leaped. Slowly, painfully, she managed to wrench open her mouth and yell, "Julian!"

PART III

Whelm

21

The Dark Lord and the King's Mage Meet Again

The vines swarmed into the cabin, ripping apart the deck. Boards cracked and thumped to the floor, but the vines made a cage over Noa's head, and she was safe.

"Noa, climb up!" Julian called. A ladder of vines undulated to the floor.

Noa tried to unclench her jaw again. "Can't," she managed. "Gabriela—"

Julian hissed, and there came another flash of lightning. The vines withered and died, and Noa realized that one of Gabriela's mages must have attacked him. She tried to fight the spell, but it was no use. She was as much help as an overturned turtle.

In the first few seconds following Julian's arrival, Gabriela sat frozen, her face white and stunned, as if she'd walked into a post. Now, though, she drew herself to her feet, her jaw set.

"Look," Noa cried. She seemed able to manage only one word at a time. "Out!"

She had no idea if Julian heard. From the deck came a series of thunderous crashes and bangs, coupled with more screaming. Some of it seemed to be coming from the water, and Noa wondered if the sailors had thrown themselves into the sea in order to be out of the way as the mages fought.

Gabriela's eyes narrowed in a thoughtful expression that Noa didn't like one bit. Rather than going up to the deck, she turned and hurried down the corridor without giving Noa another glance.

Another huge wave sent the ship listing to port. Noa tumbled over and over, banging knees and hands and elbows, until she hit the wall. For a moment, she thought the ship would fall over, and she panicked—if it did, she would simply sink into the depths. But the vessel righted itself.

She tried to yell for Julian again, but all that came out was "Mmmph." Her face was squished against the floor. Fortunately, her face was also squished against the shadow of the table. She grabbed it in her teeth and tried to pull, but she couldn't move her head enough to lift it.

The ship listed again, and Noa went into a terrifying spin with the shadow in her mouth, only this time it wrapped around her like a blanket, and as it came free it revealed the familiar door to Death beneath it. Noa fell through with a strangled shriek.

She landed in a sprawl. She felt Gabriela's spell lift—it was like having a sticky cobweb pulled off her body. For a long moment, she just lay there, dazed with relief. It felt odd to be so happy about ending up in Death, but being alive in the land of the dead was better than being dead in the land of the living.

"Otter?" she called.

"Yes?" A familiar supple shape poked its head over the edge of a boulder. "What do you want? I'm grooming."

Noa forced herself not to snap at it. She had to get back to the ship to help Julian. "But why?" she said desperately. "You're already so handsome."

The otter paused in the act of rubbing its face. "Do you think so?"

"Yes." Noa couldn't keep the frustration from her voice. "I already told you, you're the handsomest otter I've ever seen. Look, I need to get back to the ship, but I need to come out on the deck. Which shadow should I take?"

The otter regarded her unblinkingly.

Noa was nearly hopping up and down with urgency. "Well?"

The otter stood. "I've never spoken to you in my life. Are you saying you told someone else that they're handsomer than me?"

"No, of course not," Noa hurried on. "I mean—"

"Good day to you," the otter said frostily. "I hope you end up in the sea." And it flowed away.

Noa groaned. In desperation, she lifted up the nearest shadow and stuck her head through. She could see nothing except sloshing water. She turned her head and found the ship hovering only a few feet away—she was in the shadow it cast on the waves. There was a sailor in the water, swimming frantically away. His eyes caught hers, and his jaw fell open.

Not the right shadow.

Noa leaned back into Death. She tried several more shadows in quick succession, but none of them brought her onto the deck. She became aware, the more shadows she handled, of how much they overlapped, and she began to be able to sense where each one began and ended. A single ruin might have several shadows clustered beneath it, though they looked like one, and they all led to different places. Finding the right one was like sifting through papers scattered messily across a desk. In Death, everything was closer together, and two overlapping shadows might lead to places that were dozens of yards apart.

Finally, Noa found a shadow that led to the deck of the ship, and the same shadow cast by the figurehead that she had come through in the first place. Noa jumped.

Something was on fire. Smoke hung in the air, and thunderclouds clustered so low above the ship that Noa could probably touch them if she jumped. The deck was a mess of vines, alive and dead, and strange orbs hovered in the air like fallen moons. Several sailors were cowering by the railing. From the opposite end of the deck came a thunderous crash followed by a series of smaller crashes. But Noa didn't have a chance to investigate, for her muscles seized up and she toppled onto her side.

"Julian!" she managed to holler before her face seized up, too.

"Noa!"

There he was, hurrying across the deck. His hair looked singed in places, and the hem of his cloak was charred and ragged. The sailors cowering by the railing screamed at the sight of him and leaped over the side, though Julian barely spared them a glance.

"Are you all right?"

Noa just looked up at him. Her body had contorted itself back into that ridiculous posture. She looked like she was trying to run while lying on her side. "Gabriela," she managed.

"She's done something, hasn't she?" Julian touched her shoulder and murmured a stream of words in Marrow. After a few seconds of Julian trying different spells, Noa came unstuck. She sagged back against the deck. Julian helped her to her feet.

"How many mages are there?" she demanded.

"There *were* six. But I didn't see Gabriela. I've dealt with them all except for—"

"Watch out!" Noa yelled. Vines shot toward them and wrapped around Julian's mouth. A man jumped out from behind the figurehead, chanting in Briar. He advanced, and the vines snaked around Julian's arms, tightening and tightening.

Noa pulled out her pocketknife and sliced through the vines around Julian's head. As soon as his mouth was free, he spat out a spell in Eddy, and the mage went spinning backward, over the railing and into the sea. The remaining vines fell away. The deck was suddenly very quiet, except for the creaking of timber somewhere. The ship was listing and taking on water. But all its occupants seemed to be either in hiding or swimming for their lives.

"How did you get here?" Noa demanded.

"Blood spell. The same one I used before to locate you in Death. You were on the ship, so I could track the ship. I used the storm to carry me." He motioned at the roiling clouds.

Noa grimaced. "So, basically, you flew."

Julian noticed her expression. "We can take it slow on the way back. I won't mind if you're sick."

"Oh, good," Noa said. She was always sick when Julian used storms to transport them anywhere. You always got horribly damp and cold riding on a storm cloud, which made it worse. Last time, she'd thrown up on Julian's arm.

Julian raised a hand to the storm and called out a spell in Squall. The clouds reached out toward them, and a wet breeze almost swept Noa off her feet.

That was when a wave crashed over the deck.

Noa was washed over the railing. She made a desperate

grab for it, but it went by so fast that she missed it by a mile. The water was cold enough to make her gasp, and she found herself surging toward another wave that rose before her like a wall. She screamed.

The wave that carried her changed direction as some magical force yanked it back. Noa was swept over the railing and deposited, dripping, on the deck.

Julian hauled her to her feet. He was soaked, too, but had managed to maintain his footing. They both stared at the wave rising before them—and rising, and rising—and it was several seconds before Noa realized it wasn't a wave at all.

It was a figure made of water.

The figure was roughly woman-shaped, with a lot of wavy hair that seemed unpleasantly familiar. Gabriela sat on its shoulder with her knees folded beneath her, looking like a surfer riding the crest of a wave. Even though her hair was wet and plastered to her head and she had seaweed stuck to her cloak, she looked terrifyingly cool and comfortable up there.

Julian's expression darkened. His eyes met Gabriela's like lightning hitting a powder keg, and the air between them seemed to crackle. He began chanting, his brow furrowed in concentration.

"Maybe talk faster?" Noa suggested.

"This magic is incredibly intricate," he said, sounding almost impressed. "It's at least a dozen spells, woven together. I can't—ah!"

The towering water woman raised a fist and drove it toward the end of the ship, clearly set on sinking it. Julian yelled something, and a fierce wind pushed the ship out of the way just in time.

But Gabriela wasn't done. She stood, her lips moving in a spell Noa couldn't hear over the wind and waves and thunder.

Julian stepped forward until he was directly in the shadow of her gaze. "Gabriela!" he shouted. "Come down here and fight me! Leave my sister out of this."

Gabriela didn't seem to hear him. Noa wasn't sure she was capable of hearing anything. Her eyes were wild and her face was white. The water woman raised its arms and lunged at the ship.

Noa screamed. Julian was shouting spells so quickly that Noa couldn't even distinguish the languages he was speaking. To her horror, the wind he summoned was pushing them toward the watery figure as fast as it was coming at them. They were going to plow right into its stomach. At the same time, the ship's figurehead was beginning to move and stretch. It grew until it was twice its original size, and lifted its crude wooden sword.

Then they struck the water woman.

In the same moment, Julian wrapped Noa in his arms. The water closed over their heads, but it didn't touch them. They were in some sort of bubble of air, a bubble that spun round and round in the turbulent surf, so quickly that Noa would have preferred to have been in a thundercloud. After what seemed like hours, but was probably only seconds, the bubble burst, and she found herself bobbing amid the waves.

Julian was only a few yards away. The ship was no longer a ship—it was a field of debris scattered across the water. The figurehead floated on its back nearby, no longer huge and threatening, though there was something self-satisfied about its posture, as if it had just lived out a lifelong fantasy.

Noa turned. The water woman stood behind them, its head leaned forward slightly, as if it had fallen asleep. Gabriela was still on its shoulder, darting furious glances at Julian as she shouted spell after spell. The water woman lurched forward, and then it split in two, its top half melting as it fell, no longer anything other than but a wave. Gabriela screamed as she fell with it, and then Noa lost sight of her.

"Are you okay?" Julian swam to her side. "That wasn't so bad, was it?"

Noa threw up.

"Here." Julian grabbed a piece of ship and helped her clamber onto it. "We'll just rest a moment until your stomach settles. Then we really have to go."

Noa thought it would take longer than a moment for her stomach to settle, and hoped Julian wasn't wearing his favorite cloak. Then again, given that he hadn't warned her about any of that, she thought he deserved whatever he got. "Where's Gabriela?"

"With any luck, at the bottom of the sea." He didn't sound at all certain about that, though, and neither was Noa. She thought that Gabriela was probably fine, and would be on them with another terrifying spell if they gave her more than a minute to think of one. Still, that didn't prepare Noa when a head broke through the surf only a few yards away, gasping and coughing.

"Gabriela!" Noa yelped. "Julian, forget my stomach, let's go!"

Julian beckoned at the clouds, which had drifted back to their normal height, and they began to sink toward them.

Too slowly. Gabriela opened her eyes.

Julian froze for a moment, then went back to chanting. He pushed Noa behind him, though to Noa's surprise, Gabriela didn't look like she was about to attack them again. She looked surprisingly bedraggled, as a normal person would if a woman-shaped wall of water had fallen on top of them. Noa wasn't used to thinking of Gabriela as a normal person. Her cloak was in shreds and her lip was bleeding, as if she'd hit it on a piece of ship. She looked younger with her hair plastered to her head and her makeup washed away, much closer to her actual age. She flopped onto a broken door, still coughing.

Her eyes met Julian's. "Go ahead," she said hoarsely. She wiped her lip. It looked like whatever had struck her face had knocked out one of her perfect teeth, too.

Julian stared at her, either unwilling or unable to speak. He looked like he had in the days after they'd found out Gabriela was a spy, rather like someone had reached down his throat and tied his heart into knots.

Well, Noa wasn't at all sorry to see Gabriela looking like a drowned rabbit. "Go ahead and what?" she spat.

"She thinks I'm going to kill her." Julian's knotted-heart look was fading and fury took its place. "Which is what I should do, given that you've been keeping my little sister hostage. Tell me again how you're so different from me, Gabriela. How much nobler your side is."

She looked as if he'd struck her. "I—I wasn't going to hurt Noa."

"Oh, right." Noa poked her head out from behind Julian's shoulder. "You were taking me to Xavier because we're such great friends."

Julian's face was like the storm clouds. "You were taking her to *Xavier*?"

Gabriela opened and closed her mouth. "I—"

"Don't bother." Julian spoke to the sky, his voice like ice. The clouds twitched as if startled and wrapped their tendrils around Julian and Noa. Julian looked back at Gabriela. "If I was going to kill you, I would have done it already. Maybe one day you'll work out what that means. Good luck rescuing your crew with what's left of your ship. If anyone dies, you can always blame it on me."

The clouds closed around them, but not before Noa caught sight of Gabriela's face, which was pale and stricken, nothing like the careful mask she usually wore. Then she and Julian were rising into the sky, leaving Gabriela and her broken ship behind.

22

Mite Loses an Honored Guest

The storm that pounded Astrae with rain and sent the lava crickets scurrying to their burrows died during the night, and the morning dawned clear and calm. Sometime near sunrise, even Beauty went quiet, the wails that had echoed off the volcano and given the sentries raging headaches replaced by a few sniffles, then silence. Around that time, one of the mages saw a small creature that looked like a serpentine seal making its way across the open water toward Astrae. Whatever it was, Beauty shot out to greet it, and then both of them disappeared beneath the waves.

Mite opened her eyes when the dawn light touched her face. She had fallen asleep on one of the steps leading to Julian's tower. After Noa left, she hadn't wanted to go back to her room, but she also hadn't wanted to stay in the tower, given that it was filled with angry ghosts. So she had decided to wait for Julian and Noa on the stairs, holding the book Julian had been reading to her. She must have fallen asleep.

Julian hadn't come back. For the first time since Momma died, he had forgotten about her story.

Mite rose unsteadily to her feet. She left the book on the staircase and made her way to her room. Maybe when she woke up, Julian and Noa would be back. Or maybe she would wake to find that everything that had happened—Noa and Julian getting mad at each other; somebody stealing Beauty's baby; Noa leaving her alone with ghosts—had been a dream.

Mite opened her door. She was so tired and heartsick that she didn't even bother saying hello to her favorite pet, a moth named Fluffy that she had raised from a tiny caterpillar. Fluffy didn't seem to notice—he was perched in a patch of sunlight on the floor, munching on one of her sweaters.

But she didn't make it to her bed. Because the jar on her windowsill, the jar that had been Patience's home, which she had left on the sill so the spider could enjoy the view, was empty.

Mite scrambled to her closet. Her collection of pet spiders gazed back at her, each perched calmly in a nest of webs in a different corner. They hadn't been eaten, nor had the caterpillars in their cocoons, or the ladybugs marching along the stems of the giant lily she kept by the window.

Relieved, Mite set about searching for Patience. She hadn't thought the spider was strong enough to open a jar, nor small enough to squeeze through the air holes, but it looked like

Patience had gnawed at one of the holes until it grew wide enough to join up with another one, then pushed its way through. Mite would have been impressed if she wasn't so scared. The spider didn't realize that people were hunting it. And then there were the cats—though given Patience's size, Mite wasn't sure who'd win that fight.

Patience wasn't in Mite's bed, nor under it. Mite pulled out her drawers one by one and searched the contents, but found no enormous spotted spider crouched among her socks or underwear, much to her disappointment. By the time she'd finished searching, her room looked like it had been turned upside down and shaken, and her pets were disturbed. Fluffy was perched on the windowsill, wings twitching as if he could sense her anxiety.

Mite sat on her bed, trying to fight against the worry and fear inside her. *Deep breaths*, Julian always said when she got like this. *Deep breaths*. She couldn't explode now—she'd kill her pets. After breathing deeply for a few minutes, she started to feel dizzy, but at least that was better than scared.

She crept out into the hall. Reckoner was waiting for her, a forlorn look on his droopy old face. Reckoner didn't really like anyone except Julian, but he thought Mite and Noa were all right, and sometimes when Julian was away, he came looking for them. Mite scratched his ears. She was happy to have company.

Reckoner trotted at her heels as she searched the hallway

and all the rooms, most of which were empty, except Noa's. The mages lived in another part of the castle. There were no signs of the spider, and Mite was beginning to suspect that Patience had already left the castle. After all, her species usually lived on beaches and sea cliffs; they liked burrowing into the sand and then jumping out at their prey. Mite decided to go down to the beach.

She found several mages clustered in the castle foyer, deep in conversation. They had that worried, uncertain look they always did whenever Julian left Astrae, and barely glanced at her as she passed.

"—should be back by now," one of the mages was saying. "If Gabriela—"

"She's no match for him," another mage said. "If she *is* holding the girl captive, I wouldn't like to see what he'll do to her."

Mite sighed with relief. Julian must have gone to rescue Noa. He hadn't forgotten about her story after all. Stories were important, but rescue missions were more important.

She shook her head. She had told Noa that she shouldn't leave Astrae. But, as usual, Noa hadn't listened.

Mite made her way down the castle stairs to the beach, her heart a little lighter. The sunshine was warm and the sky was a pretty blue. Reckoner followed closely behind her, his busy nose sniffing at everything.

She found Tomas standing on the beach with his arms

crossed and a frown on his face. He had a big cart with him, the same one he'd used before to carry Beauty's cake. Mite's nostrils flared as she caught the scent of vanilla and pears and toasted sugar. Unfortunately, Tomas turned around and saw her before she could get close enough to peek under the cloth covering the cart.

"Have you seen your sister?" he said.

Mite found that most of the time when people spoke to her, it was because they were looking for Julian or Noa. She shook her head.

"Well, if you do, tell her I have another cake for her." He was sweaty from dragging the cart, and he sounded mad. "It's pear with mint. I hope she doesn't waste this one. It takes a long time to mix everything, you know. I have to put it all in the bathtub and walk round and round it with an oar."

Mite wanted to tell Tomas to leave the cake with her, because her stomach was growling, but she didn't want him to get mad at her, too. He picked up the handle and began to pull the cart back up the path to the village. Mite crept up behind him and managed to tear off a piece without him noticing. She scampered away with her hands full.

After she finished the cake, she let Reckoner lick her fingers. Two salt mages were patrolling the beach, but apart from them, the pale crescent of sand was empty in the dawn light. Mite decided to start her search on the grassy dunes behind the dry part of the sand. They were piled messily with driftwood that she suspected would make an excellent spider lair.

Reckoner couldn't clamber over logs, so he followed alongside her on the sand, sniffing and occasionally sneezing at the seaweed. Whenever Reckoner sneezed, he gave off a small puff of smoke. The dragon was too old to breathe fire anymore, but he still had some life left in him, as Julian often said fondly.

Mite followed the dunes to a cove just out of sight of the castle. Renne was down there, murmuring to a piece of paper. That was what it looked like, anyway. Then the paper rose into the air, and Mite realized that it was a letter, sealed with wax. Renne was a wind mage, so he could send letters to other islands, even if they were far away. The letter became a tiny dot against the blue, and then it was gone.

Renne glanced over his shoulder, and Mite was glad that she'd decided to crouch behind a big log as soon as she saw him. Renne had been in the background of Mite's life for as long as she could remember—he was Julian's oldest friend, and had been at his side constantly when they had all lived in the palace. Even though he had never said anything mean to her, Mite knew that Renne didn't like her. Some grown-ups didn't, though they pretended to.

Mite crept away, grateful for how quiet her bare feet were on the sand. "Come on, Reckoner," she whispered. The dragon turned around, but not before he let out a big sneeze and another puff of smoke.

"Maita?"

Mite thought about running, but she was a little afraid of Renne, so she waited as he made his way up the sand. Reckoner caught Renne's scent on the air and growled.

"Is your brother back yet?" Renne asked. He cast another glance up the beach. His face was pale and worried, even more than the other mages'.

Mite shook her head.

Renne yelped. Reckoner had bitten him on the leg.

"Bad dragon!" Mite said. She gave him a bop on the snout like Julian did whenever Reckoner bit someone. The dragon just growled again and skulked behind Mite's legs. He never seemed to learn, but then he did have a short memory.

"It's all right," Renne said with a sour look. "I'm used to it."

Mite swallowed a giggle. Reckoner had always disliked Renne in particular.

"Come with me, Maita," Renne said, some of the sourness creeping into his voice. "Julian won't be happy when he finds you've been wandering off again."

"I'm not wandering," Mite muttered. But Renne was the last person she would tell about her rescue mission, so she followed him back up the beach toward the castle. She sneakily walked along the logs beside the mage, pretending she was playing a balancing game when she was really looking for Patience.

They rounded the corner of the beach, and Mite stared at the horizon in surprise. An elegant sailboat was approaching.

It didn't have red sails like the king's, but it still made her nervous.

"What's that?" Mite said.

"General Lydio," Renne said. "Julian has been expecting him for some time. He's officially pledged his support for our cause."

Mite wasn't sure what that meant. She hoped it didn't mean they would have visitors staying in the castle—she didn't like visitors. They always spoke to her in syrupy voices, as if she was six rather than seven and a half.

"Are they coming to stay here?" she said, but Renne wasn't listening. One of the mages on the beach was waving at him, and he hurried off without another word.

Mite made her way alone up the castle stairs with a heavy heart. No story, no spider, and now there were strange visitors who would take up all Julian's time. She didn't think things could get any worse.

23

Noa Finds an Unexpected Ally

The journey back to Astrae passed in a haze of nausea. Noa vaguely remembered touching down, because that was when she had thrown up again, and then Julian laying her down in bed. At some point, he returned with a cool compress for her forehead and, later, a bowl of plain oatmeal. "*Merp,*" Noa managed, waving him off. The offending oatmeal vanished, and she fell asleep again.

Eventually, her stomach calmed, and she was able to sit up. From the light, she guessed it was early afternoon. She had a bath and put on clean clothes. Her old ones smelled of seawater and something deeply unpleasant that she suspected was sea serpent slime. After tossing on a fresh black cloak, she felt like herself again, apart from her stomach, which had a scooped-out feeling, like a melon rind. She went to find Julian.

The tower was empty, though. Sunlight poured through the windows and splashed upon the floor. A few of the windows had been left open, for it was a warm day, and a salty breeze flickered over the maps and grimoires and compasses. The cats were excited to see Noa. They swarmed her invisibly, rubbing against her calves and twining about her feet. It was like wading through a purring sea.

Noa waved her hands through the cat-filled air, managing to pet a few of them. She went over to one of the windows, and was surprised to find that Astrae was barely moving. They were in an unfamiliar sea between two distant walls of volcanoes. The turquoise water frothed around a scattering of tiny islets, which were lumpy with walruses.

Noa frowned. Anchored just off Astrae was a large sailboat with gaudily patterned sails. The door opened behind her, and she turned, expecting Julian, but it was Mite.

"You're finally up!" She skipped into the room. "Guess what? Julian read me two stories this morning. And he said he'll read me two more tonight." Her voice was low, as if she felt she was getting away with something.

"Whose ship is that?" Noa demanded.

Mite skipped up to the window. "That's General Lydio's. Renne said he came to wedge his support."

"Pledge his support?" Noa said. "Oh! I remember now. He sent Julian a letter a long time ago, hinting about joining our side. He's a salt mage, and he commands a third of Xavier's fleet." Noa chewed her lip. "I wonder if he really means it, or if he's just hedging his bets."

"They're going to stay in the castle," Mite said gloomily. "They have a big ship. Why don't they stay there?"

"If General Lydio can get the navy on our side, he can have the entire island to himself," Noa said. "Where are we?"

Mite shrugged. "Some place with another smelly book."

"This is Greenwash Strait?" Noa leaned out the window, but she saw nothing but rocks and walruses. She wondered if Xavier's mage had given Julian the wrong coordinates. "Where's the island?"

"There's no island. Julian said maybe the book is under water."

"But what about Xavier? Where are his ships? Maybe we're in the wrong place."

"There are two royal ships over there," Mite said, pointing. "Julian turned the island so we're facing away from them. When they move east or west, he turns it again. They don't know we're here."

Noa looked, and sure enough, she could just make out two small red smudges on the horizon. If Xavier's ships were still here, they probably hadn't found the second lost language. That was good. But Noa still felt uneasy. Even if Xavier hadn't found the Lost Words yet, that didn't mean he wouldn't. His mages had a big head start on Astrae. Who knew how long they'd been searching?

"Where's Julian?" Noa said.

"In the kitchen," Mite said. "Working on the menu with Anna."

"Menu?" Noa yelled.

Mite's brow furrowed. "For the banquet. To welcome General—"

"Xavier attacked us last night," Noa said, gesticulating at the window. "His mages are out there right now, looking for the Lost Words. And Julian is off working on *menus*?"

"It's just one menu." Mite's face brightened. "We're having sesame coconut custard for first dessert and lava surprise cake for second dessert. Julian couldn't decide, so I said we should have both."

Noa let out a long groan and flopped down on the squashy couch. She couldn't believe Julian. Imagine stopping in the middle of an important quest to throw a party! Last night, she had nearly gotten herself killed trying to save him from his own wicked tendencies. Now she had to save him from his ridiculous tendencies as well. Her head hurt.

"Go get Julian," she said without uncovering her eyes. "Tell him he needs to come and look for the Lost Words. Tell him that strategy is more important than menus." She paused. "Also, bring back some of that custard."

Mite's light feet scampered away. She returned a few minutes later with a tray laden with baked apples, urchin soup, buttered buns fresh from the oven, a neat pile of chocolate cakes, and a mug of custard. But no Julian.

"He says you're not allowed to plot anything for a while," Mite said. She set the tray down next to Noa and helped herself to a cake. "He says the last time you came up with a plot you ran off and nearly got yourself killed. He says you're not allowed to do that today."

"Oh, really." Noa's foul mood got even fouler. She sat up and stabbed at the soup with her spoon. "Well, that's a nice way to thank me for saving his stupid sea serpent. How exactly are you going to stop me from plotting, Mite?"

"Um," Mite said.

Noa swallowed her soup. She tilted her head to one side and let her gaze drift.

"Hey!" Mite said. "You're not supposed to plot."

"Hmm," Noa murmured, rubbing her chin and staring vacantly at the curtains. "*Hmm.*"

"Stop that!"

Noa pointed an apple at her. "Look, Mite. I'm going to search for the Lost Words whether you like it or not. You have two choices. You can either tattle to Julian, or you can help me."

Mite looked as if she hadn't expected that. "Help you?"

"I understand if you're scared," Noa said silkily. "The thing is, I just want to protect Astrae."

"I want to protect Astrae too!"

"Hmm," Noa said, pretending to plot as she sipped her

custard. This time, Mite only watched her avidly. "I think I know how to find the Lost Words. But I can't do it without your help."

Mite looked torn. "Julian said . . ."

"Here." Noa handed Mite the Chronicle. "Start a new entry. We'll make a list of places where the mages might have hidden the Lost Words."

Mite's eyes grew wide as teacups. Normally, Noa didn't allow her to touch the Chronicle. "You want me to write in *this*?"

Noa nodded. "This is very, very important. I know you'll take good care of it."

"I will," Mite promised earnestly. She flipped through the Chronicle, looking for a fresh page. When she found one, she took a pencil and wrote the date at the top, just as Noa always did. She seemed to be trying to be as neat as possible, so it took a full minute. Her nose almost touched the page.

"Good," Noa said. She slurped up the last of the custard and set the mug down. "Now, help me look for the map of the Ayora Sea."

They found that easily enough, and Noa spent the next hour moving Julian's telescope from one side of the tower to another, map in one hand and compass in the other. Unfortunately, the tiny islets of Greenwash were all on the map. Noa had been hoping that one would be missing, like Evert was. She told herself that the ancient mages had probably used different techniques to hide each magical language—it would be too easy to find them all otherwise. She found the coordinates Thadeus had given Julian and muttered over them for a while, but they covered too large an area to be helpful.

Mite followed Noa from window to window, taking painfully neat notes in the Chronicle. Noa was pleased by how well her ploy had worked. Mite seemed happy to go along with Noa's plots if she felt like she was being included in them. Noa wondered why she hadn't thought of that before. Mite chattered as they worked, jumping from some letter Renne had sent to how she didn't think Julian should bop Reckoner on the snout when he was bad, because he'd just forget about it to demanding with a disturbing intensity that Noa tell her if she noticed any giant spiderwebs in the castle.

Eventually, Mite settled down on Julian's bed with the Chronicle to sketch walruses, which Noa had suggested as a way of getting rid of her. She soon fell asleep.

Noa breathed a sigh of relief. Astrae had spun slightly west to remain invisible to the king's ships, so she moved the telescope to a better window. She sat down in front of it with a sextant and began going through some complicated calculations. Perhaps the coordinates themselves were some sort of riddle.

Occupied as she was, she didn't notice the shadows lengthening across the floor as the sun dipped toward the western horizon. Nor did she notice the strange icy breeze that mixed itself with the ordinary breezes and made Julian's papers rustle like dry fingers. She did notice the prickling on the back of her neck. She looked up, and then around.

A ghost stood on the other side of the tower, watching her. The ghost had the shape of a woman, and she had fewer drifting tendrils than the others. Her features were difficult to make out, and she wore a long cloak that could have been either black or gray.

The ghost brushed a strand of colorless hair from her face, and Noa froze. The gesture was painfully familiar. Noa's heart faltered. Slowly, the ghost became clearer, as if shrouded by a fading fog. The cloak was indeed black, with a cut that indicated its expense. Her face was still blurred, but Noa could see that the chin was sharp, the ears overlarge. And there was something about her eyes, the hint of wrinkles at the corners, as if from frequent bouts of laughter, that stole Noa's breath.

Noa couldn't believe it. She wouldn't. And yet—

"Mom?" she croaked.

The ghost lifted her hand. When she spoke, her voice was thin and strange, as if it were carried on a distant wind. "Noa?"

"Mom." It was half a sob. Noa threw her instruments aside and sprang to her feet. It was her mother's voice, her mother's gestures. Her mother had come back! Nothing else mattered in that moment—not Xavier's ships, not the Lost Words, not even Julian. She tripped over the telescope and was up and running again before she felt the pain.

"Stop," her mother said when Noa was still a yard away. "I'll fade completely if you get too close, honey."

Noa froze. Her face was wet with tears. Up in the loft, Mite was snoring. "Why? Did the otters give you my message? How are you—"

"They gave it to me, sweetie," her mother said. "But I'm not here just because of that. I'm here because you're in danger—all of you. He's getting close . . ."

Her voice faded in and out. Noa said, "You mean Xavier? Are his mages close to finding the Lost Words?"

Her mother said something that Noa couldn't hear. Then, "I can't stay long. I'm not strong enough. Can you come to me in Death? At midnight. Come at midnight. . . ." She flickered and nearly disappeared.

"Of course I will. I'll do anything." Noa's vision blurred. "Please don't go—"

"I know where . . . ," her mother said, "I can help . . ."

"What?" Noa cried. Her mother was fading fast. She could barely see her outline anymore. "What did you come to tell me?"

But her mother was gone. Noa was alone.

24

Beetles Ruin
the Banquet

The banquet hall was awash in light. The ceiling sparkled with tiny orbs, and every candelabra and chandelier glowed. Morning glory spilled in from the beach and wrapped around the columns, dangling its purple blooms over guests' heads. Crowding the marble floor was a motley assortment of tables, which the servants had scavenged from various parts of the castle and from the village—they didn't usually have banquets this large. The entire village had been invited, as well as all the mages and sailors, and of course General Lydio's entourage. General Lydio and his wife, Pellia, were to be seated at Julian's table as guests of honor.

Noa felt as if she was barely there. As if she was floating, drifting through the hall like a puff of thistledown. Normal things like talking and eating felt impossible, because thistledown didn't do those things—it just drifted, unless it got stuck in something, like a spiderweb. Sometimes Noa felt like she was stuck in a spiderweb, too. She just stood, staring at nothing, until the wind—or one of the guests—did something to jostle her free.

She had seen her mother.

Noa hadn't intended to go to the banquet. After her mother's ghost had vanished, Noa had left the tower and wandered around the castle in a daze. Some part of her had been looking for Julian, but instead she had bumped into Renne, who had hustled her into the hall, muttering about tardiness. If she had been able to speak, Noa would have told him that she didn't care if the banquet and all the guests went tumbling into the sea.

People milled around the cavernous hall, which opened onto the basalt bluffs at the north end of Astrae. Mite, no doubt drawn to the banquet by the promise of double dessert more than the company, stuck so close to her that she often stepped on her cloak.

She had seen Mom.

Mom had come to help them. But how? What did she know? Noa's head whirled. It had sounded as though her mother thought Xavier was getting close to finding one of the lost languages. If so, they would be in danger indeed, particularly if Xavier's mages discovered that the Dark Lord was right under their noses.

Julian hadn't joined the banquet yet, and neither had General Lydio. Noa drifted outside, where a dozen people were gathered on the rocks, enjoying the warm night and the orbs scattered over the uneven rock. Well-dressed strangers who Noa supposed were General Lydio's officers looked at her with interested gazes, clearly thinking about striking up a conversation with Julian Marchena's sister, but Noa crossed her arms and glowered, and they thought better of it.

"You don't have to stay with me the whole time," Noa said to Mite. She wished she could abandon the banquet, but even in her stunned state, she recognized how important General Lydio's support was to Julian. She couldn't risk offending him. "Why don't you go have some coconut ice?"

"That's okay." Mite looked perfectly happy to hover in the safe shade of Noa's scowl. She rummaged around in her pockets and began fiddling with a handful of small black dots that looked unnervingly like live beetles.

A young man wearing General Lydio's colors sidled up to Noa. He had a tanned, handsome face and a big white smile. "Good evening. You must be King Julian's little sister."

Noa let him bow over her hand, hoping he would go away. "You must be someone with eyes," she replied, to encourage him in that direction.

Unfortunately, the young man continued to linger. "You're a lucky girl to have a brother like him. The most powerful mage in the kingdom." He actually winked. "Not to mention one of the best looking."

Noa couldn't imagine what Julian's good looks had to do

with her, other than the fact that they increased the number of Julian's annoying suitors she had to deal with. She suspected that her life would be easier if Julian were covered in boils.

"I don't suppose you could introduce me?" the young man said.

Good grief. This was the last thing that Noa wanted to be bothered by right now. *I don't suppose so,* she almost said, but clearly the young man wasn't easily discouraged.

"Sure," she said, forcing a bright smile.

He smiled back. "Thank you. I'm sorry if I'm being a nuisance. You must get asked this sort of thing all the time."

"Not so much anymore," Noa said. "People got put off once Julian's dates started disappearing."

The man's smile froze on his face. "What?"

"Oh, I'm sure it's nothing," Noa added. "Julian jokes about how he feeds them to his sea serpent afterward, but I'm sure that's all it is—a joke. He has a weird sense of humor." She gave a sisterly laugh. "I mean, it's true that there have been a few disappearances and, you know, Beauty has been putting on weight, but they probably just get spooked. Julian can be intimidating."

"Ah, yes," the young man said. The smile was melting off his face.

"Besides, his dates don't *all* disappear." She gave him a reassuring pat on the arm. "Only the ones he doesn't like."

The young man slowly backed away. "I see."

"Oh, look! There's Julian now." Noa gave a big wave in the direction of a potted plant. When she turned back to the young man, he was halfway across the room. She gave a satisfied snort. She would have to remember that one. She leaned against a column, her eyes fixed on the obsidian clock that took up half a wall.

Four hours until she saw Mom again. She felt dizzy, then sick. Where was Julian?

"There you are!" Kell called, slicing her way easily through the guests, who sprang aside as soon as they realized who she was. "I heard you had quite the adventure last night. Wish I'd been there to see His Royal Highness give that traitor the comeuppance she deserved."

Noa nodded faintly. It felt like the sea serpent rescue mission had happened weeks ago.

"Still queasy?" Kell squeezed Noa's shoulder with her calloused hand. "You look like you swallowed a fire lizard."

Noa shook her head. The thistledown feeling faded a bit under the weight of Kell's concern. "Is Julian here yet?"

"Just arrived with General Lydio—there's a sly old fox if I ever saw one. Come on, they're waiting for us."

Noa took a deep breath. She wasn't in the mood for any of this, but part of her couldn't help feeling pleased at the prospect of sitting next to Julian at the head of the royal table while he officially welcomed an ally for the first time.

Julian was resplendent in a new black cloak with glittering dragons embroidered into the sleeves. His hair was actually clean and brushed, and he was smiling warmly as he spoke to a man with blondish hair and a pointed nose. He looked every bit like a king, and the other guests seemed to sense it, too, for they all maintained a respectful distance, even his own mages.

"General," Julian said, motioning to Noa as she approached with Mite stuck to her heels like a barnacle, "these are my sisters, Noa and Maita."

Noa wasn't sure if General Lydio could see Mite from that angle, but he greeted them good-naturedly anyway. Noa didn't think he looked much like a fox. He looked old and small, and he was wearing many layers of expensive fabric from which his head stuck out like a turtle's.

"I hear you're the brains behind the throne," he said to Noa with a wink, and Noa understood then what Kell meant, because he was clearly trying to flatter her. "Perhaps you can advise me on whether I'm making the right decision in siding with your brother."

Noa tore her eyes from the clock and forced herself to focus on the general. This man could become Julian's most important ally. "It's the right decision," she said. "Julian is the rightful king of Florean, after all. Whether it's a smart decision or not, I don't know. Which island are you from?"

General Lydio paused, as if he hadn't expected this. He

looked at Noa with actual interest, not just flattering interest. "Sevrilla."

Noa nodded. "That's close to the islands Julian already controls. You probably wouldn't have to worry about King Xavier attacking it to get revenge on you for switching sides. And of course, you would be the first general to side with Julian, so you'd be rewarded after he becomes king. Strategically, I'd say it's the smart decision."

Julian looked amused. General Lydio blinked rapidly. A slow, genuine smile spread across his face.

"Most impressive," he said. "I've been thinking this over for months, and you summed it up in ten seconds. And I suppose the little one is a whiz at economics, is she?" Mite, who had been poking her head out from behind Noa to watch the conversation, flushed and disappeared again.

"Though you've left out one thing," the general went on. "I've long been troubled by the rumors I've been hearing about Xavier. Some of his councillors whisper that he's planning to expand his campaign against dark mages. That he wants magic wiped out in Florean altogether. If that happens, I fear it's only a matter of time before one of the kingdoms of South Meruna attacks us. They hate magic, but they also fear it, and if Florean's mages disappear, all that will be left is their hatred of us." He smiled faintly. "You might guess that as a general, I spend most of my time thinking about war. But in fact, I think about

preventing it. Your brother is better for Florean than Xavier."
He grimaced, glancing across the room at Kell. "Despite the
company he keeps."

Julian's eyes narrowed. "Captain Kell is one of my most
valued councillors."

"Of course, Your Highness." General Lydio bowed his
head, though his expression was carefully blank, and Noa
knew he wasn't convinced. He wandered off to speak to a
woman even smaller than him, who Noa assumed was his wife.

"You gave our guest a turn," Julian said, smiling at her.
"Lydio says he supports me, but whether he'll do anything
about it is another question. It sounded like you gave him a
push in the right direction, my Noabell."

She felt her anger at him crumble away in the face of that
familiar smile. "Julian," she said quietly, "I need to talk to you.
This afternoon, in the tower—"

"I'm a little busy," he said, motioning to Kell. "Can it wait
until after the banquet?"

Noa glared at the side of his head. "No, it can't," she said,
pulling out her chair. "You should probably sit down first—"

"What are you doing?" Julian said.

Noa blinked. "Is sitting down not allowed at this banquet?"

"Oh—I'm sorry, Noa. That seat is for General Lydio. His
wife sits next to him, and Renne and Kell are at my right hand.
You understand—as much as the general seems to like you, it

would look strange to have children at the head of the table. Stefan will show you where you're sitting." He lowered his voice. "Keep an eye on Mite, and tell her to get rid of those beetles. Preferably outside." He turned and said something to Renne, his expression distracted.

Noa felt as if she'd swallowed ice. She numbly followed the servant to a seat at the opposite end of the table. Mite sat next to her, and beside Mite was General Lydio's son, who had the general's sharp nose and blondish hair. He was probably about Noa's age. Mite took one look at him and edged her chair closer to Noa's, as if he were contagious with something.

Noa helped herself to lemon shrimp—usually her favorite—without actually seeing it. She wasn't even sitting with the other councillors—she was sitting with the children. Across from her was Asha's granddaughter, as well as two more girls she didn't recognize who must be part of General Lydio's entourage. Their father sat next to Noa, and he kept leaning over her plate to talk to them as if Noa weren't there.

Her heart thudded in her ears. It was as if she had never been made a royal councillor. Had that even been real, or had Julian only done it to make her happy? She remembered the condescending looks many of the other councillors had given her. They had thought Julian was humoring her, his silly little sister. And now it looked like they were right. Noa sawed her shrimp into bits with trembling hands. Part of her knew it didn't make sense to get this angry over where she sat at dinner. But being angry about that made her remember that she was angry at Julian about other things, and those thoughts kept going round and round in her mind, and got louder when the man beside her leaned so far across her plate that his beard trailed in her tomatoes.

There was a clamor outside the banquet hall. Two guards entered, each gripping a man roughly by the shoulder. The men were both young, Julian's age or less, and wore General Lydio's colors.

"We caught them trying to break into your tower, Your Highness," one of the guards said.

General Lydio's face was pale. "Your Highness, I've never seen those men before."

Julian gave him a cool look, then turned to the men. "You resupplied at Hedea, didn't you? Is it possible you gained two stowaways there?"

General Lydio looked more embarrassed than frightened. Noa didn't think he was lying—if he was, he was a very good actor. "It's possible."

"Xavier's guessed you planned to join me, then." Julian's fingers tapped a slow rhythm against the table. In the silence of the full banquet hall, beneath the rapt attention of the guests, it seemed unnaturally loud. He addressed the men in a pleasant voice. "And how much did Xavier pay you to spy on me?"

The man on the left said nothing. He was shaking, with a sheen of sweat on his brow. But the other man, wild-eyed, took a half step forward before he was stopped by the guard. "I would have done it for free," he said with a laugh that went on for too long. "Monster. I'd rather die than see someone like you on the throne of Florean." And then he began to shout something in Spark, and Noa realized, too late, that the guards should have gagged the men before bringing them before Julian. The guard realized his mistake and reached for the man's mouth, while several guests shrieked and Julian's mages shoved their chairs back.

But Julian barely moved. Before any of his mages could cast a single spell, he flicked his fingers at the man and murmured something inaudible over the din. The man stumbled back, collapsing against the guard again.

His mouth was gone.

Noa's stomach lurched. "That's better," Julian said. After the eruption of sound, the banquet hall had fallen silent, eerily so.

"No," the other man murmured as he stared at his companion in horror. "No, no, please no—"

Julian wasn't even looking at him. He murmured again, and made another airy flicking motion, and the other man's mouth vanished, too. "What do you think?" he said to Renne, as if asking his opinion on the food.

Renne looked as ill as Noa felt. "Have them taken to the dungeon, of course." He glanced at the men, who were making horrible muffled sounds. "There was no need to—to do that.

Taking their voices would have been enough."

"That's not very imaginative, is it? We do have guests to impress." Several of the mages tittered. Julian leaned back in his chair, smiling at the men. His eyes had a cold glitter. "So you came here to spy on me, did you? Well . . . carry on."

He spoke a complicated series of words that sparked like flames and hummed like summer bees. It was more than one incantation, woven together in a strange pattern. The two men began to glow and shrink. They grew so bright that it was impossible to look directly at them, then slowly they rose into the air. Noa had to look away, her eyes watering. When her vision cleared, she choked on a cry.

Suspended from the ceiling were a number of lanterns that cast a cheery, wavering light over the banquet. Two of those lanterns now glowed unnaturally bright, and within them you could just make out the outlines of small, glowing faces, their eyes wide with horror as they pressed their mouthless jaws against the glass.

Noa felt as if she were back in the storm, driftwood tossed about by the currents. Mite started to follow her gaze, but Noa distracted her by spilling her drink. Mite had to move quickly to avoid getting the beetles wet.

Julian thanked the guards with one of his charming smiles, then went back to his conversation with General Lydio and his wife. Slowly, people began talking again, though their voices were hushed at first. General Lydio sat with his mouth in a line. He didn't look happy, but nor did he look surprised, and he answered Julian's questions without faltering. Noa found herself remembering, against her will, what Gabriela had said. *The only thing that can defeat a monster is another monster.* Was that what General Lydio believed? In siding with Julian, did he think he was doing the right thing, or simply choosing the lesser of two monsters?

Noa spent the rest of the banquet in silence. No one spoke to her, which suited her just fine. After what she'd just seen, her appetite had fled. A few of the guests looked like they felt the same, but most had gone back to their meals. What had happened was entertainment to them, all the more so because it had been frightening, and the glances they shot at Julian were half anxious and half admiring. The boy next to Mite decided to amuse himself by throwing oyster shells into her cup, which made the girls across the table giggle. Mite stared at her plate the whole time, blinking rapidly. Noa eventually rose, pulled on the boy's collar, and poured her sesame coconut custard down his back. He yelped and sputtered, but Noa might have gotten away with it had Mite not taken inspiration from her and dumped her beetles down the boy's shirt, too. He leaped screaming from his chair, tripped, and landed in the creamed kelp with such a splash that it spattered the guests at that end of the table. Noa was still standing up, so everybody stared at her as the boy screamed the way you would scream if you were being slowly eaten by a shark. Even Julian, miles away at the other end of the table, sat frozen in confusion. General Lydio rose to his feet and made his way over, and Noa remembered, too late, that the awful blond boy was his son.

So she did the only thing that made sense, and stormed out of the hall.

The salty wind was cool against her face, and it helped to chase away the kelp smell that clung to her hair. Noa marched along the rocky shore just outside the hall, smashing mussels and barnacles with her boots, until she became aware that she wasn't alone.

"Go back to dinner, Mite," Noa said over her shoulder. "Julian will be mad at you." This didn't make much sense, given that the sister he was more likely to be mad at was the one who had apparently tried to murder General Lydio's son, but Noa didn't care.

"I don't want to go back." Mite's face was flushed. "Can't I stay here with you?"

"No," Noa snapped. "You can't. I need to think, and you don't help."

"But—"

"Mite, for once in your life, will you *leave me alone*," Noa snarled.

Mite's mouth trembled. She turned and fled.

Noa felt a flicker of guilt, but it was no match for her anger. She kept walking, then she sat on the rocks for a while, watching the breakers. After an hour or so, she got cold, and she also realized that if Julian was looking for her, she was missing her chance to make him feel guilty. She walked back toward the castle and sat on the rocks within view of the balcony.

Julian found her a little while later. His fancy cloak was gone and his hair was disheveled again, so Noa took it that the banquet was over. He sat down beside her. "General Lydio's son has finally calmed down," he said. "You can visit him in the morning and apologize."

"For what?" Noa demanded.

"For what. He said you put something down his shirt. I know you don't spend much time with other children, Noa, but I had hoped you'd at least try to get along with Matty."

Noa glowered. Who made such a fuss over a few insects? She'd sooner put beetles down her own shirt than apologize to that crybaby.

Julian rubbed his face. He looked exhausted, and Noa wondered if he'd been hiding it before. "What was it that you wanted to tell me?"

Noa unclenched her fingers, which were beginning to ache from gripping the rock. "I saw Mom," she said in a flat voice.

Julian froze. "What?"

"I saw Mom. She came to tell me something important—I think it's about the Lost Words. I'm going back to Death tonight to talk to her."

Julian said nothing for a moment. When he did, his words were almost frighteningly calm. "Tell me exactly what happened."

Noa did.

"I don't know who you spoke to," Julian said. His face was the same shade as the distant breakers. "But I doubt it was Mom."

"What?" Noa stared at him. "Why wouldn't it be Mom?"

"Mom was happy when she died." Julian's voice was so quiet she could barely hear it. Noa couldn't remember the last time he had spoken about Mom. "She knew she was going to be with Father. You know those so-called legends I told you about? The ancient mages who visited Death? They all say that the ghosts they met linger there because they're unhappy. They're still tied to their old lives."

"She was happy?" Noa's heart thudded in her ears. "She was happy leaving us alone? I don't believe you. You're lying."

"Noa—"

"I don't believe you!" Noa cried. "You weren't there—you didn't see her. I did, and I'm going to see her again."

"No, you aren't." Julian's voice was cold. "And you're certainly not going to do the bidding of the dead. Do you know how dangerous that is? Mom would never ask you to put yourself at risk—"

"So you'll believe your books before you believe me?" Noa demanded. "Julian, it was *Mom*."

He pressed his fingers against his eyes. "If there were some way to go with you, some way I could protect you—"

"I can protect myself."

"I haven't seen much evidence of that lately," Julian snapped. "Noa, I've had enough of watching you put yourself in danger."

"Well, maybe I've had enough of being your spider!" Noa yelled.

He blinked. "My what?"

"You know. The brains. Because you hardly ever use yours." Noa leaped to her feet. "You think that because you're the most powerful mage in Florean, you can do whatever you want without having to think about anyone else. Including me." The words poured out like a river.

Julian looked stunned. "I always think about you and Mite. Everything I do, I'm thinking of you."

"Do you really believe that?" Noa gave a bark of laughter. "These days the only reason you spend time with me is because I'm useful."

Julian's face softened. "Noa, of course I—"

"That's right." Noa dashed her hand across her eyes. "I'm a magician now, so that makes me useful. I'm not just your weird little sister, somebody you can pat on the head and put on your council for everyone to laugh at. That's why you made me sit with the kids instead of the councillors tonight, isn't it? Because I'm not really one of them."

"I—" Julian stopped. "I didn't know that would upset you. I'm sorry."

"Didn't know or didn't care?" Noa's anger was leaking out, leaving behind a cold, empty feeling, like a dank sea cave. "The old Julian would have cared. The old Julian would have believed me. I don't know who you are."

She turned and ran back to the castle. Julian didn't follow her.

25

Noa Finds an Ingrown Island

Noa didn't even wait to get back to her room before she entered Death.

She ran through the banquet hall, where a handful of guests were still gathered, nursing drinks and talking in small groups.

"Noa?" It was Kell. "What's the matter, girl?"

Noa didn't want to talk to her, or anyone else. Ignoring the startled looks her red-faced appearance was drawing from the remaining guests, she grabbed the nearest shadow and threw herself into Death. Gasps followed her through the shadow door, and someone screamed. But then there was only silence.

Noa stood, brushing sand off her knees. Her entry into Death hadn't exactly been graceful, but she had certainly given the guests something to talk about.

It wasn't midnight yet, so she settled on the ashy sand

to wait. It was unpleasant and prickly, with a hungry, sucking quality, as if it were made not of ground-up rocks but ground-up teeth. Noa took off her cloak and sat on it.

An otter slithered into view. "Hello," it said, eyeing her pockets. "Do you need a guide?"

"No, thank you," Noa said. "I'm waiting for someone. Have you seen a ghost with long dark hair, wearing a black cloak?"

The otter snorted. "I wouldn't know. You all look the same to me."

Noa bit her tongue. The otter continued to gaze longingly at her pockets. She fished around and found a cake she had stowed there that afternoon, and handed it over. The otter gave a contented sigh and flopped onto its back.

"I'll keep you company," it said, as if it were doing her a great favor. When Noa didn't reply, the otter cleared its throat.

"Thank you," she said. "Your kindness is—um, overwhelming."

"I *am* kind," the otter said. "Most of us are. Not enough people know that about otters."

Noa began to shiver. The otter nibbled its way daintily but steadily through the cake, picking out the raisins and piling them neatly on the sand.

"I don't like raisins, either," Noa said.

"Too wrinkly," the otter agreed. "Is that yours?"

Noa followed the otter's black gaze. An orb bobbed in the air a few feet away.

"Ugh," she said. "That's my brother's. Ignore it. I don't want to talk to him."

The orb flickered in a sad, melancholy way. The otter said, "Is he all right?"

"He's just being dramatic." Noa leaned against something that might have been a staircase a very long time ago and closed her eyes, pointedly ignoring the melancholy orb. She must have dozed off, for when she opened her eyes again, both orb and otter were gone.

Noa stood, rubbing her eyes. She wondered if it was midnight yet—the light in Death didn't change. Her dreams had been unpleasant, but she didn't remember any of them, apart from the sensation of being balanced on the sharp edge of something, with nothing below her but stars. She promised herself she wouldn't fall asleep in Death again. It struck her as a recipe for disaster.

Someone drifted out of a nearby shadow. A flickering figure with long waving hair, her features indistinct.

Noa's legs wobbled. "M-Mom?"

"Noa." Her mother's voice was just as Noa remembered, warm and slightly rough, as if she'd just laughed herself hoarse. Mom had laughed a lot, a loud, head-thrown-back sort of laugh—Noa could almost hear it floating through the royal wing during one of her meetings with Julian, or when she was in Mite's room reading her a story. What had

Julian been thinking? Of course this was Mom. Who else could it be?

"You came," her mother said.

"Of course I did." Noa was crying. She ached to wrap her arms around her mother and breathe her in. "I miss you so much."

"I miss you, too, honey," her mother said. Her face was like something seen through frosted glass. "I've been watching over you all the time—you just haven't been able to see me. I'm stronger here than in the living world, but I still can't touch you. I'm so sorry it has to be this way."

Noa fell to her knees as close to her mother as she dared, gazing up at her. She wanted to tell her about everything that had happened since she left them. About Astrae, and Beauty, and her mission to save Julian. But she didn't know how much time they had. "Did you find the Lost Words? Is that what you meant before?"

"Yes," her mother said. "Xavier's mages have located the island. But they haven't been able to reach the book—yet. It's only a matter of time before they do."

"There's an island?"

"In a manner of speaking," her mother said. "I'll show you. But we have to be quick. At dawn, Xavier's mages will start looking again."

Noa stood. But something made her pause. "After we find

the lost language, will you—will you go away again?"

"Oh, sweetie," her mother said. "It's hard for me to manifest like this. But I'll try to visit again, certainly."

Noa's lip trembled. It wasn't enough. She wanted to stay here with her mother and never leave. Even if she couldn't see her properly, even if she couldn't touch her, or hug her, or rest her head in her lap while she brushed Noa's hair. If all Noa had was the shadow of her, she wanted to cling to that shadow with all the strength she had, even if it meant never feeling sunlight again.

And yet Julian was waiting for her. Infuriating, impossible Julian. He needed the Lost Words. If Xavier found that book first, he might never become king. And when it came right down to it, Noa would do anything for Julian, even though he didn't deserve it. Even though he *definitely* didn't deserve it, and she intended to tell him so, with details and examples, when she got back.

And that "anything" included saying the most difficult goodbye she would ever say in her life.

She drew a long, shaky breath. "Where is it?"

"I'll show you," said her mother.

Her mother's ghost led Noa around the staircase to a field of neatly arranged boulders that seemed to sprout out of the ground. Ghosts drifted by in the distance, threadbare and forlorn, but they paid no attention to Noa and her mother. They stopped by a deep puddle of dark. Noa began sifting through it, lifting different shadows like the edges of piled blankets.

"That's it, sweetie," her mother said. "If you look through that shadow, you'll see the island of Whelm."

"Whelm?" Noa said. "That's not on the map."

"No," her mother said. "It's ingrown. Has been for hundreds of years. Ships pass right over it."

Noa had never heard of an ingrown island. Her stomach was beginning to tie itself in knots. She pulled the shadow back and looked through the door.

She was looking through the shadow cast by a pillar of rock. She recognized Greenwash Strait right away—to her left was a little islet topped by a snoring walrus. She squinted, but she couldn't see Astrae anywhere. Perhaps it was facing away from her. In the distance, beyond the walrus, were Xavier's two warships, chock-full of mages. Noa bit her lip. If she jumped into the sea here, a sharp-eyed watchman could spot her.

"Can you see it?" her mother said.

Noa squinted. The wind brushing over the sea raised goose bumps on her skin. The water was black, and the sky was full of stars. She couldn't see an island, but there was a strange darkness in the water several hundred feet away. It looked like a submerged shoal, but if so, it was a very large one.

Noa drew back. Her heart was thudding. "The island, is it . . . is it *underwater?*"

"Yes," her mother said. Her hair floated in a nonexistent

breeze, framing her blurry face like tentacles. "Not only that. After the mages hid the Lost Words on Whelm, they turned it upside down."

That sounded even worse than an inside-out island. "Then how am I supposed to get to the book?"

"There are shadows underwater," her mother said. "They're finer than ordinary shadows—closer to cobwebs. If you lift the right one, you'll find your way to Whelm."

"Okay," Noa said slowly. "But I can't breathe underwater."

"The book is in a cave," her mother said. "There's a shadow that will lead you right to it. You'll only need to swim a short distance, and then come right back."

Mother would never allow you to put yourself at risk. Noa balled her hands up—they were trembling and clammy. She thought again of that cold, black sea. How much colder and blacker would it be deep beneath the waves?

"Don't worry, honey," the ghost said. "I'll be with you the whole time. You'll just go in, grab the book, and then come right back out. It will only take a few seconds, I promise. I know where it is."

"How?" Noa said.

"Because Xavier's mages know," her mother said. "I've been spying on them."

Noa shook her head. "If they know where it is, why haven't they swum down to get it?"

"It's deep, deep down. The light mages have been able to

locate the cave, but no one has managed to reach it—yet."

"Salt mages are excellent swimmers," Noa pointed out. "Surely there are salt mages on those ships."

"There's more than one spell hiding the book," her mother said. "Just as there was more than one hiding the language of Death—not only was Evert inside out, but you could only reach it by sailing backward. There's a spell on the cave preventing salt mages from reaching it. Salt mages can't even see Whelm."

"Oh," Noa breathed. That meant that Julian wouldn't be able to get to the book, even if he did find the island. She drew a shaky breath.

"All right," she said.

Unfortunately, finding the right shadow was every bit as difficult as Noa feared. The shadows that led underwater slipped through her hands, less like cobwebs and more like kelp dragged along by a powerful current. After an hour of struggling, she hadn't managed to hold on to one.

As time passed, her mother grew fainter and fainter, as if she was having a hard time holding her shape. "Try picturing the place you want to go," she said. Her voice barely sounded like her own anymore—it was as soft as a whisper. "It's a shallow cave with a high ceiling half covered with anemones. The book is in a wooden chest on a ledge."

Noa wiped the sweat from her brow and focused. She pictured the place her mother had described, and plunged her hands into the shadows again. This time, one shadow in particular drifted toward her—as if the shadows sensed what she wanted and moved to obey. Noa dug her nails into it before it could slip away, and lifted.

Darkness. She could see nothing through the door below the shadow. Water sloshed against the edges of the door but didn't spill into Death. Noa brushed the water with her hand and instantly recoiled. It was like touching ice.

"That's it," her mother breathed. Her hand went to her chest in a gesture of relief. "That's the entrance to the cave. Oh, my clever girl, you found it."

Noa swallowed. "I don't see a chest."

"It's close, honey. You only need to swim a few feet, pop your head into the cave, and you'll see it. I'll stay here and hold the door open for you."

Noa nodded slowly. She couldn't afford to be afraid—this was too important. "You're sure it's just beyond the door?"

"Positive," her mother said. "It won't take five seconds for you to fetch it. Trust me, sweetie. I wouldn't think of suggesting this unless I was certain."

Noa felt her uncertainty wash away. "I know, Mom."

She removed her cloak and boots, and also her socks—she had a strong suspicion that she would want dry socks when she got back. She paused at the edge of the shadow door. The last thing that she wanted was to plunge into that icy darkness. She looked back at her mother, and could have sworn she saw, through the blur of her features, the hint of an encouraging smile.

Noa dove.

It was like striking stone. The force of the cold shocked Noa to her bones, and it was all she could do not to gasp in surprise. She treaded water, so startled she couldn't think of anything but the cold, let alone the directions her mother had given her. Finally, she realized that her eyes were closed, and she opened them.

Darkness all around. Looming before her was a huge shape that tapered down and down to a rounded peak.

It was the island.

Whelm had probably been a small volcano at one point. Its caldera looked like a mountain with a scoop taken out of it, and it was small, as islands went, perhaps half the size of Astrae. For a second, Noa simply stared at the impossible sight: an island growing *into* the water rather than out of it. She felt a little sorry for Whelm, as she had felt sorry for Evert—it seemed like a waste of a perfectly good island. Then she remembered her mission. She glanced over her shoulder, and was relieved to see the door back to Death floating in mid-water. Noa decided that if she thought too much about that, or about Whelm, her head would explode.

There was a cave in the flank of the island only a few yards away. She swam toward it, trying not to focus on the fact that she could barely feel her arms anymore. Noa felt her way inside the cave with her hands, which slipped on the slimy, weedy stone. She could barely see anything in the cave, though she felt the sea anemones nestled into the floor—or, depending on how you looked at it, the ceiling.

She turned to the right, feeling as she went, and was relieved beyond words when her left hand struck a sharp wooden edge.

Noa pulled on the chest, but it didn't move. She felt a moment of panic—was the chest too heavy for her to lift? Then she realized that a layer of barnacles had crawled up the wall of the cave and glued the chest to the rock.

Noa swam backward so that her feet were pointed at the chest. She kicked with all her might.

Nothing.

She kicked again. Still nothing. Her lungs were beginning to ache. Normally, Noa could hold her breath for several minutes, but the chill of the water had weakened her. She kicked again, a desperate kick, and finally the chest came free. Noa grabbed it and swam out of the cave so fast, she banged her head against the rock.

She swam back to the shadow door, which seemed to grow farther and farther away. She focused all her might on gripping the heavy chest. If she dropped it, it would fall to the ocean floor, which was lost in the deep-sea gloom. She looked up and realized that she couldn't make out the surface, either. The water pressed down on her. She heard—and felt—the eerie, wavering cry of a blue whale ripple through the sea. Noa began to panic. The whalesong only drove home how far she was from everything and everyone she knew. She didn't belong in this world.

For a moment, it seemed as if the shadow door *flickered*, and Noa almost screamed. She couldn't be trapped here. She couldn't. She kicked frantically, and surged through the opening, shoving the chest ahead of her. She landed in a sprawl on the sand, coughing and sputtering.

"You did it!"

Noa's mother was less distinct than ever. "Are you all right, sweetie?"

"I—" Noa coughed up more seawater. She was trembling so hard it felt like her bones would shake apart. With difficulty, for her hands could barely close on it, she wrenched off her sodden tunic, revealing her thin undershirt, then wrapped her dry cloak around herself. She immediately felt better. She shoved her feet back into her socks.

Noa forced herself to crawl over to the chest. The bronze fittings were rusted through, and there were barnacles still clinging to the side. It had clearly been submerged for a long time. It was hard to imagine anything, let alone a book, surviving inside it.

The chest was locked. Noa tried hitting the lock with a rock, but it wouldn't break. She found a larger rock, so heavy she could hardly lift it, and dropped it onto the wooden lid.

She had to lift it and drop it half a dozen times, until her arms ached and sweat trickled down her neck, and then finally the lid cracked in two.

She peeled the wood back. There, nestled in a silk wrapping, was a large book with a plain leather cover. It was perfectly dry and showed no signs of damage, apart from a musty smell. It looked almost identical to the book Julian had found on Evert. But unlike that book, Noa didn't feel strange when she looked at it. What language had she found?

Her mother drifted over to the broken chest. She stretched out a hand like a tendril of fog and lifted the book.

"Thank you, Noa," she said in a strange voice. "It's done."

"What's done?" Dread settled in Noa's stomach. "Mom?"

The ghost laughed, and the laughter wasn't her mother's. "King Xavier will be so pleased."

26

Marchenas
Are Always First

"Xavier?" Noa sat frozen, one shaking hand still on the chest. "What are you talking about?"

"I'm sorry, Princess," the ghost said, though she didn't sound sorry. She sounded exultant. "But I couldn't pass up the opportunity to get back at that wretched boy."

Noa clung to one last ember of hope. "Mom?"

The ghost was coming into focus now. She was nothing like Mom. She was younger, for one thing, and her hair was auburn rather than black. Mom's eyes had been warm and creased at the corners from laughter, but this woman's eyes had a sly twinkle. The last time Noa had seen those eyes, they had been frozen in a look of pure horror.

"Esmalda," Noa whispered.

"It was a cruel trick to play on a little girl," the mage said. "But you're not exactly innocent, are you, child? You're a Marchena, and you're all rotten to the core. 'Marchenas are always first,' are they? First to betray an ally? First to murder a friend? You'll be just like them in a few years."

Noa couldn't think, couldn't breathe. "Them?"

"Your mother," Esmalda spat. "And your brother. I was always loyal to her. And how did she thank me? By throwing me into prison. And Julian!" She gave a frightening bark of laughter. "Dear, handsome Julian. He charmed me into thinking he was different from her. But as it turned out, he's even worse. I've killed plenty of people in my day—oh, yes. For gold. For revenge. But I do it honorably." Her voice was silky. "What Julian did to me had no honor."

Noa knew she should have been furious at being tricked. But all she felt in that moment was grief colder than the bottom of the sea.

Her mother hadn't come back to her.

"Do you know what it feels like to be turned into a statue?" Esmalda's voice was horribly pleasant. "To feel the blood freeze in your veins? To choke on the metal rising in your throat?"

Noa backed up a step, feeling sick. "I don't understand—"

"You don't understand how I tricked you." She laughed again. "I knew your mother well—I served her for years, after all. Impersonating her wasn't difficult. And it's not hard for a ghost to spy on Xavier's mages, learning everything they knew about this book and its undersea hidey-hole. Come now, I thought you were the smart one! Julian's clever little sister, always saving him from himself. . . . Well, let's see if you can save him now. I'm going to give this book to Xavier's mages. They'll surely be surprised to find it on their ship, but I doubt they'll spend much time puzzling over the mystery. Do you?"

Noa's head spun. "Why . . . why didn't you just get the book yourself?"

"I'm a *ghost*," Esmalda spat. "We can manipulate objects in the living world, but only to a point. I couldn't have opened that chest. Nor, for that matter, could any of Xavier's mages— do you know how many times they tried to swim to that cave? Well, I tracked down one of the dead mages who hid the book, and she told me the truth: Xavier never had a chance of finding it. No, the book could only be rescued by someone of royal blood."

"Royal blood?" Noa whispered.

"Yes." Esmalda's lip curled. "The ancient mages were terrible snobs. They didn't want this book found by the common riffraff, but if a future king or queen of Florean needed it, well, that was all right with them. Groveling fools."

Noa felt as if she were still under the sea, its weight pressing down on her, harder and harder, until she would surely break apart. "What language is it?"

"Oh, that's the best part." Esmalda stroked the spine of the book as she drifted just out of Noa's reach. "It's fear."

Noa froze. "Fear?"

Esmalda's voice took on a singsong quality. "Oh, Princess, you're not going to like what's coming to you. But it's nothing less than what you and your brother deserve."

Noa's heart thundered in her throat. Steeling herself, she leaped at the ghost. But Esmalda drifted away, laughing.

"Wait," Noa cried. "Wait—*stop.*"

The last word came out in Shiver, a sharp sound like the crunch of bone breaking. Esmalda froze, her face contorted in fury, drifting several feet off the ground. Noa was astonished—had she done that? She launched herself into the air and managed to grab hold of the book. But before she could get a better grip, Esmalda shook herself, and Noa fell to the ground with only one ripped page in her hand.

"Stop!" Noa cried again, but her voice was broken by a sob.

"I don't think so," Esmalda said. She began to fade, and the book faded with her, until all that remained were her feverbright eyes and the hint of a grinning mouth. "Good night, Princess. Tell *King* Julian I said hello."

Noa sat frozen, unable to think. Eventually, an otter appeared and offered to lead her home. Something about its nosy, whiskered face unstuck something inside her, and she was able to stand.

"Bad news, that one was," the otter said. "We keep away from the bad ones. You should do the same. Oh, did you hear that? I just gave you advice, and I didn't ask for anything in return. Only the noblest of creatures would do that."

Noa didn't say a word. When they came to the place where

Noa had entered Death, she grabbed the first shadow she touched, and simply fell through. Not surprisingly, this didn't turn out well. She ended up in the ocean. There was Astrae a few hundred yards away, yet she couldn't bring herself to swim toward it. She could barely bring herself to tread water.

Just my luck, a distant part of her thought. *I'm going to die escaping from Death.*

She laughed. Once she started, she wasn't able to stop. She was still laughing—and coughing, because by that time she'd breathed in a certain amount of seawater—when a strong arm hooked under hers and pulled her toward the shore. Noa supposed that a sailor must have seen her from the beach and swum out to save her. It was dawn, and the sky was full of pinky-purple clouds. As they drew near the island, Noa heard shouts and applause. Great—that was just what she wanted right now, an audience. Her laughter had died away to noisy, embarrassing hiccups, and she thought she might also be crying. It was hard to tell. Before, Noa had felt as if she had been hollowed out, but now she felt as if she had been hollowed out and then filled up again with small, sharp things, like thumbtacks and crab claws.

Once he reached the shallows, the sailor tossed her over his shoulder and carried her to the dry sand. As soon as he put her down, a wrinkled snout tipped with cold nostrils pressed against her face, snuffling. Its breath was an odd combination of campfires and tuna. Reckoner! Was he her rescuer? But he didn't have hands. For a moment, Noa thought she was going to start laughing again at the image of the dragon heroically dragging her back to shore, but then a familiar voice said, "Get off her, you smoky old lump," and Reckoner's face was replaced with Julian's. He was dripping wet, his shoes were gone, and his face was very pale.

Noa burst into tears.

Julian pulled her to his chest, murmuring soothing words. "Black seas, Noa, you're freezing. Everyone, move back. Give her some space."

"I was underwater," Noa said. "That's why I'm cold. It was deep, deep underwater, and there was a whale. . . . Mom told me to swim to an ingrown island, but it wasn't Mom after all, it was Esmalda. She made me give her the language of fear, and I'm sorry, Julian, I thought it was Mom, but she lied. . . . She wanted to hurt you. . . . I'm sorry. . . ."

She wasn't sure how much of this Julian understood—the words kept mushing together with her sobs. She was dimly aware that they were surrounded by a circle of staring faces, mages and sailors and villagers, but they all moved away quickly after Julian cast a black look in their direction. He stroked her hair until she had no tears left, which took a while.

"What's wrong with Noa?" said a hushed voice. Mite's face popped into view behind his shoulder. "Did the ghosts attack her?"

"Mite, go back to the castle," Julian said, pushing a hand

distractedly through his sodden hair. "The servants will get you some breakfast."

Mite's small face slowly got redder and redder. Then, out of nowhere, she yelled, "No!"

Julian turned back to her, astonished. "Mite—"

"I don't want breakfast!" Mite yelled. "I don't want to go back to the castle! Why do you keep telling me to go away? You can't make me! I'm staying right here!" She began to cry.

"Maita, Maita, it's okay." Julian looked from Noa to Mite, trying to figure out which sister was more in need of comforting. Since Noa was not currently crying, he gathered Mite into his arms. "You can stay. I just thought you might be hungry—"

"I'm not hungry!" Mite yelled through her tears. Noa didn't think she'd ever heard Mite make so much noise, except when she exploded. Julian gave Noa a *help me* look.

"It's my fault," Noa said glumly. "I told her to go away. Mite, I'm sorry. I didn't really want you to go away."

Mite glared through her tears. "Yes, you did. You always do!" She buried her face in Julian's shoulder.

"No, I don't," Noa promised. She wiped her nose on her sleeve, which was already a little slimy. "I want to be alone sometimes, but that's not the same as not wanting you around. Last night I just wanted to see Mom again."

Mite lifted her head. "You saw Momma?"

Noa would have cried again if she had any tears left. "No.

You were right, Julian. M-Mom didn't come back to see me. I just thought she would miss us . . ."

"Noabell." Julian tilted her chin up. "I know that Mom's thinking about us, wherever she is, just like we're thinking about her. So is Dad, though I know neither of you remember him much."

Noa sniffed. "I remember some things. He wore glasses that were always falling down his nose. And his beard was scratchy when he kissed me."

Julian laughed. Then, to Noa's astonishment, he began to cry.

Mite looked from Julian to Noa, clearly astonished, too. Noa hadn't seen Julian cry in years. Mite wrapped her arms around his neck, and Noa wrapped hers around his chest, which probably made it hard for him to breathe, but he didn't complain. After a moment, he pulled away, wiping his eyes on his sleeve.

"Do you miss Papa more than Momma?" Mite said, her eyes wide and serious.

Julian smiled faintly. "I miss them both."

Noa wondered why she had never thought about the fact that Julian was the only one of the three of them who could remember both their parents' deaths. Noa remembered some things about their father, but the only memories she had of his death were a room full of people talking in hushed voices and Mom's face crumpling once when she thought Noa wasn't looking. The memories of their mother's death hurt bad enough that it was hard to imagine having to carry around ones of their father's death, too.

Julian blew his nose on a handkerchief. He pulled out a second one and used it to clean up Mite's face. Then he turned back to Noa. "Noa, part of the reason why Mom wouldn't have lingered in Death is because she knew I was looking after you two. She made me promise that I'd take good care of you."

Noa thought this over. "That wasn't fair," she said slowly. "You were only sixteen."

"I'm the eldest," Julian said, as if that explained everything. "Besides, I would have done it anyway." He sighed. "Only I'm afraid I haven't been doing such a wonderful job of looking after either of you these last few months."

"That's not true!" Noa said passionately. "I shouldn't have said those things before. You were right about that ghost. I should have listened to you. I'm sorry, Julian—"

"You have nothing to apologize for." He let out a long breath. "You said you don't know who I am. Well, sometimes I don't, either."

He looked so pale that Noa hugged him again. Mite was frowning. "*I* know who you are, Julian," she said.

Julian smiled. "All right, Maita. If I ever need a reminder, I'll ask you. Deal?"

Mite nodded. "Deal."

Julian took Noa's hand. "I'm sorry I don't listen to your

advice as often as I should. I really did put you on the council because you belong there, Noa. You must know how clever your ideas are."

Noa puffed out a bit. She did know, of course, but it was nice to hear someone say it.

"And I'm sorry you two had to sit next to Matty at dinner. He's a truly dreadful boy."

Noa giggled.

"*I* knew that!" Mite said, shaking her head.

"He kept the servants up half the night, running back and forth to fetch salves and cookies and who knows what else. Claiming the whole while that he was probably poisoned. If his father wasn't my most important ally, I'd send Matty back to Sevrilla right now. Or make him spend an hour in Mite's closet, maybe."

"No!" Mite looked aghast. "He'd step on the crickets."

Julian turned back to Noa. "If I understood you correctly, you found another magical language."

"Yes," Noa said, swallowing. "Then I lost it."

Noa told them the whole tale, though it hurt. The hope she had felt when she saw Mom was still there, but now it was a broken, jagged thing that she didn't like to think about. When she thought of Esmalda, she felt an anger so bottomless, it scared her.

"What are you going to do about Esmalda?" Noa asked.

"I've already done enough where she's concerned." Julian's face was drawn in a way Noa had never seen before. "This is my fault. I'm sorry."

Noa couldn't tell if he was apologizing to her or wishing he could take back what he'd done. What had happened wasn't all his fault, but some of it was, so she didn't argue; she just hugged him. His cloak smelled of seawater and smoke, probably from some experiment he'd been working on. She wished she could stay tucked in his arms forever and not have to face whatever was coming their way. But at least Julian wasn't going anywhere, and neither was Mite. They would face it together, like they always had.

"I always knew Esmalda resented Mom," Julian said. "I shouldn't have put her on my council. I knew she would do anything for power, and that she was completely ruthless toward anyone who wronged her." His gaze was distant, and Noa thought she could guess what he was thinking.

"You're not like her," she said.

"No?" He gave her a tired smile.

"Well . . . sometimes you are," Noa said slowly. She remembered something. "Gabriela said that Mom destroyed her village when she was little. Did you know that?"

Julian's face was blank with surprise. "No—she never told me."

"It doesn't sound like Mom."

Julian sighed. "Mom faced a few rebellions during her reign. All kings and queens do, because it's impossible to get everyone on your side, and sometimes things go wrong that aren't your fault. Harvests fail. Sea serpents prey on your harbors. Mom dealt with more rebellions because she was a dark mage and people distrusted her. I'm not saying what she did was right. But it was what all the other kings and queens of Florean have done. In fact, many of them did worse than burn villages."

"Gabriela also said she doesn't believe in heroes," Noa said. "She said that you and Xavier and Mom are all monsters, and the best anyone can do is side with the least monstrous monster."

"I don't know what to say to that," Julian said, "speaking as a monster. But I think Gabriela does believe in heroes—after all, she sees herself as one. Maybe she's wrong about the rest of it, too." He rubbed his eyes. "Sometimes, when everything seems to be going wrong like this, I wonder what Mom would have done. She always seemed to know what she was doing, no matter how bad things got."

"Maybe you don't have to do what Mom would have done," Noa said. "Maybe you can do better than her. Better than all of them."

Julian didn't reply. He looked pale and young, not like the Dark Lord at all, or even a prince, but a boy recently turned eighteen who didn't know what lay ahead of him.

Noa glanced up the beach. The crowd hadn't dispersed,

but was simply watching them from afar. Some of the mages seemed to be pretending to patrol the beach while sneaking glances at the Marchenas.

"What are we going to do?" Noa said. "Esmalda will give that book to the king's mages. What if one of them can speak this fear language? They're only a few miles away."

"They don't know we're right under their noses," Julian said. "That buys us some time. Can I see that page?"

Noa pulled it from her pocket and handed it to him. It was perfectly dry. Julian unfolded it, his brow creasing. Mite and Noa crowded around him. It seemed to be some sort of title page, for the writing was large and spaced out. That was all Noa could deduce, though. The words careened around the page like dancing ants. She couldn't read one letter.

She watched Julian, holding her breath. After a moment, though, he sighed.

"Nope," he said. "Well, this whole quest has been rather humbling. Just last month, I was the only mage in history who could speak all the languages of magic."

"I'm glad you're not a fear mage," Noa said. "You already give people nightmares. It would definitely make you go bad, and so much for my mission."

Julian stared at her blankly. "What?"

"Ah—nothing," Noa said. "*The* mission, you know. The Lost Words. Do you think there are other magical languages out there?"

"Probably," Julian said. "But we've exhausted our only two leads. Come on—we need to get you some dry clothes. And breakfast."

Mite trailed at their heels. "Julian," she said in a worried voice, "I didn't mean what I said. I *am* hungry. Can I have breakfast, too?"

Julian and Noa laughed.

The
King's Spider

After a hot bath and a breakfast of goose eggs and fried tomatoes, Noa felt, if not entirely herself, then at least partway there, and a freshly baked chocolate cake brought her even closer. She slept the morning away, and would probably have slept longer had she not been awoken by a strange sound.

She lay among her pillows, trying to work out what had pierced her dreams. Was Beauty howling about something again? But then the sound came a second time, and she knew it wasn't Beauty. It sounded rather like a foghorn, but deeper. Darker.

She went to the window, pushing back the curtain. She blinked, certain her eyes were playing tricks on her. But no— there on the horizon was the strangest cloud Noa had ever seen. At least, she thought it was a cloud. It didn't really look like one, but it looked more like a cloud than anything else. The main problem was that it seemed to be rising out of the water and reaching up to the sky, rather than the opposite. It was huge and dark, and sparks danced across it like lightning.

If it was an approaching storm, where were the cool breeze and the choppy waves? The sky was a pure blue, and the sea was still. Noa shivered.

She threw on a clean cloak and hurried outside, muttering as she tripped over an invisible furry shape. Everyone seemed to be gathered on the beach, watching the bizarre cloud looming on the horizon.

Noa hurried across the sand to Julian, who stood with Asha, Kell, and several other mages, his brow knitted. "What do you think?" Asha said. "Some kind of storm?"

"Let's hope so," Noa said darkly. Her thoughts were on the Lost Words, and the book Esmalda had taken from her. She exchanged a look with Julian.

"Should we try to outrun it?" Kell said. "Whatever it is, it doesn't look like it's traveling very fast."

"There shouldn't be a need to outrun it," Julian said slowly. "Astrae is facing away from it. If it's only a storm, we have nothing to worry about. If it's sentient, it can't see us."

"I've seen storms that could shred your nose hairs. Never seen one like that." Kell sounded grim. "Why's it look like it's headed right at us?"

"Should we send out the scouts?" Asha suggested. "They can get as close as possible, then report back."

Julian nodded. "In the meantime, let's head up to the observatory. Noa?"

She shook her head, still watching the cloud. "I'll stay here."

"All right. If you see Renne, send him to me," Julian said. "We can't find him."

"Renne?" Noa said, but Julian was already striding away.

"Maybe he went to send another letter," Mite said from a hole she was digging in the sand.

Noa frowned. "A letter?"

"He sent one yesterday." Mite tipped more sand off her shovel. "It looked like a secret letter. He kept looking over his shoulder."

Noa's heart was beginning to thud. "You mean he sent it on the wind?"

"Yeah." Mite unearthed a sulfur clam and set it carefully aside. "I told you yesterday. Don't you remember?"

"Oh no," Noa murmured.

Her thoughts flashed back over the last few days. Someone had let Gabriela know that Beauty liked cakes. Renne had been on the beach with Kell when Noa had told her that Beauty had taken a fancy to them. Julian had thought Esmalda was a spy—but what if someone else had been the author of that first letter to Xavier? What if, rather than discovering Esmalda writing it, Renne had been caught with it himself and blamed her? Noa thought of how furious Esmalda had been with Julian, how she'd accused him of betrayal—that didn't make sense if she'd betrayed him first.

And Julian . . . of course Julian would believe Renne's word over Esmalda's. Renne was Julian's oldest friend. Who would believe that he'd been passing information to Xavier?

A murmur was rising on the beach. Mages backed away from the water's edge, their eyes wide. The mysterious cloud was suddenly closer to Astrae—much closer. Close enough that Noa could make out shapes within it, or rather through it, towering shapes the color of blood.

"Xavier's warships," she breathed. "They're hiding behind the cloud!"

The ships were much farther away than the cloud was. As Noa watched in horrified fascination, the cloud began to writhe and twist, and then it spilled across the water and covered the beach.

"Mite!" she shouted. "Back to the castle! Now!"

Her shouts were drowned out by screams. As the cloud spread across the beach, it touched the horde of sea iguanas snoozing atop their favorite basking rock. An eruption of startled snorts filled the air, and the creatures began to stretch and grow. Noa had to stifle her own scream as one of the iguanas leaped into the air with an echoing roar, spreading broad wings no iguana should possess.

The iguanas had become dragons.

Mite screamed and dove into the hole. Noa stood frozen, her logical brain fixated by the impossible sight. The other onlookers had no such hesitation, though. People were fleeing, including most of the mages. The dragons were young and healthy, nearly twice the size of Reckoner, and they all seemed to be taking to the sky, soaring over the beach, skimming people's heads. One breathed a cloud of fire that a mage barely dodged. The fire touched a pile of driftwood, and Noa threw herself on top of Mite, waiting for it to explode into flame.

But the wood didn't ignite. Nor was the sand scorched where the flame had passed over it. Noa watched another dragon breathe a cloud of fire at a mage as she fled. But the mage ran on, as if she wasn't even aware of the fire, let alone hurt. One of the scouts shot an arrow at a dragon, and the beast fell to the ground with a surprisingly gentle thud given its size. A dark mist rose off its body, and it was an iguana again.

The dragons weren't real. It was all an illusion. But how?

A dreadful roar interrupted Noa's thoughts. On the steps leading up to the castle crouched an enormous jaguar. The mages who had been running up the stairs to seek shelter in the castle turned on their heels and ran back down again. Another jaguar happily chased a screaming sailor along the beach. The huge cat seemed to bore after a while, and pranced back up the sand. Then it simply vanished, winking back into view next to a pelican, which squawked and flew off.

Noa looked from the jaguars to the dragons, still wheeling across the sky and breathing fire while the few stragglers remaining on the beach cowered and screamed—but not, Noa noticed, doing any actual harm. Nobody had been eaten, or burned, or even lightly charred. People were running because they were afraid, not because anything terrible was actually happening to them.

"Fear," she whispered. She looked back at the ships. The strange cloud had dissipated after it passed over Astrae, but whatever magic it contained hadn't.

Someone on King Xavier's side could speak the language of fear. That was what the cloud had been—a spell that made people's fears come true.

Julian came racing down the castle stairs, followed by Asha and several other mages. The jaguar leaped at him, placing a paw on each shoulder, and then—

It nuzzled his neck. Because it wasn't a real jaguar—it was one of the island cats. The huge beast flopped at Julian's feet with its belly in the air.

Julian hopped over the cat. Noa dragged a protesting Mite out of the hole and ran up to Julian. "Julian, I think one of the mages on those ships—"

"Speaks the language of fear," he finished for her, his voice grim. "Yes, I think you're right."

Noa's eyes welled with tears. "This is my fault."

"It's not your fault." Julian's voice was firm. A dragon skimmed his head, and he ducked with a shout. They seemed to be enjoying themselves almost as much as the cats were. Noa couldn't really blame them—iguanas were ordinarily about as intimidating as barnacles. Julian murmured a spell, and a fierce wind rose, pushing the dragons down the beach.

"You shouldn't waste your magic," Noa said. "They're just iguanas—they can't hurt anyone."

"Unfortunately, they seem to have most of my mages convinced otherwise." Julian froze.

Noa looked. The king's ships were almost close enough to launch boats. On the deck of the nearest ship stood a familiar straight-backed figure, her red cloak and dark hair billowing in the wind.

"Gabriela," Noa murmured. Of course she had survived the destruction of her ship. Gabriela could survive anything.

"Who's that man with her?" Mite asked.

Noa had hardly noticed him—compared to Gabriela, he cut a much less striking figure, being skinny and so pale he seemed to fade into the background like a wisp of cloud. It was hard to tell from that distance, but Noa thought he was smiling.

"That's Xavier," she said, feeling faint. "Why would he come here?"

Julian didn't reply for a moment. When he did, his voice was dangerously flat. "I can only imagine it's because he wants to watch me fall." He motioned to the salt mages, and they hurried down to the water, already chanting a spell that stirred up the waves and would make landing boats more difficult.

"Call Beauty," Noa said. "I bet she can sink at least one of those ships."

"I would, but she can barely move," Julian said. "Being separated from her daughter almost killed her. That was Xavier's plan, after all—to incapacitate my greatest weapon, and then sweep in and destroy us all when he found the Lost Words." He ran his hands through his hair. "How do they know we're here?"

"Renne," Noa said, her voice grim. "He's a spy. Mite saw him sending a letter yesterday. That must be how Xavier always seems to know where we are."

Julian looked as if he'd been struck. "Oh, Renne," he said. On the deck of the ship, another man came to stand by Gabriela's side. Even at that distance, Noa could see the worshipful look he gave her.

"I knew he had feelings for her," Julian said. "He was furious when I abandoned her on that island. I just never thought . . ."

Gabriela raised her arms, her lips moving. Another dark, glittering cloud coalesced out of thin air and floated toward Astrae.

"It's her," Noa murmured. "She can speak it. What have I done?"

"What have you done? Well, you foiled Gabriela's last plot," Julian said. "And provided me with excellent advice, and saved the island numerous times. I could go on." He let out a breath of laughter. "So, Gabriela's a dark magician, is she? I wish I had time to gloat properly."

He turned to Asha. "Have the salt mages keep at it. And

send someone to round up the others. I won't have my mages cowering before Gabriela's specters." Asha nodded, and he turned to Noa and Mite. "We have to come up with a plan."

"What is there to plan?" Noa said. "Move the island. They've passed the shoals, so they can see us now, but if we move away from them, your spell will hide us."

"I don't want to run away." Julian's jaw was set. "Not this time. This time, we finish it."

"Julian—" Noa began.

"Noa, if we run, they'll come after us again." He met her eyes. "And again. And again. You know that."

A dozen arguments rose to Noa's lips. There would surely come a time when they were better prepared to fight Xavier. When they had more allies, more mages. But Noa realized that she didn't want to wait for that time. She thought of Gabriela's betrayal. Xavier storming around the palace as if it had always been his.

She wanted to fight now.

To her surprise, it was Mite who piped up. "Can't you throw a storm at the ships, Julian?"

"No, Maita." Julian rubbed his eyes. "All Xavier's warships are defended against magical attack."

"*Magical* attack . . . ," Noa murmured. Calculations flitted through her head. Astrae's coordinates, the date, the season. If she was right . . . Julian and Mite watched her with nearly identical hopeful expressions.

Noa nodded. A smile was breaking across her face. "I have an idea."

"Finally!" Mite said with what in Noa's opinion was an unnecessary degree of exasperation.

"Follow me," she said, and raced up the beach.

They ran across the hillside and onto the path that led to the Nose, the same place from which Noa had observed the mysterious island they had crashed into. It felt like years ago but had actually been only a few weeks. The shade cast by the scalesia forest was a welcome change from the beating sun, and the branches were alive with finches and warblers and fly-catchers going about their day-to-day business, oblivious or indifferent to magical battles.

"We have something better than warships," Noa said, panting. "Something Xavier will never expect. If you can reach them."

A few minutes later, they arrived at the top. Noa leaned against the rock that crowned it, out of breath. Mite's cheeks were bright red. She flopped facedown in the shade. "My side hurts!"

Noa turned slowly, peering in all directions. The mountaintop afforded a view of the entire island, as well as King Xavier's warships. The dark cloud had completely covered the beach, and the wind carried the sound of screams all the way up the mountain. Noa wondered what new horrors the mages down there were dealing with. Had Gabriela made the walruses on the rocks look like ravenous sea serpents?

The cloud could reach anything above the water, change it, warp it. But it couldn't touch anything *below* the water—it was a cloud, after all.

"Julian," she said, "call the whales."

He looked at her as if she'd lost her mind. "What?"

"Astrae is close to one of the migration paths," Noa said. "I know where they are—at this time of year, there are hundreds of them heading south. If you can get one to collide with Xavier's ship, you'll capsize it!"

"Noa," Julian said slowly, "I can't *call the whales*. I can't speak *whale* language."

She grabbed his hand. "You don't have to. Just—just lure them here. They follow the krill, you know."

"I don't, actually."

"Julian." Noa yanked on his arm, hauling him down so they were face-to-face. "You can make bees out of water. You can make your own reflection jump up and run around! You do this sort of flashy, show-offy stuff all the time! Now there's actually a need for it."

Julian's eyes narrowed. "'Flashy, show-offy'?"

"Oh, come on!" Noa said. "Just do it!"

"All right," he said, after staring at her a moment longer. "But I want you to know that of all the mad plots you've come up with, this takes the cake."

He turned to the sea and began to chant. It was the most ridiculous spell Noa had ever heard—he sounded like he had a lot of bubbles stuck in his throat, bubbles that fizzed and whistled and popped. Mite actually giggled. But after a moment, the sea around Xavier's ships began to darken, as if a cloud was rising through the water. The cloud made the water writhe and foam, because it wasn't a cloud at all but a swarm of tiny krill.

"That's it!" Noa said. The cloud spread out from Astrae, forming something that resembled a path. Julian was creating the illusion of a feast the likes of which no whale would have seen before. Noa didn't see how they could resist.

And indeed, one of them couldn't. After only a few minutes, Noa caught a glimpse of a familiar shape off the coast of Astrae—a broad back curving out of the water like a wave given form, a hint of something massive and ancient, more force of nature than animal.

"You did it!" Noa shouted.

A smile spread across Julian's face, the dark sort of smile he wore whenever he tossed someone to Beauty. "Now let's see if we can't give Xavier the surprise of his life."

Bigger than any ship, bigger even than Beauty, the blue whale glided toward the island and the great krill cloud. Noa watched in helpless fascination. The whale exhaled, sending a tremendous geyser into the air. It was the most beautiful thing she had ever seen.

"Noa," Mite said, tugging on her sleeve.

"What?" Noa said distractedly.

"Noa." Mite yanked hard enough to pull her cloak off her shoulder.

Noa turned. The dark fog was creeping up the mountainside, and birds fled in a cacophony of chirrups and squawks. The trees near the foot of the mountain began to rustle, as if something very large was moving through the forest. Noa felt certain that some huge, horrible beast was making its way toward them. She shook her head. *No.* It was an illusion. It wasn't real.

"Ignore the fog," Julian said. He let out another stream of fizzy-bubbly words, and the krill began to encircle Xavier's ship. "Nothing it shows us can hurt us."

The fog swept over them. Noa tried to ignore whatever was moving through the trees, slowly yet surely getting closer and closer to the mountaintop. But it was harder this time. There was something different about this fog. Every time she took a breath, awful images rose in her mind. She saw Gabriela attacking the village, Xavier's cannons tearing the castle apart. Julian gagged and chained, paraded across the deck of a ship while the king's mages jeered at him. Mite locked in a dungeon. Her heart thundered, and she felt sick.

Mite, crouched at her side, was whimpering. Julian's chanting faltered. Noa could see that King Xavier was lowering boats full of mages from his warships.

"Julian." She went to his side. "What you're seeing isn't real. You have to keep the ships moving."

"He's hurting you," he rasped, his eyes wide and unseeing. "He's hurting you and Mite. And I'm—I'm gone. I can't protect you. Gabriela—"

"It's not real." Noa shook him, even as another powerful vision overwhelmed her. She saw Xavier's mages setting fire to Astrae. She saw the forest burn, and the apple orchard. The tidy houses in the village reduced to blackened shells. The tortoises, birds, and lizards all fleeing the flames that gobbled up everything they touched until Astrae looked like Evert before Julian had turned it right side out, a barren, lifeless thing.

No. This was what Gabriela wanted. She wanted them to lose the ability to think or plan, to feel nothing but fear. Noa was afraid. Her hands were shaking and it felt like there was some cold, clammy creature crouched on her chest, weighing her down, making it hard to breathe.

But she could still think.

The fake krill vanished, then reappeared again. The blue whale let out a long, melodious cry that had a querying note in it. Xavier seemed to have seen it, and was trying to move his ship away. Julian crouched on the ground, his head in his hands.

"Julian, remember when Mom was sick?" Noa said. "Remember how scared I was? You told me it was okay to be scared. That it was okay to feel whatever I wanted. But to also remember that you were there and you weren't going to leave me. Remember?" She touched his shoulder. "Me and Mite aren't going to leave you. Whatever happens, we face it together. Just like we always have."

Julian lifted his head. His gaze was unfocused, but at least he seemed to be listening to her.

"One step at a time," Noa said soothingly. "Just stand up first." She helped him to his feet. "Now look at the whale. Can you lure it underneath Xavier's ship?"

Julian drew a breath. He repeated the incantation, and the krill stopped flickering in and out of existence. They drew together like a wave.

"Good," Noa said, even as another horrible vision filled her thoughts, this time of the assassin from the palace creeping toward her with the long knife. She forced herself to focus on Julian. "Keep doing that."

Julian's hand was squeezing hers far too tightly, but Noa didn't protest. He continued to chant, his voice low and uncertain. The blue whale dove deeper and deeper until it was barely a shadow beneath the waves. But even as she rejoiced, Noa became aware of a crashing sound in the forest.

She screamed.

A huge spider emerged from the trees. Its limbs were black and furred with hairs thick as rope. On its back was a red splotch like an eye.

Mite took a step toward the spider. "Patience!" she shouted. Her face broke into a grin.

Julian wasn't looking at Xavier's ship anymore. He was staring at the spider, his face frozen. "Mite, get back!" He ran toward her, and the spider reared up on its back legs.

"No! Bad Patience!" Mite said in the same sort of voice Julian used with Reckoner when he wet his blankets. Then she said something else in a language Noa had never heard before. It was a strange, whispery language—almost musical, but in an uncomfortable way, like a lullaby sung backward. The huge spider froze, its many eyes fixed on Mite. Then, in a puff of black fog, it disappeared.

"Patience!" Mite ran forward. She leaned over something in the grass. "There you are! You're all right." She turned to Julian and Noa, beaming. "I knew I would find her! Although . . . I guess she found me."

They stared at her.

Mite frowned. "What?"

"Mite," Julian said in a wondering voice, "I think you can speak the language of fear."

"Really?" Mite's eyes were round.

"Could you . . . could you read the page I brought back from Death?" Noa said.

"Yeah," Mite said with a shrug.

Noa gritted her teeth. "Then why didn't you *say something*."

"You didn't ask," Mite said. She paused. "Does this mean I'll explode more?"

Noa burst into laughter. It had a wild edge, but the sound was a balm, and Julian smiled, too. She looked down at the beach, and her heart started thudding again. There was another cloud of fog moving toward them. "Mite, see if you can tell that fog to go away. Can you try?"

Mite set her jaw. "Okay." She turned to the fog and yelled something at it. But even though she was yelling, there was still a whispery quality to the words. The fog seemed to tremble. It didn't dissipate, but it froze at the base of the mountain.

"She's holding it off!" Noa cried. Julian was already chanting again, and they watched as a second blue whale appeared in the distance, drifting closer to Xavier's fleet. Xavier's ship gave a sudden jolt, as if something enormous had brushed up against the bow. Several mages were so startled that they fell overboard, and sailors raced back and forth across the deck.

Julian's chanting grew more confident, and the krill cloud grew thicker. In the second before it happened, Noa saw Gabriela dive overboard, abandoning King Xavier as he stared, motionless in his confusion.

Then King Xavier's ship simply tipped over.

Noa had been expecting something more dramatic. The whale rising up from the deep with its mouth open, smashing a hole in Xavier's ship, or slashing its tail down and cleaving the bow in two. But the whale didn't even lift its head above the waves. Noa saw only the curve of an enormous back that lifted the warship several feet above the water and then sent it slamming back down on its side. The whale may not have even known the ship was there.

The other warships were making a run for it, but the captains were so frantic that two of the ships rammed into a third. Noa wondered if they thought the whale was some new monster Julian had tamed. The second whale arrived, slamming its tail against the water to stun the krill. The wave it created washed over one of the warships, sending several mages into the sea.

Julian began chanting a different spell that struck Noa as familiar, but she couldn't place it—as usual, the words fell out of her head right after she heard them. Julian collapsed against the rock, his face gray, but kept chanting. The warship rolled and floated for a moment upside down, and then it slid below the waves.

Noa shook Julian's shoulder. "What if Xavier's still alive? He'll swim ashore!"

"No, he won't," Julian said darkly. Noa blinked, then turned back to the sea. Now that she thought about it, the other warships were getting smaller far too fast. And the ripples that marked where Xavier's ship had sunk—those were shrinking, too. She turned to look at the row of volcanoes on the horizon, and found that they were moving. But no—they weren't moving.

Astrae was. Away from Xavier and Gabriela and the ruins of their ship.

As Noa watched, the ripples and the cloud of krill grew smaller and smaller, as did the foam churned up by the whales' hunt. Mite leaned her head against Julian's shoulder, and he put his arm around her. The clouds Gabriela had summoned dissolved, streaming off the island like rainwater after a storm.

Noa knelt at Julian's side. "You did it," she said wonderingly.

"Me?" Julian gave her a serious look. "I think you're forgetting someone."

"Well," Noa said, puffing out, "I guess I—"

"Mite, obviously," Julian said. "It's quite clear that *she* did it."

Mite's eyes grew even rounder. Noa glared at Julian. But she was smiling, too, which made for an awkward glare, and Julian, seeing her face, began to laugh. The three of them sat together on the mountaintop and watched the sea churn in Astrae's wake.

28

Noa Figures
Some Things Out

"What will you learn at magic school?" Mite said. "Nobody else can do your magic."

"I expect I'll learn the rudimentary theory," Noa said in a misty voice, because she didn't actually know.

They were in Noa's bedroom, packing—or, more accurately, taking everything out of Noa's wardrobe and chests and laying it on the floor in categories so she could decide what to pack, and checking quantities against her list in the Chronicle.

It was a month after Xavier's death, and the Marchenas were back in the palace at Queen's Step. With General Lydio's ships—not to mention all his mages—they'd retaken the heart of Florean without too much trouble, given the disarray in Xavier's forces after he died. Xavier didn't have an heir, so there was nobody to give his soldiers and mages orders apart from the generals, and the generals didn't know what to do. Julian had sailed Astrae right to the palace and demanded that the council surrender. When they didn't, he had told Beauty to pound her tail against the cliffside below the councillors' apartments. As the rock began to crumble and the apartments grew perilously close to tumbling into the sea, one of the councillors had emerged to inform Julian that they would surrender, provided none of them were fed to Beauty or burned alive by Reckoner. (Just as there were exaggerated stories about Julian, there were also exaggerated stories about Reckoner, and many people in Florean believed that the Dark Lord's dragon was an enormous beast that could breathe flame so deadly it rivaled a volcanic eruption. Noa and Julian had laughed themselves silly at the look on the councillors' faces when they saw Reckoner for the first time.)

None of this meant that the Marchenas had won the war altogether—there were a few islands where Xavier's mages had holed themselves up in castles and whatnot and refused to surrender to the magician they still called the Dark Lord. But most of Florean belonged to Julian now, and Noa knew he'd soon capture the rest.

Noa wouldn't be there to see him do it, though, because she was going to Northwind Island.

The headmistress had written to Julian soon after he'd retaken Queen's Step to say that she'd heard about Princess Noa's unique powers (apparently the whole of Florean was buzzing about her and Mite), and that since she was around the right age, she could come and study at Northwind if she wanted to. Noa had dug out her suitcase before Julian was finished reading the letter.

Renne was dead. Gabriela, characteristically, had escaped. There had been no whisper of her anywhere, but Noa was convinced she was biding her time until she could get revenge on Julian. Julian pretended not to care where she was, but Noa had discovered that he'd been about to send word to her family that she'd get a full pardon if she surrendered. It was the first time Noa had needed to talk him out of doing something out of kindness rather than wickedness.

Mite furrowed her brow. "Will you learn how to boss the ghosts around? Julian says bossing people around is your special skill, and he doesn't know why dead people should be any different."

"Mite," Noa said with dignity, "why don't you go down to the kitchens and have a cake? Tomas's father sent over some fresh ones. Licorice spice, your favorite."

"Oof." Mite flopped onto the bed, looking green. "I don't think I can eat another cake. I might be sick."

"Now I've heard everything."

Julian poked his head into the room. "My Noabell," he said, surveying the organized wreckage of Noa's bedroom, "only you could make packing a suitcase look like a military campaign."

"Can I go to magic school, Julian?" Mite said.

"Maybe when you're older, Mighty Mite." Children

usually attended Northwind when they were twelve or thirteen, though some went when they were younger. It depended on when their parents decided they were ready or when they got fed up with the side effects of having a magical child who didn't understand their magic, such as explosions—though Mite was really the worst-case scenario. Students usually stayed for a year, or until they mastered their powers. Noa was confident she could master hers more quickly.

"But I want to go with Noa. Maybe they can teach me about Hush," Mite said. Julian had let her name the language of fear, and Noa couldn't think of a more appropriate name for a language she wished to never hear again.

Julian settled on Noa's bed, surveying her progress with bemusement. He looked more relaxed than Noa could remember seeing him, which probably had something to do with the fact that after the battle with Xavier, he had taken Astrae to the Iskial Sea for a few days. Iskial was the nicest of the thirteen seas, in Noa's opinion, being a sunny blue expanse dotted with over a hundred tiny islands of white sand and scalesia trees. There Julian and Noa had spent their time swimming and lounging about and generally avoiding work altogether, while Mite had spent her time collecting crabs (Mite's interests were expanding from bugs and spiders to bugs, spiders, and things that looked like spiders), and everyone was in agreement that it had been a splendid holiday.

Noa started as a sock jumped out of her suitcase and

flopped across the floor like a woolly worm. It flopped purposefully toward the wardrobe, where several cats had their lairs, and when Noa picked it up, she was rewarded with a telltale hiss from an unseen source. The invisible cats had migrated from Astrae to Queen's Step along with the Marchenas, though Noa often wished they hadn't. Packing was a difficult task with invisible cats. To be fair, though, most things in life were more difficult with invisible cats.

"Does everyone at magic school dress like that?" Mite said dubiously.

"Probably," Noa said, though she secretly hoped not. She wanted to stand out—she was a rare and powerful death mage, after all. She adjusted her sleeves, which were intimidating but not overly practical. She had asked Petrik, the village weaver, to make her a cloak that befit her new powers. It had an enormous, dramatic hood that could cover her entire face if she wanted it to (good for scaring people, but only if you stood in one place and didn't try to walk anywhere) and drapey sleeves that resembled bat wings. Obsidian beads ran along the hem and cuffs and made an eerie clacking sound if you twirled around, which Noa did often. She paired the new cloak with a hairband woven with whalebone and black garnet. When Julian had received the bill, he had asked if Noa had purchased the entire shop.

"I have something to show you two," Julian said.

"Are we moving back to Astrae?" Mite said eagerly. Mite

asked to move back to Astrae almost daily. Noa understood why. As much as she loved her old royal home, it was strange to live on an island that didn't move again. She missed the resident sea lions that sometimes got left behind when Astrae took off, and followed in its wake, roaring indignantly. She missed the winds that buffeted Astrae from all sides and made the confused trees grow crooked. She even missed the little jerky motions the island made after it passed through a whirlpool, as if all that bubbly water had given it the hiccups.

"Not exactly, Maita," Julian said. There was a mischievous glint in his eye that Noa knew better than to trust. He led them through the palace and out the smaller rear door, which opened onto a winding stair down the back of Queen's Step. It was fine weather—the salt spray caught the sunlight like handfuls of pearls. Guards bowed to them as they walked, and Noa held her head a little higher. Her attempt at magician-like dignity was spoiled somewhat by her drapey sleeves, which kept catching on the railing.

"Here we are," Julian announced when they came to the bottom of the stair. A few hundred yards off Queen's Step was Astrae, rotating slowly in the jewel-blue water. A path led around the side of the crag, up and down the uneven basalt until it came to the harbor, which was now full of General Lydio's warships.

Julian's warships, Noa corrected herself, and felt a little rush of self-satisfaction. The novelty of seeing Julian as king of Florean—even if it wasn't all of Florean yet—hadn't worn off. Surprisingly, though, Julian didn't act much like a king. He performed all his kingly duties, of course, but he did them in ordinary clothes and without feeding anybody to a sea serpent. He spent as much time talking to ordinary sailors and mages as he did with his councillors, to the point where most people he met went away only mildly scared of him, as opposed to terrified. Noa could see that something about him had changed since those terrible moments on the Nose, when their minds had filled with dark visions, though whether the change was permanent or not, she had no idea. It would certainly make her life easier if it was. She had other things to worry about besides Julian—starting with getting her sleeves taken in. They trailed in the seaweed on the rocks, and she would have a hard time impressing anybody covered in seaweed.

"I know you both miss Astrae," Julian said. "I have to say, I do, too. After all, there are a lot of advantages to a moving island. So!"

He lifted his hands and released a stream of bubbly, gritty, windy words. Astrae gave a little hop, and then it began to move toward them. A fishing boat off the coast of Astrae rocked in the wake the island left behind. Astrae picked up speed, the forest blown back like windswept hair.

"Uh, Julian," Noa said.

"It's all right," he said breezily. He spoke another

incantation, and the island slowed. Not enough. It was going to slam right into them! Screams filled the air as the inhabitants of Queen's Step came to the same conclusion.

"Julian!" Noa yelled.

"Hold on!" he said. He grabbed Mite, and Noa held on to the rocky cliff for dear life. And then—

Shwump.

Astrae struck Queen's Step with an oddly underwhelming squishy sound, as if the islands were made of mud rather than rock. The impact rolled through Queen's Step like a gentle wave, and Noa kept her feet. A cascade of salt spray fell across the island, drenching them.

When Noa dashed the water from her eyes, she saw that the northern promontory of Queen's Step had fused with one of Astrae's sea cliffs. What's more, Queen's Step no longer seemed to be anchored into the water. It rocked when Astrae rocked, bobbed when Astrae bobbed.

"There," Julian said, a little flushed. "That wasn't so bad."

Noa doubted this was the majority opinion on Queen's Step. No one seemed hurt, but the air was still punctuated by screams. Servants and courtiers leaned out of palace windows, gaping, while mages ran hither and thither, clearly under the impression that the palace was being attacked, but lacking any sense of what to do about it. A man standing on a balcony fainted, landing with a thump that Noa could hear all the way down at sea level.

"What do you think?" Julian said.

"It's *great*," Mite said, hopping up and down.

Astrae began to rotate, and as Queen's Step was now joined to it like two cakes smashed together, the palace rotated, too. A fresh chorus of screams echoed across the water. Noa began to feel nauseous.

"Hang on," Julian said distractedly. "I can get the spinning to stop."

"Oh, why?" Noa said. "This is such a delightful way to travel."

Julian muttered another stream of nonsensical incantations. Slowly, the horrible spinning ceased, and the island of Astrae/ Queen's Step gave a shudder that rattled Noa's teeth. Then, with a sound like an avalanche of rusty cutlery, the island surged forward, before settling into a calm, southward glide.

"Right," Julian said. "A few kinks to work out. I'll speak to Kell about it."

"What?" Noa was bent double against the rock with her hands over her ears.

"Oh, come on," Julian huffed. "I think it turned out pretty well."

"I think," Noa said, "that you could warn people before you go gluing islands together. Do you *want* everyone to keep calling you the Dark Lord?"

Mite grabbed his sleeve. "Can we go to Astrae now, Julian? I want to visit Patience."

"Of course, Maita," Julian said, looking put out. "It's nice to know that someone appreciates immensely difficult feats of magic."

Noa snorted. She felt an odd wave of sadness. Though she was secretly happy that they could go on living on Astrae—in a manner of speaking—it made it all the harder to leave. Of course, she wasn't really leaving Astrae behind, for how did you leave a place that could follow you wherever you went? And she wasn't leaving Mite and Julian, either—if either of them needed her, she would come back. They were Marchenas, after all. And Marchenas were always first.

Julian had to stop a few times on the lumpy, slightly soft middle ground between Queen's Step and Astrae to smooth out fissures and ripples in the earth. Several people had waded into the water to gawp at the new bay that had formed between the islands. A towering dark shadow bloomed near a knot of chattering nobles, but Julian swept them to safety with a wave just in time.

"Beauty!" Julian shouted.

The sea serpent's huge head surfaced. A smaller head surfaced next to hers, an identically murderous gleam in its eyes. The baby serpent, whom Mite had named Lovely—sea serpents didn't abide with names, and they had to call her something—stretched her mouth wide, revealing a freshly grown row of jagged teeth.

"I thought I sent you away," Julian snapped. "Shouldn't you

be somewhere in the Untold Sea by now, terrorizing pirates?"

"You didn't really think you'd get rid of me so easily, did you, dear?" the serpent cooed. "I've sworn to have my revenge on you for keeping me captive, and I keep my promises. One day, dear Julian. One day, you will let your guard down. And the air will fill with the sound of your screams as I feast upon you bone by bone. . . ."

Noa folded her arms. "How about instead of all that, Tomas promises to bake you a cake once a month?"

Beauty fixed Noa with a long stare, her tongue flicking across her teeth. "*Two* cakes," she said finally. "Provided one's lemon-lime."

Acknowledgments

Thank you to my brilliant editor, Kristin Rens, for making this and every book ten times better than what it would have been; thanks as well to the team at Balzer+Bray. Huge thank you to my agent, Brianne Johnson, who is the most talented and enthusiastic advocate any author could hope for. Thanks to Allie Levick, for always being on top of everything, and to Julia Iredale for crafting the perfect cover. Thanks again to Kim Ventrella, Claire Fayers, and Ruth Lauren. Thanks to all the librarians, teachers, and book bloggers who supported this book and who champion children's literature online.

Thank you to Shannon Grant, Ross Conner, Rebecca Larsen, and Stephanie Li for reading early drafts of *The Language of Ghosts* and providing advice and encouragement. Thanks to Tanis Cortens and Jane Cortens for the advice on chapter titles, and to the local writers' community here on

Vancouver Island. Thanks to my family, particularly my dad, who provided feedback as well as general nautical insights and is thus responsible for any related errors present in this book (kidding!).